THE LUCKY ONES

FELICE STEVENS

DEDICATION

To my family. I'm the lucky one to have you.

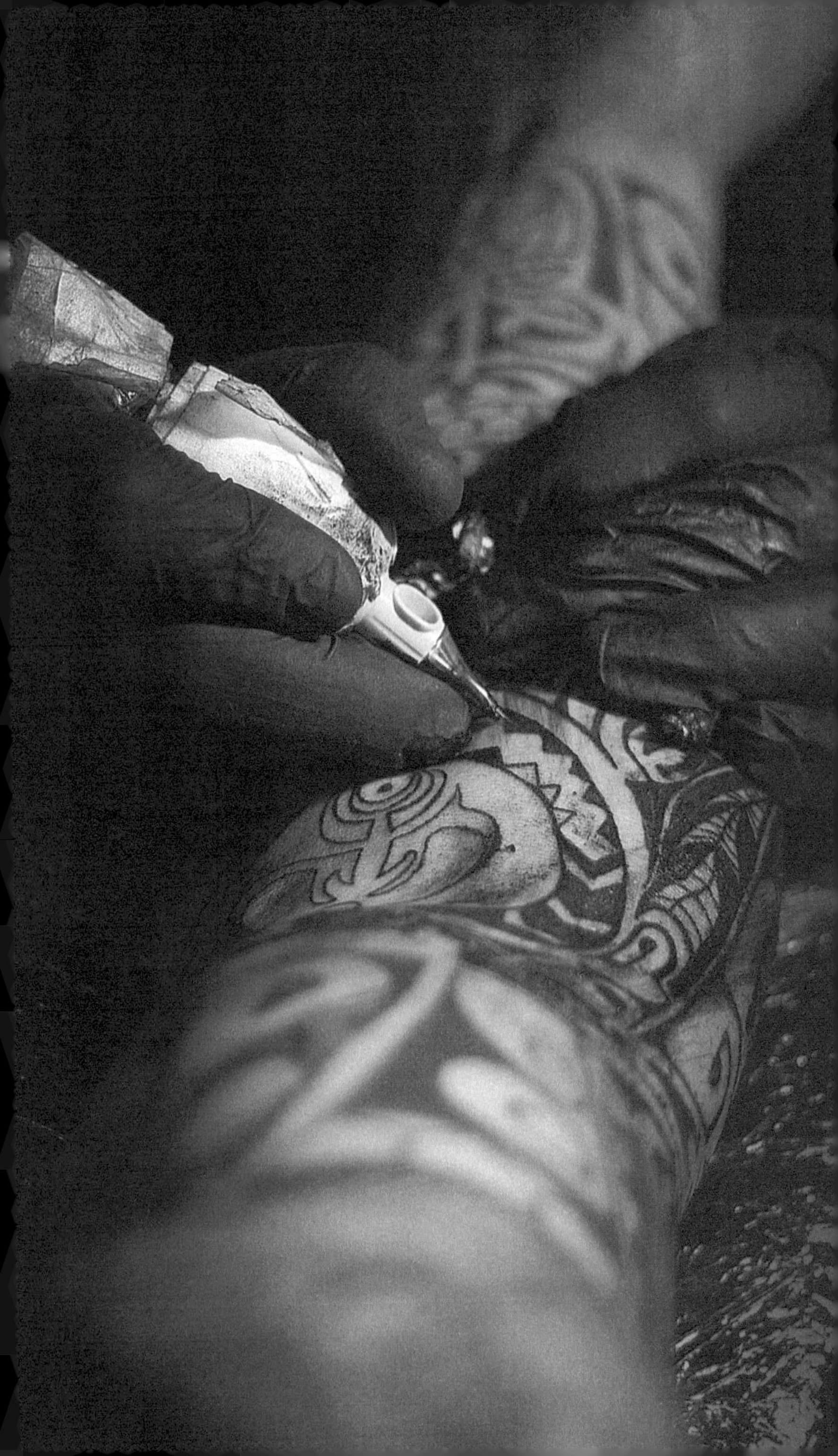

ACKNOWLEDGMENTS

Thanks to my fantastic editor, Keren Reed. To Hope and Jess from Flat Earth Editing, you are the best. To Dianne, from Lyrical Lines, I couldn't do it without you. And to Reese. Thank you for everything and more.

And always, every day, to the readers who choose to pick up my books, thank you for making my dreams come true.

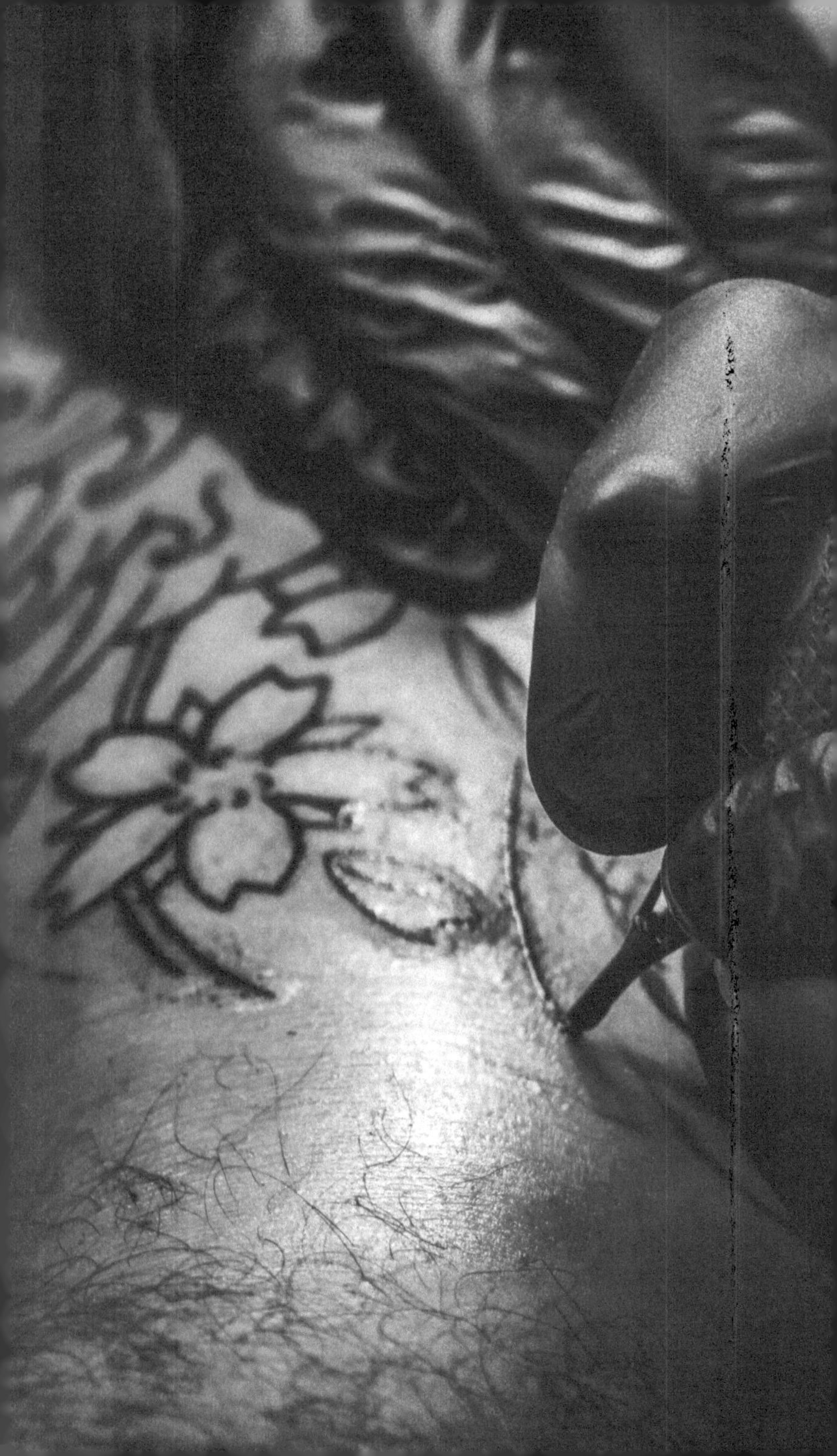

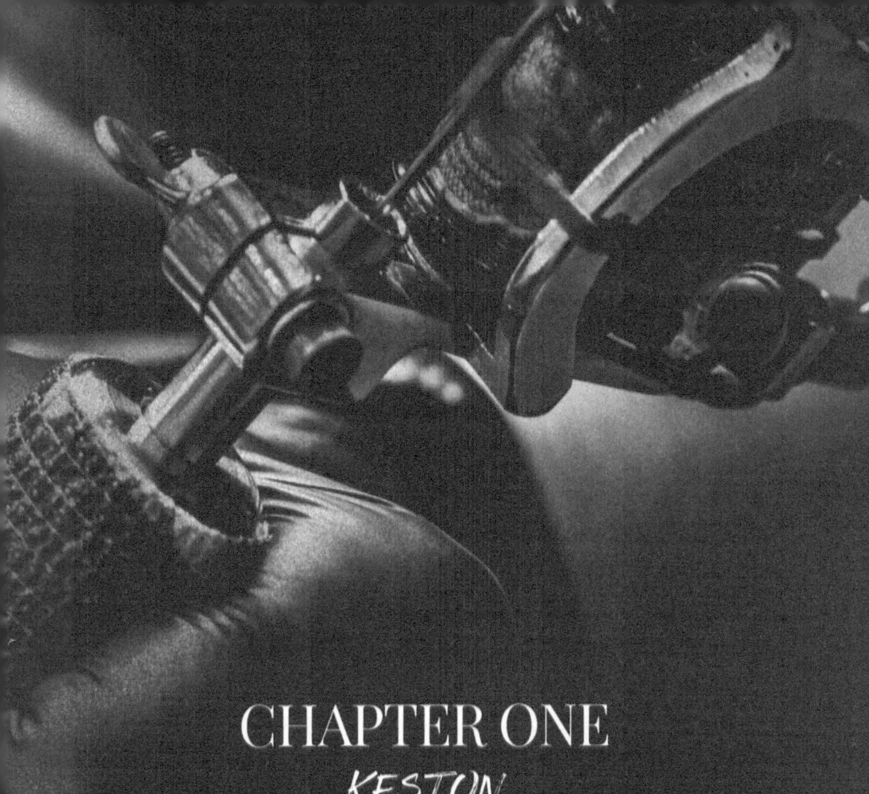

CHAPTER ONE
KESTON

I spend my days peering at half-naked bodies.

Not for fun and games, unfortunately. As a tattoo artist, I've had all kinds of customers—eighteen-year-olds who loved thinking they were being defiant against Mommy and Daddy, grandmothers who wanted their grandchild's name on a discreet patch of skin. And of course, the couples who came in together, desperate to have their names inked on each other's bodies forever...then returning not a year later, begging me to erase that mistake from their lives.

I entered my tattoo shop, Inktastic, and as I did every morning, closed the door behind me and stood for a few moments in the semidarkness. Soaking in the quiet. Reveling in it. Until I'd left my foster home at eighteen, I'd had no idea what solitude was. Five foster brothers and sisters had meant little time to myself. Someone was always in my space, in my face.

I walked across the shop, scanning the photos of our more intricate designs, displayed so the customers could see the type of work we were capable of. Early beams of sunlight streamed in through the window, and the street began to wake up. Inktastic was on St. Mark's Place in the city, and the neighborhood high school kids loved to think they could fool me by pretending to be eighteen. I constantly had to turn those little idiots away. I understood wanting autonomy, and God knew I'd been a rotten little bastard at that age, but I wasn't going to contribute to the delinquency of a minor.

My phone buzzed, and I smiled. My brother, Grady, loved to send me morning affirmations, knowing they made me laugh.

Smile, motherfucker. Don't color outside the lines today.

Snickering, I replied:

But I like to live just over the edge.

I'm sure you do, but your clients might not appreciate it.

Of course, he had an answer. We'd both inherited the sarcasm gene. We just didn't know from whom.

My clients love me. Wanna come clubbing tonight?

Sure. Lauren's busy. I'll swing by after work.

I was gonna text him: *Girlfriend got you on a leash?* but decided not to be a dick. I slid the phone into my back pocket, and not a minute later, Ambrose walked in.

"Dude, what the fuck are you doing here in the dark?" Tall, skinny, and covered in ink, he squinted at me through his red-framed glasses before flipping on the light switch. "You got a guy hidden here somewhere?" he joked but peered around nonetheless, as if half expecting a naked dude to run past him.

I rolled my eyes so hard, they hurt. "Why the hell would I do that?" The shop opened at ten, but we all arrived earlier to set up our stations. I also needed to check our online appointments, which comprised more than half our business.

"Got plans for the weekend?" Ambrose asked as he set out his instruments.

"Going out with Grady tonight. Gonna hit up that new dance club my client Jeff owns on Second Avenue. Wanna come with us? I've got passes."

"Nah. Me 'n Carly are going to the movies. Tomorrow we got an anniversary party for her parents, and on Sunday a baby shower for her best friend."

"Aww. So sweet. Look at you being all cute and domestic."

"I don't mind it." Ambrose shrugged. "I'm thirty-five. I want a kid—a family. We're savin' up to buy a house."

The thought of having to wake up in the morning and make small talk with the same person every day for the rest of my life was fucking unimaginable. I mean, I was a moody son of a bitch on a good day, and I didn't even want to talk to myself. Why would anyone else?

I set up the schedule. It was going to be a busy day, just the way I liked it. "I've got five appointments for you. That okay?"

"Yeah. The more the merrier, as in a happy bank account."

As a kid, I'd always been fascinated by ink, and to all my foster parents' despair, would draw designs on my arms and legs with ballpoint pens. The kids in school would make fun of me, and I'd lash out, first with my mouth, then with my fists. After getting suspended repeatedly, and a few arrests for smashing windows and swiping stuff from bodegas resulting in a stint in juvie for six months, my foster family put me in art therapy as a last-ditch effort. My doctor was friends with Carlos Reyes, one of the top tattoo artists in the city, and had invited him to look at my sketches. He'd offered me a summer job in his shop, where he taught me everything about the business. I'd worked for him after school and every summer until I graduated from high school. That had been almost twenty years ago. Learning the art of tattooing–and meeting Carlos–had saved my life.

Funnily enough, I wasn't covered with tattoos like Ambrose. I had a small heart on the inside of one wrist, with the inscription "Me" inside it, and the word "TRUE" in script like a bracelet on the other. I'd gotten them on my eighteenth birthday, to celebrate leaving the foster care system. I was finally free. The silhouettes of two doves with an infinity symbol and the date of Carlos's death underneath were on my left biceps. A rising sun on my right.

I'd taken over Inktastic after Carlos passed and left me as his sole benefactor. He'd been my first lover, taking care to not even talk to me about sex until I was sixteen. It was from Carlos that I'd learned about using protection and the dangers of the club scene. Whom to trust and whom to keep away from. He needn't have worried–I was crazy about him but too afraid to make a move on a man twenty years older than me. On my eighteenth birthday I kissed him, right here in the shop and I'd known I wouldn't need to look for anyone else. Worried I might be missing out on dating guys my own age, Carlos made us wait two years to make sure I was ready to be with him. No one had ever treated me with such respect and kindness. Carlos had helped me with my anger and kept me out of the system and on the right path.

We'd only had ten years together before some punk put a bullet in Carlos when he left to make a bank drop of the day's take. His death left a hole in my heart and in my life I didn't intend to ever fill again. Sex was sex and there for the taking, but I wasn't about anything permanent anymore. A kid like me, bounced from home to home since I was born, should've known better than to think about believing in *forever*. That was for fairy tales. Same as happily ever afters.

The one exception was my brother. Accepting I had someone who gave a damn about me besides Carlos had taken some time, but Grady became the one person I truly trusted. He had no other motive to be with me aside from love.

The day sped by with some quickies and an intricate design I'd started a few weeks earlier—a woman wanting to honor her firefighter husband who'd died from complications due to working on the pile in the aftermath of 9/11. Wendy had been to the shop for other ink and loved to talk while I worked. She liked to think she knew me because of that, but I'd perfected the art of listening and not sharing anything personal.

"I met someone," Wendy told me. "For the first time, I'm ready to think about the future. That's why I wanted this tattoo. So even if I do marry this new man, I'll always carry something of Frank with me."

That brought me out of my intense concentration, and I stopped for a moment. "And he doesn't mind?"

Wendy's eyes teared up. "No. He understands you can have more than one love in a lifetime. And that moving on doesn't mean forgetting the past but learning from it."

"I never was the best student." Only Carlos and Grady had tried to teach me the things that mattered—love and family. Things I still struggled with on the daily.

A line bisected Wendy's forehead, and to my shock, she put her hand on my arm. "You own a business. Obviously, something went right."

I forced a smile. "You're too much of an optimist. It's killing my vibe."

"You're being foolish," she huffed.

Without answering, I picked up my instrument. I finished as much as I thought she could take for the first part of the design, and she made a follow-up appointment. By that time, the shop was closing, and Ambrose and I began our cleanup, sterilizing the equipment and putting away the inks.

When Ambrose and I had met at juvie, we'd formed a bond of friendship that only two kids lost in the system could forge. I'd asked Carlos to hire him, and God knew I'd needed him after Carlos was killed. Without asking, Ambrose had stepped in and taken care of everything for the months I'd been lost in a fog of anger and pain. He and Grady had helped bring me back to life.

After so many years together, we had our system down and we worked seamlessly. Jodi had joined us three years ago and brought her clients from a Brooklyn shop that had closed. She specialized in what we called sweet designs and a lighter aesthetic, which I hoped would bring in new clientele. We were doing okay, but every month the shop teetered on a thin line between running in the black and sliding toward red, and it freaked me out.

Backpack in hand, Ambrose bumped my fist. "Catch you later. Have a good one." Ambrose didn't come in on weekends—Jodi did, plus Mondays and Tuesdays. I was at the shop all the fucking time. Kept me busy, out of trouble, and out of my head.

"See ya."

Another hour, and I closed the shop. My apartment, which had been Carlos's that he'd deeded to me in his will, was off St. Mark's and a quick stroll home. I showered and put on my club attire—black leather pants with a matching vest and no shirt underneath. A couple of silver chains and rings, and I was done.

The buzzer sounded, and I peered at the video camera—we'd had it installed after a slew of push-in robberies and a rape. Grady stood in his suit and tie, and I hit the button to let him in.

"Dude, you're sharp." He smirked, and I snickered.

"And you look like a fuckin' lawyer. Lose the suit and tie, man. You're gonna drive away potentials. Guys are gonna think I'm with my PO."

Brown eyes twinkling, he snorted. "You're an ass. I'm not there to pick up a date. I have my woman."

"I know a few dudes who wouldn't mind showing you around the world."

Grady was a handsome guy, big and muscular, with tattoos up and down his arms. The lines etched on his face gave the impression that he'd seen it all but had made it through the fire.

"I've already had that offer from a friend of a friend. Plus, I think Lauren might have a problem with that."

"Ready?" I slid my wallet, phone, and keys into my pockets. "It's only a few blocks away."

Side by side, we walked to the club, and I could see the line outside the door. I gave my passes to the bouncer, and he checked his list and nodded.

"Go on in."

A wail of protests rose from behind us as he lifted the rope and we walked in past the waiting hopefuls. I recognized a few regulars from other places I frequented. About to step inside, I heard the murmur of a deep voice.

"Now that's an ass I'd like to grab."

I peered at the crowd to see who'd spoken. Dark, messy hair fell over a pair of laughing blue eyes. A sexy smile curved full lips. The man's gaze grew heated as I contemplated his words and allowed myself a slow grin.

"Find me inside, and we'll see if we can make it happen."

I left him and spotted Grady near the entrance waiting for me.

"What happened?" he yelled over the pounding music. "I thought I lost you."

"Just checking out the scenery."

Amused, Grady knocked my shoulder with his. "Come on, lover boy. Let's get a drink."

We were given a table in the VIP area, and Grady ordered a bottle of vodka. The space was packed, but I saw my client behind one of the bars, sipping what I knew was club soda, since he didn't drink.

"I'm gonna go say hi to Jeff. Wanna come?" I stood and waited for Grady.

"No, I'm good, thanks."

"I bet you are, honey." A willowy, pale blond in a harness passing by, stopped in his tracks and bent down. "Wanna show me?"

Grady chuckled. "Thanks, but I'm just here for him."

Disappointment clouded the blond's face. "Well, if you decided to make it a threesome, come find me." He wiggled away.

"I'm tellin' you…" I winked, and Grady snorted.

"Go find a hottie."

I weaved through the crowd and caught Jeff's eye. He waved me over and hugged me. He'd been coming to the shop to get his ink even before I'd met Carlos.

"Lemme get you a drink." He ordered me a vodka on the rocks. "It's been a long fuckin' week."

"Same, dude. Same."

Drink in hand, I scanned the floor, checking out the scene, and picked out a few guys I wouldn't mind getting naked with, but it looked more like a banking convention than a gay dance club.

"You got a lot of suits in here tonight. What's going on?"

Jeff laughed. "Sorry. I know that's not your type. But the Gay Lawyers' Guild was having an annual meeting, and I couldn't say no."

"Not saying no can be trouble." I cackled. "I can attest to that."

"Is that so?" The voice at my shoulder had me peering to the right, and I found myself once again caught by those blue eyes I'd seen outside. "Does that mean you'll say yes to me?"

CHAPTER TWO
BAILEY

Yum, yum.

I'd had little hope of finding the gorgeous, leather-clad stud I'd ogled outside, but Lady Luck was on my side, and I was ready to have my lever pulled. I gulped my Scotch and licked my lips. Leather-man reached out and plucked the empty glass from my hand.

"What's the question?" That husky voice sent a shiver through me, straight to my groin.

"How about we get on the floor and find out?"

He slid a muscular arm around my waist. "I'm not that much of a dancer."

I grabbed hold of that fabulous ass. "I am. You can stand there and look pretty."

His deep chuckle rumbled, and the floor was crowded enough to allow him to do exactly what I'd said while I pressed up against him. The rock-hard bulge in his pants matched mine, and I rubbed my cheek to his stubbled one. He carded his fingers in my hair and twisted it tight. I drew in a sharp breath, not from pain but pleasure.

"Am I pretty enough yet?" he asked. "Because I'm about ready to get you naked right here if you don't say yes."

I was drowning in the blue pools of his fierce gaze. "I live uptown."

"And I live down the block. Let's go."

His firm, calloused hand grabbed my wrist, and I followed him. He stopped by the VIP section, where a man sat with a bottle.

"I'm out. Talk to you tomorrow." My partner picked up a glass and finished it in one smooth swallow. I watched his throat bob and imagined what he'd taste like and how he'd feel in my mouth.

"That didn't take long."

Hold up. I knew that voice. "Grady?" I peered at the table.

"Bailey. I see you've met my brother."

My jaw dropped. "Your brother?" I blinked.

"You know Grady?" My leather-clad hottie stared at us in confusion.

"Yeah. We have friends in common."

He crossed his arms, lip curled in a sneer. "Of course. You're a lawyer."

I grinned. "You say that as if it's a dirty word."

"It has been sometimes."

"Keston." Grady's voice held a slight warning. "Bailey's cool."

A dark brow arched high. "Your name is *Bailey*? Damn. I picked the WASPiest guy in the city to go home with."

With that attitude, my good mood vanished, and I stuck my face in his. "Didn't anyone ever tell you never to assume,

Keston? Both those statements are wrong: I'm not a WASP, and you just lost your shot at bringing me home with you." I patted his cheek and trailed my fingers across his sharply cut jaw. "And I'm a great lay. Too bad you'll never find out."

With Grady's cackle ringing in my ears, I left Keston standing and strode out of the club. It took me a moment to reacclimate myself to the relative quiet once I was outside, and I called for a car. I glanced back, maybe hoping Keston would follow me, but I dismissed that almost immediately. The guy was supermodel gorgeous. He didn't need to grovel to get someone in his bed.

Besides, he was a bit of a dick. Although I could admit I'd been ready to give it up right away. Maybe the universe was trying to tell me, *Hey, Bailey. You don't need to fuck someone to make them like you.* But even after years of therapy, old habits were hard to break.

I might've acted too quickly, but there was little I could do about it now. No way would I return to the club. My car arrived, and once we were on our way, I got on my phone and saw a text from Grady.

> *My brother can be an ass, but he's a good guy.*

I rolled my eyes.

> *Yeah, I could tell.*

> *No, seriously. He's still here bitching about how you left him.*

> *And that means what?*

I was such a needy bastard.

> *You caught his eye, and he can't forget you.*

Yep, there it was, that thrill of knowing someone wanted me, but I had to play it cool.

You must be smoking something.

Waiting for his response, I chewed my lip.

Nah. He's just complicated.

I snorted as my fingers flew.

Who isn't?

Grady sent a laughing emoji followed by:

He owns a tattoo parlor on St. Mark's. Inktastic.

Why did that not surprise me?

And you're telling me this why? Do I look like I have tattoos?

I wouldn't know. TTYL.

At home, I undressed and showered, running my hands over my body. My very lonely, untouched body, without a single tattoo. I sighed, knowing I'd missed out on a night of hot, wild sex with the best-looking guy I'd ever seen. I toweled off, put on boxers and a T-shirt, and flipped on the television for background noise.

My phone buzzed with a text from Weston.

Brunch on Saturday?

I had nothing going on, so I might as well hang out with friends. It beat being alone.

Sure.

Good. There's a new guy at the firm I think you'd hit it off with. I could ask him, if you want.

I groaned.

Told you already. Not interested in a setup.

Of course Weston didn't bother to answer me. Now that he had Brenner, he thought the entire world needed to be coupled up and be as disgustingly in love as they were. I tossed the phone aside and tried to pay attention to what was on the TV screen, but all I could see were sexy, arrogant lips and hot blue eyes.

I picked up my phone and scrolled to Grady's text.

"*Hmm.* I haven't been to the Village in years."

**

It might be Saturday, but I had an entire day's worth of case files to finish before I could make my way to St. Marks Place. It was now close to six, and I must've walked by the tattoo parlor at least twice.

"Get your head out of your ass and go inside." When I opened the door, a young blond glanced up from the customer she was working on. Her eyes were heavily rimmed with black liner and blue shadow, her lips a shocking pink, but her smile was bright and friendly.

"Hi. Have a seat. Someone will be with you in a few." Her voice was a nasal combination of Long Island and Brooklyn, reminiscent of the neighborhood I'd grown up in and curiously comforting.

I scanned the walls, taking in the tattoo art. I'd never had any desire to mark my body, and I watched the artist, both fascinated and squeamish knowing a needle injected ink into the person's skin. I preferred firm body parts, not sharp, pointy things poking into me, but I could admire the artistry that created the designs. The client was a twentysomething guy who was having a small skull and a crow placed on his biceps. I'd had numerous lovers with tattoos and had never really paid attention to them. The process was interesting, though, and going by the pictures on their walls, Keston and his coworkers were extremely talented.

The artist finished with the young man, washed the area carefully, then dried it thoroughly. A clear adhesive wrap was secured around his arm. She handed him a printed sheet. "I've also emailed this to you. Take care of it, and don't get it wet for five days. After that, moisturize a ton, don't pick or rub at it. Keep out of the sun, and don't get it sweaty."

"No problem. Thanks." He paid and left, and she squinted at the screen.

"Sorry you had to wait...*hmm*, do you have an appointment? I don't have anything on here for you..."

I wondered what I was doing, waiting for this random guy when I should've just ignored Grady's text.

"Well, I–"

From the rear of the shop, Keston walked up to the front counter. "What the hell are you doing here?"

Not exactly the greeting I'd have liked, but I probably shouldn't have expected more.

"Nice to see you too," I smirked. I'd taken care with my outfit today—a tight blue shirt that showed off my hard-won ripped body and a pair of joggers that rested low on my hips and showed off my ass. Not that I could compete with the leather pants Keston had been wearing the night before that had featured in the filthiest dream I'd had in years.

"I'll handle this, Jo," Keston said, his gaze latched to mine. "You can take off. See you tomorrow."

Her curious eyes darted from Keston's hard face to my mild one, and she nodded. "Okay. Night." She grabbed her purse from a drawer and walked out. The door shut with a *click*.

I faced Keston. Damn, he was even hotter today, in a tight black T-shirt and low-riding sweats. In the bright overhead lights, I could now see the ink on his arms and circling one wrist. "So, this is your shop?"

"How did you find me?" he growled, and that gravelly sound went straight to my dick. He huffed. "Never mind. My brother, of course."

"Don't blame Grady. But I mean, you were kinda rude."

Heat kindled in those laser blue eyes. "Rude? What're you talking about? You bailed on me, *Bailey*."

That snide tone wasn't going to wash with me, and I advanced on him and poked him in his very hard, muscled chest. "You're still making assumptions about me."

His lip curled. "So you're not a lawyer?"

"I never said I wasn't. So what?"

"They're nothing but trouble for the most part."

My lips twitched. "It depends on what kind of trouble. Some can be more fun than others."

He scowled. "I'm sure Grady's told you about our past. I don't exactly have fond memories of the legal system."

"Yeah. We all have shit we've dealt with. I prefer to leave it in the rearview mirror. Live in the present." Aware of the heat pouring off him and the scent of his sweat, my heart rate kicked up, and I was seconds away from melting into a puddle of want and need.

He backed away into the recesses of the shop, where I saw two other chairs and a long table on a wooden platform.

"Why are you here?" He positioned himself behind the table, and I leaned a hip against it and ignored his question for one of my own.

"Is this place yours, or do you work for someone?"

I should've known that would get his ire up.

"Why?" A brow rose. "You don't think I can run my business?"

"Damn, you're defensive." I ran a hand over the smooth tabletop. "I didn't say that. I'm thinking you could do whatever you want."

And whomever. Like me. You could do me in a second.

"Are you interested in getting a tattoo?" That searching gaze scanned me, head to toe, leaving me breathless. "I don't see any, unless they're hidden under those clothes."

My face heated. "I've never had one." I paused. "Yet." I circled the table, and his expression darkened.

"Is that why you came here? To suss me out about getting ink?"

"No." I crossed my arms, fixing him with what I hoped was a fierce scowl. "I didn't like your assumptions. That I'm snobby and rich and a WASP. Which I'm not. I'm Jewish."

"So what?"

I narrowed my eyes. "What does that mean, so what? You made this assumption that because my name is Bailey, I'm a rich, snooty WASP. I'm telling you I'm not."

He shrugged. "Okay. You're not. Why does it matter what I thought?"

Damn. Keston should've been a lawyer–the way he twisted arguments into knots. "It doesn't, but I didn't like your insinuations. You don't know me at all."

His lips kicked up in a smile that rendered me speechless. Something that never happened. "I think I do. You come from a nice, middle-class home. Mommy and Daddy love you. You've always had a house, and your own room, and you've never had to worry where your next meal is coming from or how to pay your bills."

I didn't bother to dispute his assumptions because it wouldn't matter what I said. "And you didn't have any of that."

Without answering and with a face filled with fury and pain, Keston strode off and into the room from which he'd first appeared.

Grady had spoken frankly and often about his youth, how he and Keston hadn't known of each other's existence and that their mother had put them into foster care. Until they'd become emancipated, neither had led an easy life, but where Grady freely opened up about his experiences, it looked like Keston had no such desire.

I had two choices: either walk away and forget about the sexiest, most intriguing man I'd ever met, or follow him and push his buttons to see what would happen next.

I found him standing in the darkened office, staring into space. He whipped around, his expression a dangerous storm of emotions.

"What the hell are you still doing here?" he asked, but his hands were already reaching for my face, and I melted into his touch.

"Damned if I know," I murmured. His hot mouth slammed on mine, and I sucked his velvety tongue. I fisted his shirt and rubbed up on him. Our tongues teased and danced, and he bit my lips. Desperate, I shivered with desire. "Oh, God." I clutched his heavily muscled shoulders and buried my face in his neck, sucking at the rapidly pumping vein. "Fucking hell."

"Which is it, God or hell?" His wicked smile sent me reeling. "Opposite sides of the spectrum."

"Are we getting it on or having a philosophy lesson?" I panted. "Who cares?"

My hands slid under his waistband and shimmied those sweats and briefs past his hips until they puddled at his ankles. Perfect washboard abs. That delicious V leading to the most beautiful dick I'd ever seen greeting my hungry eyes. Where only moments ago his eyes glinted black with anger, they now turned hazy with lust as he tugged my joggers down. I dug my fingers into those powerful biceps and pulled him closer. He dipped his head and took my mouth, bruising my lips with his hard, demanding kisses. I wrapped my fingers around his cock, which pulsed beneath my touch.

"Fuck, your mouth is fire," he grunted, hips thrusting, his leaking cock sliding in and out of my hand. He yanked down my briefs and tugged my shaft. "Give me your dick."

That bossy tone turned me on, and I rutted into his fist, moaning his name.

"Keston, fuck me, Keston." I nipped his shoulder, and he stiffened and came hot and heavy, coating my hand. He increased the pressure along my throbbing length while sucking my tongue, and my vision blurred as I broke apart in the most intense climax of my life. He held me tight, fingers stroking my naked skin while I regained my equilibrium.

We stayed locked to each other, our hearts pounding. I was sleepy and content and laid my head on his shoulder. His teeth scraped against my jaw before taking my earlobe and sucking it. My swirling brain came together, and I wondered if he was going to kick me out or fuck me.

"I'm just around the corner," he whispered.

"Are you inviting me home with you?"

"Unless you want me to do you here," he growled, and I could have sworn my dick twitched.

"*Mmm*, I'm not sure. Could be sexy, me bent over the table." His breath hitched, and I licked his collarbone. "What do you say?"

He reached for me, and I heard a noise from the front of the shop.

"Keston? Are you here? Keston?"

He pushed me off him and jumped away, eyes wild with shock. I stumbled several steps, my feet tangled in my clothes. Keston pulled up his sweats and wiped his hands on some paper towels.

"Stay here."

I nodded and reached for my briefs and pants while he slipped out of the office and shut me in. With my clothing straightened and my hands clean, I carefully opened the door a crack, and peered out. A lanky man stood near the front of the shop. Their quiet voices didn't reach far enough for me to hear what they were saying, and I grew more frustrated by the minute as they continued to talk, Keston laughing as if I wasn't standing and waiting for him.

Why the hell was Keston hiding me in here?

CHAPTER THREE
KESTON

My body still buzzing from that mind-blowing orgasm, I collected myself and forced an easy smile to my lips.

"What're you doing here? I thought you had plans."

Seeing Ambrose in the shop freaked me out a little. Frankly, the fact that I'd just had sex in my shop did as well, but this Bailey guy flipped my switch. I'd had to touch him, and when I did, it was as if I'd become possessed. The more I had of him, the more I wanted.

"Carly's got a stomach bug, so we had to cancel our plans. She's moaning and groaning and told me to leave her alone, so I was heading to your place to see if you wanted to grab some dinner. Then I saw the lights on. What the hell are you still doing here? It's, like, over half an hour after closing."

Thinking fast, I shrugged. "I had a late walk-in, and we got to talking after I did his work. I was cleaning up and decided to do some paper work." That sounded plausible. I hoped. Meanwhile I could smell Bailey on me and wondered if Ambrose could as well.

"So what do you say? We could get some Italian or maybe Indian? I'm down for anything."

What I was down for was dark-haired, blue-eyed, about six feet, one ninety, with a killer tongue and a dick I wanted in my mouth. But that wasn't gonna happen now.

"Yeah. I was just in the middle of something I gotta finish. Get us a table, and I'll be there in like ten, fifteen minutes, tops."

He settled against the front counter. "I can wait. It's no big deal."

Fuck.

"All right. I'll be ready in a few."

How the fuck was I gonna sneak Bailey out of here? I couldn't tell Ambrose I had a guy with me in the shop. Not only was it unprofessional, but Ambrose hated lawyers with a passion, especially since his brother, Lucas, had gotten convicted in a drug possession case and was serving time. I'd asked Grady to take a look at it, and he said criminal law wasn't his specialty but from a cursory inspection of the file, the lawyer should've probably had Lucas plea to a lesser charge. Ambrose didn't like that answer, insisting his brother was innocent.

I returned to the room, where Bailey had gotten dressed and was waiting for me with an annoyed face. "Why am I hiding in here?"

I put a finger to my lips. "*Shh.* Listen. That's Ambrose, my coworker. I-I can't have him thinking I'm hooking up in the shop." I left out the lawyer part.

He smirked but kept his voice to a murmur. "Glad to know you don't make it a habit. So how do we do this? I'm assuming there's no back door?" Bailey winked. "Except mine."

Damn, I still wanted him, bad jokes and all. It was the only reason I came up with the craziest fucking idea. "I'm gonna trust you because you're Grady's friend. If I give you the keys to the shop, could you lock up after Ambrose and I leave? You can meet me here in like a couple of hours, okay?"

My heart sank when he narrowed his eyes. "No. I don't think so." Surprising me, he put his hand on my nape and yanked me to him, whispering against my mouth. "But you can come to my place, and I'll give them to you. Along with something else I know you want." He rocked his hips, and I had to stifle a groan. I remembered what he felt like, which was why I agreed to his ridiculous plan.

"Yeah, okay. Give me your address." Reluctantly, I pulled away from him, took the extra set of keys from the desk and handed them to him. "Better give me your number too, in case something gets fucked up."

"The only thing getting fucked tonight is me." He cupped the bulge in his pants.

"Yeah," I grunted. "Got that right." We exchanged numbers, and he texted me his info. "Okay. There are two locks on the front door."

"What about an alarm? You don't have one?"

"Yeah, but you can leave it off for one night." As hot as he was, I wasn't about to give Bailey the alarm code.

Frowning, he scanned the space. "Not a smart move. You've got valuable equipment here."

The last thing I needed was some uptown guy telling me how to run my shop. "Listen, you take care of your fancy-ass clients, and I'll handle my business." But he did have a point. "Fine, set the alarm. Here's the number." I smirked. "In case you're wondering, I'll be changing it in the morning."

Steady blue eyes met mine. "Got it."

"I'll see you later." I hesitated, then kissed him. "Bye."

I left him standing there with his brow furrowed.

"I'm ready, Ambrose. Let's go."

We walked out, I locked up, pretended to punch in the alarm to not raise suspicion with Ambrose and we headed down the block.

"What're you thinking?" I asked him. "Indian?"

"Yeah, sounds good."

We walked to what was known as Curry Row—the block in the East Village where all the Indian restaurants were congregated. Though most were good, our favorite spot was Veeray da Dhaba. The waiter recognized us and brought us each a Kingfisher beer and our usual assortment of appetizers. While I munched on a samosa, I listened to Ambrose talk about his brother's continuing legal problems.

"Can you believe I'm still getting bills from that fucking lawyer? I swear they're vultures, man. Bloodsuckers, all of them." Ambrose had been in and out of the system throughout his teens and didn't trust a lawyer as far as he could throw one.

"What're they asking for?" I took a drink. While no fan of the legal system, I didn't hate all lawyers, considering my brother was one. He and I had gone through a few tense years when we'd first connected, but we were okay now. It wasn't his fault he'd been the one to have gotten the more stable home life. Luck of the draw.

"He got billed for the parole hearing. Which was denied."

The waiter took our order, and I waited for him to depart. "I mean, it's not a guarantee, is it? And the lawyer did show up, didn't he?"

Ambrose rested his chin in his hand. "It just sucks, man. I know Lucas was set up. The cops planted those drugs on him. And his shit-talking girlfriend? He never laid a hand on her. They're all lying. You know how it is."

I knew nothing of the sort. The times I'd met Lucas, I'd pegged him as a smooth-talking SOB. It wasn't hard to figure him out. When I was younger, I'd gotten in enough trouble with his kind to see through his bullshit. A man who didn't seem to work but always had money to burn—what the hell did he do? That, along with the numerous complaints about domestic violence I'd heard over the years, was enough for me to know he was a piece of shit who used Ambrose's blind devotion to get what he wanted.

"When is his next hearing?"

"Not until next year."

I tuned out Ambrose's bitching, wondering if Bailey was going to keep his promise or if I'd made a mistake by giving him my keys. Then I laughed at myself. That guy would never dream of crossing the line. He probably never even jaywalked. I could spot his type a mile away, someone who thought hooking up with a guy like me was walking on the wild side. And God knew, I was happy to oblige and get as wild as he liked.

"Keston, hey." Ambrose's fingers snapped in front of my face. "What's wrong? Did you hear me?"

"Huh?" I blinked and found him staring at me. "Sorry. What did you say?"

"Could you do me a favor and have your brother look at his case again? Maybe he missed something."

Doubtful. "I could, but he was pretty sure there wasn't anything problematic about Lucas's arrest."

"So you're on the lawyer's side? I should've known you'd change your tune because your brother's one of them."

I narrowed my eyes. "Don't be a fucking asshole. Grady's the best, and if he says there's nothing he can do, I believe him."

Ambrose's shoulders slumped. "I just wanna help him, you know? Like we wanted people to help us."

"I know, but if Grady says there's nothing you can do..." I shrugged, but Ambrose didn't want to hear it.

"Maybe he's wrong. I know he's your brother, but that don't mean he's perfect." He thrust out his jaw, challenging me to react, but I kept quiet, letting him rant. "Lucas said his public defender barely knew his case. You know these Legal Aid lawyers suck." He checked his phone. "Carly needs me to come home. I'd better go."

He left, and I gazed at my half-eaten plate. I wasn't too worried about Ambrose. I never took offense at what he said—I didn't blame him for not trusting authority. Neither did I. Yet here I was, getting it on with a corporate type. A lawyer, no less. The universe worked in fucking crazy ways.

I took out my phone, searched for Bailey's address, and called for a car. I'd expected it to be in Tribeca or Chelsea, but it was on the Upper West Side. I didn't know the area, and when the car pulled up on the tree-lined block of 85th Street between Amsterdam and Columbus, I had to admit it was...charming. I'd figured a corporate type like Bailey would live in a huge, modern apartment building, but these were brownstones. Mostly three or four stories, with bay windows and flowerpots on the windowsills. I checked the number, found the building, and mounted the steps. Bailey Marks lived on the second floor. There was one of those high-tech cameras like I had in my building, and I hit the buzzer. A moment later the lock clicked, and I mounted the stairs, not bothering to wait for the elevator.

A shirtless Bailey stood waiting for me in the doorway. I strolled up to him and held out my hand. "First things first. My keys?"

A smile curved his lips, and he held them out to me. "Come and get 'em." And he took off running into the apartment.

"Little shit." I kicked the door shut behind me and caught up with him in the living room. I tackled him to the couch and pinned him underneath me. My mouth found his, and I plunged my tongue inside. He sucked it like a fucking lollipop, and I ground my hips into his.

"Fuck, Keston," he panted, digging his fingers into my shoulders.

"Yeah, that." I pulled off my shirt and watched his eyes widen, a hungry light kindling in their depths. Those full lips fell open, and a red flush rose to his cheeks. "Let's get to the bedroom."

I knew that was what he wanted. A bad boy like me giving it to him hard and fast. But Bailey surprised me by wriggling out from under me. "What's the rush? Want a drink?" He licked his lips, and my dick jerked. "I taste curry. I have beer if you want."

My breathing now under control, I nodded. "Yeah, sure."

This wasn't one of those ultra-modern apartments. It was older with original floors, crown molding, and had a beautiful bay window overlooking the leafy trees lining the street. I wandered around the living room, taken in by the warm atmosphere. Again, this wasn't the picture I'd already developed in my mind.

"Here." Bailey reappeared and handed me the bottle. He had a glass of Scotch in his other hand. "*L'chaim.*"

I tipped the glass. "What you said." I took a swig and set it on the coffee table. "So you locked everything up?"

He smirked. "It was two locks and an alarm. I managed."

I glanced at his front door, where there were numerous locks. "I guess you think I'm lax in my security."

The teasing light in his face vanished. "You can't be too careful." He took a drink. "I've seen too many cases of people who trust blindly, to their detriment."

"Your clients? You do criminal law?"

Lost in thought, Bailey didn't answer me, and I studied him. Angular jaw, dark with stubble, high slash of cheekbones, and a strong nose. He must've felt my stare, because he raised his gaze to meet mine. "What? Oh, yeah. I'm in general practice. Solo. I do a little of everything."

"Not many of those left. All the lawyers I've known are with firms." My lips thinned. "Or Legal Aid."

"Overworked and underpaid," Bailey said. "I did a stint with them for a while out of law school." He finished his drink and set the empty glass by my beer. "Are we sharing résumés?" His mouth kicked up in a sexy grin. "Or body parts? I vote number two." His fingers twirled the silver chain hanging from my neck and tugged gently. "I've been waiting for hours for what you promised me."

The air rose heavy with heat and the potential of sex. My cock thickened, and I cupped his cheek. "I was ready when I walked in."

Bailey's eyes glinted. "I tried to be a good host. Didn't want you to think I was only after you for your body."

"I don't care," I growled, rough and ready, and he laced our fingers together and pulled me with him to the shadowed bedroom. Like before, he tugged at the sweats and my briefs, but this time I kicked them off completely and stood naked.

"Fuck, you're perfect," he rasped as he undressed. Even in the dimly lit room, I could see the fire in his eyes, and I grasped my cock at the base.

"You want this, don't you?" I stroked myself, watching him grow lust-drunk. His dick rose stiff and full, and the ache of desire tightened in my belly. I loved giving head, and I couldn't wait to taste him. "C'mere." I held out a hand, and he moved closer until our chests touched and I could feel his lips hovering over mine. Normally I was in and out, looking to get off as quickly as possible, but I had plans to savor Bailey. I sank to my knees, and at his harsh intake of breath, I slipped my mouth over the leaking crown of his dick.

"Oh God, oh God," Bailey moaned, his hips thrusting. I clutched his hairy thighs, holding him in place while my lips and tongue played on his hot shaft. I sucked hard and fast, listening to his cries and whimpers rise in the stillness. Bailey shook under my touch, sweat dripping down his face, the pungent scent of him intoxicating. My head swam with desire.

"Keston, fuck me," he yelled, tightening his fingers in my hair as he pumped out his load. Greedily, I swallowed every drop, and when he was finished, I sat on my heels and licked my sticky lips.

"Bed," I croaked and helped him walk on shaky legs. He lay with his face in the pillow, and I ogled him while playing with the smooth, hard globes of his ass. My fingers teased along his crack, and he sighed. I ran my nose between his cheeks and held him wide to lick the tight little hole in front of me.

"Oh God, you're killing me." Bailey's muffled voice spurred me on, and I slid my tongue in deep before sucking at the wet opening.

"Taste so fucking good. Can't wait to stick my cock in here. You want that, don't you?" I put a finger in my mouth to wet it, and eased it inside him.

"Yes, please. More. *More*," he cried out, working himself on my finger.

"This is only one finger. Imagine what my dick is gonna feel like in there."

"Stuff is in the drawer. Do it already."

I reached out and found the lube and condoms. I'd never sheathed and slicked myself so quickly. Bailey positioned himself on all fours, and I circled the damp hole, then sank into him fully, grinning at his hiss.

"Like that?" Damn, he squeezed me like a fucking python. An explosion of heat wrapped around my shaft, and I willingly walked into that inferno. I rolled my hips, and Bailey rose higher on his knees and elbows. I grabbed him, and we fell into a rhythm where I gave and he took. There was no doubt that Bailey controlled the pace, meeting each push into him by tipping that gorgeous ass higher.

"Harder. Yeah, like that. Harder."

"I should've known you'd be mouthy as fuck," I grunted and pumped hard and fast. His moans of pleasure rose loud, and it was a fucking turn-on.

"Oh yeah, that's it. Do it. Fuck me till I'm done."

I dug my fingers into his hips to hold him steady as I slammed into him over and over, my dick swollen and aching. "Like that? Feels good, doesn't it?" Sweat blinded me, and my heart drummed a pounding beat. Everything centered at this moment. The bed creaked as I thrust into him, and my dick swelled, trapped in that slick passage. "You like that, don't you?" Funny how it wasn't only about my pleasure and getting off. I needed to know Bailey was feeling it too. "Don't you? Tell me," I demanded, driving in deeper.

"Yes, oh God, yes. Keston," he wailed. "Fuck, oh fuck. I'm coming again." The feel of his twitching body beneath me broke me apart and I came, white light blinding me. I collapsed on top of him, still buried in his ass.

"Jesus, am I dead?" I muttered. My head buzzed as if a swarm of bees lived inside it, and I couldn't move.

"I hope not. You're too heavy to move."

I cracked an eye open. With my breath finally steady, I slid out of Bailey, making sure to get the condom and toss it into the garbage.

"That was...something," Bailey murmured.

Something else, I wanted to say.

"Stay the night?" he asked on a yawn.

I'd usually say no, but the bed was damn comfortable, and I had a feeling I wasn't done with Bailey Marks yet.

CHAPTER FOUR
BAILEY

The workweek was made so much better by having a hot weekend to reminisce about. And Keston had made it an inferno. I'd lain in bed, worn out from him pushing me to the edge, over and over, leaving me a quivering ball of nerves, half-dead from pleasure when he'd finally entered me.

And while I'd slept, he'd left, without waking me or leaving a note to say…what? Thanks? I didn't know what I'd expected, but I'd hoped he'd want to see me again. With a gorgeous guy like Keston, I suspected if I wanted that to happen, I'd need to make the first move.

The phone rang, and I had to shelve my salacious thoughts to earn my keep. My secretary was busy on the other line, so I took the call.

"Hello, Bailey Marks. Can I help you?"

"Hi, Bailey, it's Dr. Sharpe."

Automatically, I checked my calendar. "Hi. We don't have a session until the end of the week—Thursday, at one thirty. Am I right?"

"Yes, but I'm afraid I have to reschedule. Would you have any other time free this week?"

"Now?" I joked.

"I'm free if you are," she deadpanned. "We can do a video conference if you want."

"Even better."

"All right. Give me a minute, and I'll send you a link."

I hung up and closed the files on my computer. The link popped up, and I clicked it. Dr. Sharpe's face appeared.

"Hello, again, Bailey."

"Hi."

"How was your weekend?"

I thought about it and decided to tell her about Keston.

"It was good. I met a guy, and we hooked up." I had no qualms getting into my sex life with her. I wasn't a monk, and she wanted my truth, warts and all.

"Oh? Where did you meet him—an app, club?"

"At a club, but it turns out he's the brother of an acquaintance."

Her lips curved in a smile. "So you'll be seeing him again?"

I thought about waking up alone, to a cold bed, with no note or text. "Honestly, I'm not sure. He left, and I haven't heard from him."

She set her pen on the desk. "We've talked about that. You have to stop waiting for other people to make your happiness happen. Your joy is dependent on you. If you want to see him again, you can make the first move."

With another guy, maybe, but Keston was a prickly son of a bitch. "This guy—Keston—he's different. A loner. He and his brother were given up as kids to foster care. Neither knew of the other until they were grown."

"*Hmm.*" Her brows drew together. "That's pretty unusual. They like to keep siblings together."

"I know, but from what I heard, the boys were born four years apart, and his brother was given up first. They had no chance to be adopted together. I don't know much beyond that. Anyway, he's not much of a talker."

"Do you like him? If you want to see him again, don't let his behavior stop you. Take charge. You never know—maybe he also thinks you only want something casual, and he could be afraid to take that step."

Keston afraid? Unlikely. "He's pretty blunt. I doubt he's afraid of anything."

"Often the people who are the quietest or most closed off are the ones with the most fear. They know that if they reveal one scar, more wait in the wings. Like you were."

I winced. "I've told you everything. My father, mother...all the random guys." I spread my arms wide. "That's me. The real Bailey."

"Do you really think that? Do you only associate yourself with the trauma in your life?"

Sweat broke out on my brow. And I laughed although it was uneasy. "The guys aren't traumatic. They're tons of fun."

Her gaze was piercing, and it reached out to me even through a computer screen. "I have no doubt they are, yet you're alone. Still searching. For what?"

"I don't know, all right?" I threw up my hands.

"I think you do." Her calmness was irritating.

"Isn't that what I pay you for?" I snapped, and when she didn't respond, I sighed out loud. "Sorry. That was rude. I-I guess, I'm hoping I'll meet someone who'll want to see me again, even if it doesn't lead to sex. Someone who'll care about me. Maybe fall in love with me because I'm a nice guy."

"How do you feel saying that?"

"My stomach hurts." I rubbed my nape. "But less tense, I think."

"That's good. Why do you think people don't love you?"

My smile was thin. "Gee, maybe because everyone I've ever loved has left me. My mother, every guy I slept with. Even my dad left." My voice caught.

"Bailey, you had no control over your parents. Your mother's abandonment was a selfish act of her own, and your father's death was a tragedy. You're seeking to fill the void with random men, but it's not helping."

"I always think, maybe this guy...and then they leave, and I never hear from them."

Dr. Sharpe fixed me with her steady gaze. "Yet you keep repeating the same self-destructive behavior. Now you've done the same with Keston. Try and arrange a date with him, and don't have it end in sex. Ask to see him again, but say good night, no matter what."

After the session, I thought about everything she said, and though it made me cringe, I figured why the hell not? Better to exorcise him from my system now, before I fell harder for him. But all that had to be shelved until later, as I had several court appearances and a closing on a co-op.

By the time I got home, the last thing I was thinking about was sex. It was six o'clock, and I was hungry and tired.

And yet...I picked up my phone and texted.

> *Doing anything?*

My text remained unread, so I decided to take a shower and figure out what to order for dinner. I came out of the shower, rubbing my hair with a towel, when I saw my phone light up. I couldn't deny the thrill that ran through me.

> *I was. Bottom half of a full sleeve.*

I chewed my lip.

> *Feel like dinner? I can come downtown.*

I waited, my hopes draining with each passing second.

Sure. Meet me at Temakase at 7:45.

I stuck my fist in the air for the win.

Ok.

I put on jeans and a button-down over a Henley. Casual but not sloppy. The car dropped me off in front of the restaurant, and I spotted Keston walking toward me from the second he turned the corner. Black jeans, white sweater, and a battered leather jacket. Effortless and completely gorgeous.

I gave a small wave. "Hi. How's it going?"

"Good. Hungry." He pulled open the door, and after a five-minute wait, we were shown to a table. A young woman in her twenties gave us a practiced smile as she approached.

"Hi, I'm Janessa, and I'll be your server. Can I get you a cocktail, beer, or anything else to drink?"

Reading the menu, Keston nodded. "Sapporo, please."

"Same for me," I said.

"Great. I'll be back in a few."

After she left, I waited a moment before speaking. "Surprised to hear from me?"

"Not really." He smirked and pulled off his jacket. "I figured we have to eat."

The teasing grin on his delicious lips left no doubt that he thought he was getting lucky later.

We studied the menu. "I've never been here. What's good?" I asked, hoping to start some kind of conversation, as I figured he wasn't going to make much of an effort. Keston came alive when we were having sex but was a man of few words otherwise.

"Everything. Usually I'll pick something up to bring home. I don't eat out much in restaurants."

"I only do when I have an event or meeting friends."

That wicked smirk ticked up the corners of his mouth. "Event, huh? One of those where you pay a thousand bucks to dress up like a waiter and eat lousy food?"

I chuckled. "Well, I don't pay that much, but in my business, sometimes you gotta play the game."

"Do you do a lot of game playing?"

I arched a brow. "Only in the bedroom."

I hadn't lied to Keston. I rarely went out to dinner during the week. By the time I battled the subway to my apartment after a day at the office, I was tired and wanted nothing more than to stretch out on my couch like a slug. Of course, if I had a networking get-together after work, I put on my Bailey-happy-face and presented myself, but the truth was, if I had a steady boyfriend, I'd have liked nothing more than to be home with him.

But Keston didn't play along. "Why did you want to be a lawyer?"

I sipped my beer. "I'm a Jewish guy. We're allowed three professions—doctor, lawyer, or accountant." When he didn't laugh at my joke, I sighed. "I really like helping people, and I believe I'm a good problem solver. Being a lawyer helps me accomplish that."

That brought a reaction. "Oh yeah, sure."

Hmm. I sensed sarcasm. "Not a fan of the legal system, I take it?"

I watched the play of emotions over his face—anger, pain, loss. "How could I be? It kept me with people where I was only wanted for the money the government gave them. And then there're the cops." His blue eyes narrowed to slits. "They've got nothing better to do than harass kids for tagging or swiping a damn doughnut from the bodega 'cause maybe they're hungry."

"Is that what happened to you?" The restaurant was filling up, but it was as if we were the only two people in the world. Knowing how self-controlled Keston was and that he lived inside his head, I could see him formulating an answer, his memories falling into place, lining up like soldiers on a battlefield.

And I wanted to be his armor and shield him against the world.

His jaw tightened. "Forget it."

"No, I don't think so. Grady told us he had a few brushes with the cops as a teenager and that's why he became a lawyer. So kids like him would have an advocate."

An ugly sound escaped Keston. "Listen, I love my brother, but he's not much different from you. Working in a fancy office with a view, pulling in a big six-figure salary."

"First of all, he and I are nothing alike. Aside from him having a PhD as well as a law degree, Grady works at a large firm. I'm a solo practitioner, hustling for each and every client. Grady started his career working with kids who grew up like the two of you. He's been in the trenches of child welfare."

"You don't have to tell me about my brother," Keston growled.

"Maybe I do, if you're dismissing him and all the hard work he put in to get where he is as a partner in a law firm. And don't give me that snarl. You don't scare me."

"I don't need this shit."

"And I don't need to be your booty call. If you want to see me in bed, you'll have to deal with me out of it. And that means talking."

Nerves dancing and heart pounding, I waited for him to get up and walk away. I half expected him to. Keston had that "it" quality that drew men to him. When you looked like him, honey had nothing on his vinegar. Everyone wanted a taste, and they'd willingly take the bitter with the sweet.

"Fine, whatever," Keston grumbled. "But Grady and I, we live in different worlds. He's being nice to me—"

"Because he loves you. Do you know how lucky you are to have found each other and to have a great guy like Grady as your brother?"

Our server returned, and we each ordered three rolls. Keston once again fell silent. I took a sip of my beer. How could a man so loud and vocal during sex have so little to say across the table? It was like pushing a wheel up the mountain only to have it slip halfway down. I could take this dark and broody act for so long—I'd never been a fan of *Jane Eyre* or *Wuthering Heights*. I was looking for a real-life man, not a Rochester or Heathcliff.

"So, uh, is there a most popular tattoo? Like a starter that people who haven't gotten one usually pick?" Was my question as stupid as it sounded? Keston's brow furrowed, so I guessed not.

"Depends. Some girls and women like a flower or a heart. If they've had a new baby, they'll get the birthday with maybe a little footprint. Or paw prints for their dogs or cats. Guys will go for skulls, or maybe the flag—US or their country. The eagle is popular." He grinned, transforming his moody features into a thing of beauty, and I couldn't help returning his smile. "Why, Uptown? You thinking of getting some ink?"

"Maybe. I don't have any."

Those blue eyes blazed hot. "I noticed. Pure, virgin skin."

I snickered. "The only part of me you could call virginal, that's for sure."

Our rolls came, and we both demolished them, Keston giving me his extra ginger and pointing his chopsticks at me.

"You eating all the wasabi?"

I scooped up a dollop of wasabi and plopped it on his plate.

"Here you go, hot stuff."

When the bill came, I scooped it up. "My treat. I invited you."

He shrugged. "Thanks."

Once outside in the cool air, he took my elbow. "My place is this way."

Here goes nothing.

"I'd better get home. I've got a court appearance in the morning. But maybe we can get together again? Like over the weekend?"

In high school, I'd never been in the popular crowd. I hadn't been invited to hang out on the weekends at the mall, go to the movies, or play video games, and I wouldn't have had the money for any of it anyway. Now, at thirty-nine, I was reliving my teenage era of insecurity. I might have the ability to do what I wanted, but I still yearned for the right person to do it with. Being with Keston brought me right back to those days of wondering if I'd ever find someone who'd want me.

And apparently, I'd startled Keston with my question. He'd been certain I was a sure thing, and that convinced me I'd made the right decision.

"I work both days."

Buoyed by the fact that he hadn't blown me off, I jumped to answer. "I do too. But maybe after? You can decide what we do, if you want."

"I'll let you know."

Not exactly what I'd hoped to hear, but I was determined to stand up for myself and not be so easy.

"All right. Well, have a great night. I'm going to call for a car."

His gaze was unreadable. "Night."

He took off down the block, and I waited for my ride. It was an uneventful trip to my place, and once I got home, I brushed my teeth and got into bed. Dr. Sharpe would be proud, and it might be a good thing to be strong, but that wasn't going to be of much comfort in the middle of the night when I reached out for someone. I was still alone.

The week plodded along, and I had my head in my work, but not my heart.

"Jerk," I muttered that Friday evening. I sat on my couch and my phone, again, remained frustratingly silent. Each night,

I scrolled through dating apps, but no one caught my eye enough to make a connection. Not like I'd had with Keston, although given his silence, it was all one-sided. Dr. Sharpe was right. I was nothing more than a vessel for Keston to have sex with. A willing, eager participant. So, so eager that the hot shame of embarrassment flushed through me, and I tossed my phone aside.

My buzzer rang, but I ignored it. It rang again and again. Annoyed, I stomped over to the intercom.

"Who is this? Stop ringing my bell."

"It's Keston. Wanna go for a ride?"

CHAPTER FIVE
KESTON

I had a need for speed that night. To escape the walls closing in on me.

Along with the apartment, Carlos had left me his Harley. And though I rarely took it out, there I was, zipping up FDR Drive, then across town to Bailey's apartment. I'd had a shitty week, and seeing Bailey would put me in a better mood.

It didn't look like he was of the same mindset, though, as he slowly walked down the steps of the brownstone to meet me on the sidewalk.

"A motorcycle?" He eyed it with suspicion. "What do you expect me to do with that?"

I tossed him a helmet, and he caught it reflexively. "You? Nothing. I do the driving. You just have to hold on."

"Guys like me don't ride on motorcycles," he muttered. "I think that's the Eleventh Commandment. *Thou shalt not do stupid things that can cause broken bones.*"

"Don't worry, Grandma. You'll be fine."

All week a dark fog suffocated me, things beyond my control filling me with self-doubt, feeling like that worthless kid again. It had put me in a funk that had me snapping at people like Jodi, which in turn had made me angry at myself because she was innocent and just happened to be in the way of my nasty mood.

All that ugliness lifted at the sight of Bailey's outraged face. Damn, he was cute. And just the person I needed to wash away the shame of my bad behavior. I straddled the bike.

"Come on."

He slid onto the seat behind me and gingerly put his arms around my waist. I started the bike, and he jumped and tightened his hold.

"I am so gonna kill you if I get killed," he shouted in my ear as I traveled toward the park. I grinned.

"You're gonna love it."

He remained quiet until we got on the West Side highway. "Where are we going?"

"Someplace I know."

"Thanks for narrowing that down."

The sun had begun its descent, and the city lights brightened the sky above the Hudson River. I could feel Bailey's warmth through his jacket and his breath on my neck. It was only a short ride to Fort Tryon Park, and I pulled into a parking spot by Margaret Corbin Circle and cut the motor.

"This is it." I slid off the bike and pulled off my helmet, and Bailey did the same.

"Where is 'this'?" He craned his neck. "I have no idea where we are."

"Not that uptown, are you, City Boy? Haven't you ever been to the Cloisters? It's in here—Fort Tryon Park. Let's go this way." When I realized he wasn't at my side, I stopped. "What's wrong?" I retraced my steps to where he remained.

"Why am I here?" Bailey asked, jaw resolute.

After our dinner earlier that week, after Bailey had deliberately pushed my buttons to get me to talk, I'd decided to forget him. I had no desire to bare my soul—I was only interested in getting naked. I'd avoided relationships for exactly that reason. I'd been fine on my own, and I was satisfied. It didn't mean anything that on a particularly stressful day, I'd reached for my phone to text Bailey to see if he wanted to get together. Halfway through, though, I'd remembered he wasn't interested in ending up in bed with me, so I'd deleted the message and gone home, alone and frustrated.

Then I'd started getting my income and expenses together for quarterly taxes, and the decline in the shop's take was worrying. Jodi's clients had kept us busy initially, but that had slowed significantly during the year. I'd never had to rely on marketing or advertising—word of mouth had always been enough. But numbers didn't lie, and I needed to figure out something because I didn't want to have to lay anyone off. Ambrose had been with me since the beginning, and Jodi was a single mom with two kids and depended on her income from here, as her piece of shit ex had bailed when their second kid had been diagnosed with autism.

I had no one to talk to about my fears. If I confided in Ambrose, he'd think I was hinting he might be on the way out. And I wouldn't tell Grady. I couldn't. He was so damn smart and such a success, I didn't want him to think less of me. Be the brother who couldn't make it. Carlos had run the shop with no problems, all on his own, and had entrusted me with its legacy.

Bailey might understand, but still I hesitated. I loved having sex with him, and he was funny as hell to talk to, but I didn't want him to think we were getting close.

And yet...I couldn't help thinking he was the one I needed, so instead of calling or texting and risking him blowing me off, I'd decided to take a chance and simply show up at his place.

"I-I'd like to talk to you. I need some advice."

"Oh." Obviously, he hadn't expected that, and immediate concern rose in his eyes. "Sure. Whatever you want."

We walked through the parking lot and sat on a low rock wall. A smattering of stars lay like one of those diamond necklaces against a black velvet background, and we could hear the *whoosh* of cars on the highway. Lights from across the Hudson glowed, shimmering hazily on the surface of the water. All the people in those buildings, living their lives, never knowing we were out there, hanging by a thread. Maybe they were as well.

"It's the shop. I'm getting close to running at a loss for the first time, and I don't know what to do about it." A nervous sweat broke out on my brow.

"How bad?"

"Not terrible yet, but I'm afraid if I don't stop the bleeding, I'm gonna have to fire someone, and I...can't."

Saying the words broke me, and Bailey put his hand over mine. "I'm sorry. Really. Tell me the details."

I pulled up the info on my phone and explained. He listened carefully and took some notes on his. When I was finished, he frowned.

"What's your advertising budget? Do you run specials or do anything to entice customers?"

"I've never had to." The thought made my stomach hurt. "Do you think it can help?"

"Sometimes, but it's not a cure-all. The economy ebbs and flows, and the ones who play it smart are the ones able to ride it out and stay successful. We have to learn to roll with it or go under. The city is a jungle, eat or be eaten."

"That's for damn sure," I muttered.

"Here's what I'd do. Run a new-client special to start. Get friendly with the local merchants, especially the ones you frequent, like the neighborhood coffee shop and sushi restaurant, and ask if they'd be willing to have your cards in their places in exchange for you having their menus in yours."

"Do you think that can help?" I was willing to try anything to keep us running. "People have been coming to me for years, but now I'm only getting a trickle of new clients."

Bailey thought for a moment. "You know, sometimes you're around for so long, you become part of the landscape and people almost forget you're there. They pass by your shop but don't see you."

Unfortunately, that made sense.

He gave my hand a comforting squeeze. "Don't be so worried. We can work on it. Today the world is driven by social media, especially businesses concentrating on artistic expression. Do you know anyone who could do it for you?"

"Between Jodi, Ambrose, and me, we can figure it out, I bet."

"I'm surprised you don't already have an Instagram or some online presence. It's made for creatives like yourself. But you're definitely not too late. Set up an Instagram account and put your best designs on there. Mention the new-client special—I have no idea how much a tattoo costs. What is it, twenty or thirty bucks on average for a small one?"

Instead of being insulted, I busted out laughing. "You're kidding, right?"

Seeming a little lost, Bailey lifted a shoulder. "What? Too little? What the hell do I know?" He pulled up his jacket and sweater sleeve. "Remember? Virgin skin."

I eyed the swirls of hair on his forearm and the thin, blue-green lines of his veins. My mouth dried, and I forced my gaze away, looking anywhere but at him.

"A basic tattoo, the smallest, is a hundred. A full sleeve can run into the thousands for the work, plus I charge for my time." As I spoke, Bailey's eyes grew wide.

"Jesus. I'm in the wrong profession," he joked. "I had no idea."

"Yeah, well, there's the drawing of the piece, the transfer to the skin, then the needlework and filling in the color. It's intense, precise work that can't be rushed." Maybe I sounded defensive, but I wanted him to understand that although I might not've gone to college, I was still smart and capable.

"I know." His eyes—filled with questions—met mine. "If you think I'm doubting you, you're wrong. I have complete faith in your abilities. I saw the photos of your art in the shop. You're extremely talented and smart as hell." A smile tugged up the corners of his lips. "After all, you're here with me. And I'm a catch."

I had no response, and despite the coolness of the air, we sat for a while, the sky darkening above us. On occasion, other people would walk by, their conversations muted, but they left us alone and found their own spots.

Still holding my hand, Bailey turned it to expose my wrist and the small heart. "I noticed this the first time we were together. What does it say inside? The writing's so tiny, I can't make it out."

No one had ever asked me. I tried to keep it hidden, and it was small enough to be barely noticeable. But Bailey had, and now he waited, the moonlight reflecting in his eyes.

"It says 'Me.' Carlos did it on my eighteenth birthday."

Bailey's fingers slid upward to trace the outline. "You finally loved yourself," he murmured, shocking me with his insight.

We sat staring at each other until the scream of fire-engine sirens broke the peace of the night.

"You've never been here?"

Bailey shook his head.

"No. The farthest I've been uptown is Columbia for something law-related. And of course, the Bronx Zoo, but I haven't been there in years."

"Carlos was from here." I had no idea why I shared that with Bailey. "He taught me everything about tattooing and the business. He was murdered by some punks while walking to the bank to deposit cash. I told him to wait and we'd do it together, that it wasn't safe to walk alone with that much money, but he laughed at me and said I was acting like an old lady."

Bailey pressed his leg to mine, the warmth from his skin a balm to my frozen heart. "I'm so sorry. Did they ever catch them?"

I nodded, lost in the past. "The next day. Dumbasses used his credit cards." Bailey's hand on my knee hurt because for the first time, my heart wasn't bleeding with pain but pounding with the need to be held and comforted, and I didn't know what to do about it. I squeezed my eyes shut for a moment. "What I am today is because of him. He left me the shop, his apartment...everything. His family kicked him out years earlier when he told them he was gay. He said I was his family."

"And you loved him."

I felt the weight of his eyes on me and met his gaze. "Yeah."

"You were lucky to have him."

"I know. I can't let him down."

"You haven't, and you won't. From what I've seen, you've done an amazing job keeping the shop in business. And busy. This is probably a minor blip, and if you get past it, you'll be fine." He chewed his lip. "If you need my help with anything, I'm more than happy to lend a hand. Like I said, your talent is obvious, and I'm not saying that simply to get you to come home with me."

"Is that an offer?"

Bailey's teeth flashed white. "Are you accepting? If you say yes, that's a contract and I can force compliance."

I leaned in close. "You wouldn't have to force me." I was ready to give this man anything he wanted.

A slow smile crept across his face, and I pulled out the keys to the Harley. "Ready?"

He held out his hand, and I took it. Bailey's fingers twined with mine, and it was nice to hold someone's hand again. I wasn't one for PDA, but Carlos had been the demonstrative type and used to tease me that he wanted to show off he had a young, hot boyfriend.

We walked back to the bike, put on our helmets, and this time, he pressed up against me and hugged my waist nice and tight. It was a swift ride to his place, and I eased up in front and cut the engine. He got off, but I remained in the seat.

"You got used to the bike pretty quickly."

He held on to the helmet. "Yeah. I was scared at first, but then it was kind of a thrill." He dangled his house keys. "Can I interest you in another kind of thrill ride?"

I slid off the Harley and followed him up the stairs, my desire increasing with each passing step. I'd barely entered his apartment before he took my mouth in a bruising kiss. His tongue and lips were everywhere, licking and sucking, his breath hot and heavy. I ran my hands over his body, touching him everywhere, and pushed the jacket off his shoulders. I shrugged out of my jacket and sweater, leaving them in a heap on the floor.

"It hurt riding with a hard-on," he whispered and bit my earlobe, sending a jolt through me. I cupped his bulge.

"I'm ready to ride you. Let's go."

Our clothes came off, landing in all directions, and I devoured his naked body as he stood in front of me. He palmed my dick, and I groaned at the touch, precome slipping through his fingers.

"Fuck me, Keston. I need this."

"On the bed," I ordered, but first he got out the lube and condoms. I coated my fingers and pistoned them into his quivering hole, stretching him. The wild noises coming from Bailey were almost enough to make me shoot my load, but I gritted my teeth and withdrew to roll the condom down my shaft. As desperate as I was to have him, I couldn't begin without kissing the soft skin where the base of his spine dipped and rose to the plump, smooth globes. I spread his cheeks and sank into his waiting body.

"Oh God," Bailey moaned. "Harder, harder," he demanded, and I complied, my fingers digging into his hips as I thrust deep and buried myself in his white-hot passage. Lust consumed me, and I was catapulted into a swirling abyss of hungry need.

My head spun and my heart thundered as Bailey swallowed me into his body, and I shattered as he squeezed my throbbing cock. We collapsed on the bed, my sweaty body plastered to his.

"Don't leave," Bailey mumbled, and I smiled against his neck.

"I don't think I can move."

The scary thing was, even if I could, I didn't want to.

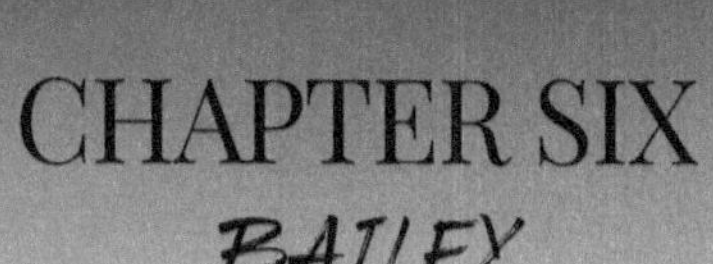

CHAPTER SIX
BAILEY

I awoke with a start, darkness swallowing me. Sweat dampened my brow, and I blinked to clear the shadows from my mind. My watch glowed 5:25 a.m. on the nightstand. My usual wake-up time during the workweek, but not on a weekend for damn sure.

Next to me, still sleeping, was Keston. It had been a shock that he'd agreed to stay. I'd figured after that night of confessions, he'd want to fuck me and forget me, but it was nice to know we'd most likely have another go-around before he left. Yeah, my ass ached like a bitch, but I sure as hell wasn't going to say no.

Keston sighed in his sleep and turned on his back, the sheet slipping, allowing me to devour his naked body. I'd been having sex since I was a teenager, but no one I'd ever been with possessed his pure physical perfection. And while it was usually about the sex, Keston's dry wit was also a turn-on.

Fuck it, who was I kidding? I had the hots for the whole gorgeous package.

Itchy from dried sweat and Keston's come, I decided to take a shower and slipped out of bed. I closed the door behind me to keep the sound from disturbing him and turned the taps on. Steamy hot water poured down on me, and I luxuriated in the heat. I drizzled body gel in my hand and spread the foamy bubbles everywhere. It had cost me a fortune, but it was an indulgence I didn't mind splurging on. When you grew up watching every penny, the little luxuries in life meant everything.

I finished and toweled off, wondering if Keston had any plans for the day. I realized what I was doing and I grew angry with myself. There I went again, puppy-dogging. I'd already ignored Dr. Sharpe's advice by having sex with Keston. The least I could do was not follow him with my tongue hanging out.

"Dumbass. He got what he wanted all along, and you fell for it." Yet the despair in his eyes from the previous night was real and not a pretense to get me naked. He'd come to me with a real problem. Not his brother or a friend. There had to be something there, aside from sex. Or maybe I was too damn hopeful.

It was why I'd been in therapy for over fifteen years. Low self-esteem from my mother's abandonment, filling that void with sex, always falling for unattainable men, hoping someone would love me. I was almost forty and damn tired of the scene. I'd become *that guy*. The regular at all the clubs. The one they could always count on for a quick blowie in the bathroom. The extra, fun gay to round out their dinner parties or brunches. That was what they saw because it was all I let them see. But fuck...this past year, seeing Grady fall for his girlfriend and Weston and Brenner coupled up, so nauseatingly in love, I wanted what they had.

And if I thought maybe I'd found someone who might be interested, he usually was. Only not with me. They wanted someone younger. Richer. Hotter. I'd tried it all—dating apps, lunch meet-ups, dinner dates, cruises....God, it was pathetic. I was pathetic. Was I ever going to realize I'd missed my chance and should let it go? Some people were meant to be alone, and I was one of them.

Keeping quiet, I dressed, letting Keston sleep. But being awake meant needing coffee, so I fixed myself some and took it to the seat at the bay window. I finished my first cup and refilled it, returning to the window. As I sipped, I stared out at the street, mostly empty, aside from parents with strollers, and dog walkers.

"Any of that left for me?"

Keston stood in the archway between the living room and hallway, wearing only his briefs and a half smile. God, I wished I could frame that picture because if anyone ever asked me what my perfect man looked like, Keston half-naked and sleepy-eyed, and with all that messy, dark, silky hair would be who sprang to mind.

"Uh, yeah. Sure. I'll get you some. How do you like it?" I put my mug on the ledge.

"Black as sin."

I poured it out and brought it to him. He drank it in one long swallow. Fascinated, I watched him lick his lips.

"Speaking of sin..." He turned around, and as if tethered to him, I followed him to the bedroom. He set the empty mug on the night table, and with one hand pushed me to the bed.

I gazed up at his serious face. "What?"

"I'm thinking how I want you. On your knees or on your back."

"Stay here all day, and you can have it both ways."

Those blue eyes gleamed. "Yeah? You're not busy, Uptown Boy? No brunchie brunch with your lawyer buddies?" He eased off his briefs, and his dick sprang free.

"Yeah, so what? Come with me." *Whoa. That slipped out.*

Keston snorted. "Oh, sure. Your friends would really go for that."

My temper spiked. "Hey. You don't know them. They're good people, down to earth and nonjudgmental. Seems like you're the one with the hang-ups."

"I like seeing you get all riled up. It's hot." Keston crawled on the bed with me. "I want you face-to-face so I can shut that mouth of yours."

Annoyed as I was, the moment his lips brushed mine I lost the ability to form a coherent sentence. But it wasn't only me affected. I could see by his widening eyes, their blue turning bright as sapphires. How his nostrils flared. The rapid beat of his heart when I rested my hand on his chest. His dick dripped precome, joining the mess I'd already made on my stomach.

He rolled on the condom, and I braced myself for him to ram it in me like he'd done the previous night, but no. Not this time. Keston inched in. Slowly. Taking his time, placing kisses on my face and neck while he slid in. I wanted it hard, and I dug my heels into the bed, tilting my hips.

"Fuck, Bailey, you're sucking my dick into you. I wanted to take it easy because of last night."

"Screw that. Give it all to me. Make me feel."

His brows drew together, but I slid a hand around his nape and locked my ankles behind his waist, burying him completely. He moaned, his eyes fluttering shut.

"Dammit. I swear it's like my dick's on fire every time it's inside you."

"Burn, baby, burn." I snickered, until he touched my prostate and I cried out with pleasure-pain. "Oh, fuck." I worked my dick furiously, each brush against it sending white-hot bursts of electricity through my blood.

Realizing he'd hit that spot, Keston thrust hard and fast, pushing me to the edge. I lost sense of where and who I was other than a throbbing element of lust, need, and desire. He pounded into me, and my aching cock exploded in my hand.

I quivered and shook on his shaft, my body squeezed so tight, I could feel each hot pulse as he emptied into the condom. His mouth settled over mine, and we breathed life into each other.

"I don't think I even said good morning," I whispered.

"It sure as hell is." Keston pulled out slowly, got rid of the condom, and got to his feet. "Can I take a shower?"

"My water is yours."

I watched him leave and sighed. I could cancel brunch and spend the day with Keston, but dammit, what was I going to therapy for if I was going to ignore everything my doctor said?

But Keston reappeared, naked and gleaming, dark hair wet and hanging in his face, and I sat up and blurted, "I was serious, you know. You could come to brunch. We do it almost every weekend. It's Grady's friends—West and Brenner. I think you've met them. It could be fun—" I stopped, seeing his frown.

"Sorry. I'm working. Gotta get downtown and go home to change first." He dressed, then circled the bed, leaned over and kissed me, much softer and sweeter than I'd anticipated. "Thanks for the advice last night. I'm gonna look into it. Bye."

No mention of getting together another time. Dammit, he could've at least pretended he wanted to see me again. I watched him walk out, and when I heard the *click* of the door lock, I fell back on the bed with a sigh. *Another one bites the dust.*

**

"So what'd you do last night? Did you have a date?" West poured me a mimosa. He and Brenner had ordered a spread from Citarella, and there were the usual bagels, lox, cream cheeses, and all kinds of sides.

I sipped and debated whether to say anything. Keston hadn't said to keep what happened between us a secret, and I was the type who lived for shock value. Being so friendly with Grady, it was possible Weston and Brenner knew something more about Keston than I did. Sure, he was fucking gorgeous and had a magic dick, but I wanted to dig below the surface to the layers of pain built on a foundation of hurt and betrayal.

"Not exactly." My teeth sank into an everything bagel with a healthy schmear of cream cheese and piled high with lox. "*Mmm.* You two know how to throw the best brunch."

Ignoring my comment on their brunch prowess, Brenner rolled his eyes. "Not exactly? What does that mean? A wild sex party?"

I finished chewing. "I hooked up with Keston. And it wasn't the first time." I waited for the explosion and was not disappointed.

Brenner's jaw dropped, and his blue eyes popped wide. "Keston? As in Grady's brother? *That* Keston?"

"Bailey, you dog." A wicked grin kicked up Weston's lips. "How the hell did that even happen? I wouldn't think you two ran in the same circles."

"Well, that's not snobbish at all, West," I remarked, my tone mild but with enough of a rebuke that he flushed bright red.

"I didn't mean anything other than from what Grady's told me, Keston's pretty much a loner, and I know you're big into the pickup and party scenes."

Ouch. Those words, though unintentional, still hurt. More than I'd ever let on, but that was me. King of hidden emotions. I took another sip of my drink. "Well, aren't differences what make the world go around? Are you and Brenner exactly alike?" I held up a hand. "No, don't answer that. You are. Both lawyers, great-looking..."

"That's surface stuff." West frowned and glanced at Brenner, who shrugged. "Part of why it was hard for us to get together was that we were too busy living in the past and concentrating on why we didn't like each other."

"Maybe so," I agreed. "But you sure changed quickly once you got together."

"I guess we realized what we had in common was more important than our differences."

At his pat phrase, I mentally rolled my eyes. Weston could give up the practice of law and write greeting cards.

"So why can't that be the same for Keston and me? Despite our differences, we found something in common."

Brenner made a face. "Sex?"

"I didn't say it. You did. And I must say, you two seem very hung up on it."

"Come on, Bailey. We're just confused, is all. From what we've seen, your type is...well...guys like you. Nice guys, white-collar professionals, straight arrows. Keston ticks none of those boxes. He's...different. Foster care treated him rougher than it did Grady. It took the two of them a while to trust each other, and they're brothers."

This brunch was becoming tedious, and I had places to be. I drained my mimosa, popped the last of my bagel into my mouth, and wiped my lips. "Guess you don't know me like you think. Keston ticks all my boxes, which is what matters. You two have been together for what, a little over a year? Yet you think you're gonna lecture me on relation-ships?" I rose to my feet. "Thanks for the bagel and booze, but I have to go."

I walked away, Weston and Brenner on my heels, protesting.

"No, Bailey, please, come on. Stay."

I held up my hand. "I'm not mad at you. I'm being honest. I really do have someplace to be."

Brenner followed me to the door. "Bailey, you know we're only concerned because we care about you."

"So much uproar because I bumped uglies a few times with Keston. I wouldn't worry about it. It was fun, but now it's finished. Like you said, we're not each other's type. I took a walk on the wild side for a change. Talk soon."

I left and called a car to Brooklyn. With Saturday traffic, it would take me about forty-five minutes to reach my mother, which gave me plenty of time to ruminate over our upcoming visit. Good thing I'd already lubricated myself with a few mimosas, although I might need a whole bottle of something stronger by the time I finished.

Instead of thinking of what was to come, I chose to sink into the pleasure of the previous night. I'd mentioned walking on the wild side, and I hadn't been kidding. Keston had unlocked something primitive inside me I'd thought had died years ago. That total abandon to the most elemental part of me.

Desire. Lust. Need.

Too many weekends had found me getting screwed by guys who were in it for themselves, and once they got off, zipped up and were out and gone. Did I make it easy for them? Yeah, but a guy got lonely, and sometimes anything was better than nothing.

The car pulled up to my father's house. Now my mother's. The word tasted bitter on my tongue. When it came to her, I would've been a hell of a lot better off with nothing.

"Thanks," I said to the driver and stood on the sidewalk, gathering strength, courage, and my sanity before putting one foot after the other and unlocking the front door.

"Who's that?" she called from the living room.

Of course the television was on—it played continuously from morning until she left for the evening. Dinners with wealthy men she found on dating apps she claimed she used to keep the loneliness at bay.

"It's me."

I entered the living room to see her lying on the couch, feet up, a cigarette between red-tipped fingers. A half-empty bottle of vodka sat on the coffee table, the glass drained save for some ice cubes. A plate filled with ashy butts was next to it. The air smelled stale. I coughed.

"Hello, Jennifer. Isn't it a little early for the hard stuff?" I sat in the threadbare club chair.

"Judgmental much? It's only my first drink." She took a drag and blew out the smoke. "I have a dinner reservation at six, and I always have one while I get ready."

I had to hand it to her. She looked damn good—almost sixty, yet she could pass for twenty years younger, thanks to facials, fillers and Botox, glossy hair extensions, and dieting.

"Why don't you cancel and have dinner with me?" I could predict the answer, and I was correct.

"I would if I could, but Marshall is taking me to Jean-Georges, and you *know* how hard it is to get a rezzy there." She splashed more vodka into the tumbler. "I couldn't disappoint him." Thick lashes fanned down for a moment, and then she turned the full force of luminous blue eyes on me. "He's such a generous man. Look what he had sent over for me."

She held out her arm, and the lights picked up the gleam of gold on her wrist. Her lips curved upward in a smile. "It's so nice to be appreciated by a man for once."

Inwardly I seethed at the not-so-subtle dig at my father.

"What're you doing this week?" I asked, attempting to make conversation. "Have you looked for a job?"

She stubbed out her cigarette. "No, and you can stop harassing me. I have enough from your father's pension and the World Trade Center payment for his 9/11 sickness that I don't need to stand on my feet for seven hours a day. I still don't understand why you work for yourself, when you could make twice as much with a big law firm."

Because they'd never divorced, my mother was entitled to my father's pension, as if it were a line-of-duty death. I resented it, not because I wanted the money, but because she didn't deserve it. Not to mention, she'd blown through the money all her ex-boyfriends had given her. Her whole life had been spent figuring out ways to weasel money from people.

Dramatic as always, she huffed and threw her hands in the air, the dark waves dancing past her shoulders. "Just like your father. No ambition."

"Leave Dad out of this," I warned. "I don't want to hear it."

But she ignored me. "He never looked to climb the ladder, make detective or anything higher."

"My father was a people's cop. Working within the community. Not someone who wanted to sit behind a desk. Besides, he—"

"He was a loser." Finished with her drink, she rose to her feet, her silky robe swirling around her thin frame. "I have to get ready for my date."

"Loser?" I spat, jumping out of my chair, shaking with rage. "You call a man who stepped up when his wife walked out on him and his four-year-old child a loser? Someone who gave his life for the city? That's no loser. That's a hero."

As usual, she didn't bother to pay attention and walked past me toward the stairs. "Call me soon, Bailey. We can do lunch." She disappeared up the landing.

I wished I were the type who could give no fucks, walk out, and say to hell with her. But my father's dying words stuck with me.

"I know she let you down, but she's back now. She's all you have left. I don't want you to be alone after I'm gone."

That was the problem. Having a mother like Jennifer was no better than being alone.

In the car on the way home, my phone buzzed. Seeing it was Keston, my pulse accelerated.

Feel like hooking up?

I laughed, shaking my head. Keston had no qualms about getting straight to the point. But I guessed that was what a fuck buddy was, and considering I didn't think I'd be hearing from him again, seeing him later was the best way to finish off the day.

I'm hungry. How about dinner first?

K

Yep, definitely a man of few words.

I'll meet you at your shop.

No. I'll come to you. Have to change first.

That worked for me. Seeing Keston would dull the pain and anger of the visit with my mother. Hopefully by the end of the night, I wouldn't remember it at all.

CHAPTER SEVEN
KESTON

I paced the sidewalk in front of Bailey's brownstone, wondering if the fact that he wasn't home was a sign that I should bounce while I could. What the hell was I doing, getting involved with one of Grady's friends? A guy who probably never missed a credit card payment and was on a first-name basis with his dry cleaner. A lawyer, for Christ's sake, with expensive body wash in his shower. Not my kind of guy at all.

So why was I here? Why did I want to see him so damn badly? He made me laugh, set my body humming with pleasure. And after our talk at the Cloisters, I'd felt this connection to him like no one else—since Carlos. I raked my hand through my hair. Three times now I'd have seen him. This was a bad idea. I should leave. I should—

"Keston?"

I turned toward the street and watched as Bailey stepped out of a car. Damn, he looked edible. No suit and tie today for Bailey the Lawyer. Dark, messy hair falling over his brow, jaw covered by stubble, and the biggest, bluest eyes behind a sexy pair of black-framed glasses I hadn't seen him wear before. I liked it. As quickly as ice cream in the hot sun, all my misgivings about another night with him melted away.

"Hey, Bailey."

"You looked about to bolt. Everything okay?"

"Yeah." I could skip dinner and go right to dessert. "Wanna go inside?"

The look he gave me indicated that he wasn't on the same track. "I thought we were gonna have something to eat. First." His smile spoke of hot, sweaty sheets in my future.

"Okay, well, you know this neighborhood. I never come up here."

"Follow me to Columbus. Lots of places there."

Side by side, we walked down the leafy street, dodging couples wheeling babies or walking their furry designer dogs. I stuck my hands into my pockets.

"What made you want to live all the way up here?" It was nice, I'd give him that. A hell of a lot less crowded than the East Village and with a family vibe I couldn't really relate to.

"Why? Am I geographically undesirable because I live above Thirty-fourth Street?"

"I never said you were undesirable."

"Just my location. I did offer to meet you at your shop. Any reason you said no?"

Plenty, but none I was willing to mention if I still wanted to get laid tonight. "I like seeing how the other half lives." I knocked his shoulder so he'd know I was teasing. "And your bed's a lot comfier than mine."

"*Mmm*, yeah. Okay. Well, we can do burgers, sushi, Italian...you pick."

"How about pizza?"

"Sure. Right here." We stopped in front of Motorino.

"Didn't know they had a place up here. I go to the one by me in the East Village." I opened the door. "I'll grab a table."

"What kind of pie do you want?" Bailey waited on the short line. "And what do you want to drink?"

"I'm pretty easy—pepperoni, sausage, mushrooms. I'm fine with any or all of it. And water's good."

"I'm a sausage man myself." Bailey winked. Corny as his joke was, my lips twitched, and I sat, admiring his ass as he placed the order. He returned to the table with two waters. "Here. It'll be a little while." He clasped his hands around the bottle. "How was business today? Lots of people?"

Small talk was one of my least favorite things to do, but considering I'd asked him for help with Inktastic, he had that right. Bailey waited, face expectant, as if he were interested in me and what I had to say.

"Funnily enough, yeah." Instead of brushing him off, I thought about my answer. "I told Jodi about your suggestions, and at lunch she ran out and bought one of those folding boards, you know? She made a new-client-special sign and put it outside the shop."

"Great idea."

Encouraged, I nodded. "I thought so. I got a mom who came after brunch with her girlfriends and a few tourists stopping by who wanted a memento of their trip to the city. So thanks."

"My pleasure." He chugged some water. "What's this month's most popular design?"

I grinned. "Believe it or not, it's *Mom* written inside a heart. Corny, huh?"

The twinkle in his blue eyes died, and I wondered why. "Yeah. Really corny."

"I spoke to Jodi about setting up a social media profile, and she said she could do it, no problem."

Bailey brightened. "That's great. Between that and some local advertising, I bet you'll turn your problems around."

"Yeah. I hope so."

He turned silent, and I didn't push. The counter guy called out, "Bailey. Sausage pie." He didn't jump up, so I decided to leave him be and get the pizza myself.

Back at the table, he gave me a halfhearted smile. "Sorry."

"No problem. Let's eat."

I ate my slice with short, quick bites, chewing and swallowing without tasting much. The second went down the same while Bailey still worked on his first. I picked up my third, and Bailey put a hand over mine.

"Hey, chill out. We have all night."

My instinct was to snap at him to mind his own fucking business. But remembering the therapy Grady and I had taken together when we'd first met and the tools it had given me to deal with hurt and abandonment, I curbed my anger. "Yeah. Sure."

He didn't know—how could he? A foster child couldn't be certain they would have a hot meal or a bed to sleep in every night. Life was lived on a wing and a prayer. I'd learned to take what I wanted as soon as it was in front of me, otherwise someone else would. But I sat and drank my water, watching Bailey catch up.

"I'm full. You still gonna eat that?" He tipped his head toward my plate, and I realized I hadn't eaten the third slice. And didn't want to. Maybe Bailey was right, and I should slow down and taste my food. I liked watching him eat. The way his tongue licked his lips, picking up stray crumbs and a bit of sauce. How his eyelids fluttered with appreciation of how good the pizza tasted.

I raised a brow and returned the slice to the pie tray. "No. Not now. Maybe later."

"Much later." His grin sent a throb of desire through me. "After." He rose to his feet. "I'll get a box to take it home with us."

Home. Funny how that word had never had meaning to me until I met Carlos. And then it was all taken away, and I knew it wasn't meant for someone like me.

"Keston?"

Bailey waited, and I gathered up the plates and dumped them into the trash.

"Let's go."

We walked out, Bailey holding the box, and somehow my arm ended up around his shoulders. The street was even more crowded now, and a guy decked out in designer logos blocked us from moving forward. Before we could step past him, he kissed Bailey.

"Baby, what's shaking? How's it goin'?" Appreciative brown eyes raked me from head to toe. "I'm thinkin' good."

"Marco. It's been a while." No welcome vibes from Bailey, I noticed. He'd turned stiff–and not in a good way.

"I'm having a party tonight. Maybe you and your *friend* would like to come."

"I don't think so, Marco, but thanks anyway." His gaze flicked to me, and I could see he wanted to leave. Desperately.

"Ready to go?" I rumbled. "It's gonna get cold if we don't eat it soon."

"See you." Bailey pulled me along, and we left Marco standing on the sidewalk. "Fucking asshole," he grumbled as he pulled out the keys to the front door.

Amused but curious, I followed him up to the second floor of the brownstone and into his apartment. "What was that about?"

Bailey shrugged and set the pizza box on the kitchen counter. "Just a guy. Nothing special."

"Not what it looked like to me. He got to you. Old boyfriend?"

"I don't have boyfriends." Bailey pulled out a beer from the fridge and held it up in question. I nodded, and he handed it to me, then crossed the shining wooden floors to sit on the sectional in the living room.

"No? You look like the type."

Bailey's brows drew together. "What does that mean?"

I set my beer bottle on the coffee table and crawled across the sofa to him. "Do you really wanna talk? Or..."

Bailey grabbed my T-shirt at the collar and twisted his fingers in the fabric, pulling me to him. "I like the *or* much, much better," he murmured against my mouth and kissed me.

I sat and pulled him close, our lips still locked together. "*Mmm.* Me too. This is all I could think about. You on top of me. Me inside you."

"I'd like that. I must confess I wasn't sure I'd see you again after last night." Thick dark lashes swept down on his cheeks.

Damn, he was sharp. I couldn't even say why I'd texted him—except I'd wanted to see his face.

"Yet here I am."

A crooked grin kicked up his lips. "Yeah. Here you are. In the flesh." He leaned in and settled his lips on mine. That position gave me a chance to run my hands over his broad shoulders and back. Bailey rocked his pelvis into mine while plunging his tongue past my lips. I sucked hard, the need to possess this man growing by the second.

"So fucking hot, Bailey. I watched you eat that pizza, and you almost made me come in my pants."

He reached between us and squeezed our dicks. My head spun, and my cock throbbed, painfully hard and swollen.

"Let's go."

I yanked him up with me, and we tore off our clothes. What the hell was happening that every time I got near this man, I had to have him? He took off his glasses and vivid blue eyes watched me as I stroked my shaft.

"You are so beautiful."

Compliments rolled off me. I didn't need them. I'd heard them all my life, and I knew they were given easily to get me in the sack. But Bailey's made me self-conscious, and I wanted to change the subject. I hovered above him and dipped my head to bite at his nipples. Our hard cocks brushed together. "What do you like?"

His hand slipped around my neck. "You. I like you."

I reached for the condom and lube, when Bailey's phone buzzed. I hesitated. "Need to get that?"

"Fuck it," he rasped. "In me. Now."

The phone stopped and started again. It kept ringing.

"It's a buzzkill." I sat on the edge of the bed, found Bailey's pants, and handed him the ringing phone. "Just answer it."

"Dammit." Bailey took it from me, and his eyes widened when he checked the screen. "Shit. Okay. Belinda? What's the matter?"

"Bailey, I need you." Her scared, shrill voice was loud enough for me to hear.

"Calm down and tell me what's wrong." Bailey sat up and grabbed his glasses.

"It's Jonas. He's outside yellin' that he don't want me seeing nobody else. He's so mad."

I watched as Bailey morphed from a naked hot guy with a big dick to a hard-faced, sharp-eyed lawyer. "When did this happen?"

He put the phone on speaker and started to get dressed. I sighed, knowing my fun evening was ruined. I found my scattered clothes and pulled on my briefs.

"J–just now. I had a date—met this guy for coffee, and then he walked me home and kissed me good-bye. Next thing I know, Jonas is here, yelling at me, calling me a whore. He keeps banging on my door. I don't know what to do."

The fear in her voice made me sick. I'd seen enough of this shit growing up.

Bailey kept his cool and pulled a brush through his bed head. "Call the police and tell them your ex-boyfriend violated his order of protection. I should be there within forty minutes, maybe sooner."

"I-I'm sorry, Bailey. I didn't wanna call you on a Saturday, but—"

"Not a problem. That's what I'm here for. Don't let anyone in but the police or me. They'll have ID, and you know my voice. I'll see you soon."

He ended the call, and I stuck my feet into my sneakers. "I'm ready to go."

In the middle of shoving his phone into his pocket, Bailey gave me an apologetic smile. "Sorry. I can't tell her no."

" 'Course not, she's a client. No problem. We can pick it up another day, if you want?"

"What? Yeah, sure."

Or not, guessing from his absentminded answer. But I could understand that Belinda took precedence, since she seemed to be in danger. Somehow that made Bailey even more desirable. Most lawyers I'd met put their cases second to their personal life—except Grady, but he was my brother and I was a little prejudiced in his favor.

Out on the sidewalk, a car waited. Bailey gave me a kiss on the cheek. "I'll see you."

"Want me to come along? In case it gets messy?" The words tumbled out of my mouth. *Why the hell did I say that?*

Behind the sexy black frames, those big blue eyes widened. "Uh, that doesn't sound fun for you. Hopefully Jonas has sobered up and won't give anyone trouble."

"But he might give *you* trouble."

"I can handle him," Bailey muttered. "It's not the first time." He got into the car, and before I could say anything, he slammed the door and the car drove away, leaving me on the curb.

"Well, that sucks," I grumbled to myself and made my way to the nearest train station. My phone buzzed with a text from Ambrose.

> *Wanna come over for dinner? Carly made tacos, and I made margaritas.*

About to text no, I figured, what the hell. Might as well drown my sorrows in tequila.

> *Sure. Be there in about forty-five minutes.*

Ambrose lived in Brooklyn, in a small one-bedroom apartment. As a foster kid, I'd spent too many years in buildings like his, listening to people fight behind closed doors, the smell of the other tenants' cooking permeating the air, eventually burrowing under your skin so you could never get rid of it. Even now, more than twenty years later, it gave me the chills. Ambrose let me in.

"Dude, what's goin' on? Have a taco."

"Nah, I ate already, but I'll take that margarita." I glanced around the small living room decorated with the miniature ceramic people Carly collected. Every time I visited, I got the willies thinking I was being watched. "Where's Carly?"

"Right here." She stuck her head out of the kitchen, then came to give me a hug. I'd known her almost as long as Ambrose, and though she constantly bugged me to meet people and date, I still liked her. With her platinum bleached hair and colorful skull-tattoo sleeves on both arms, she and Ambrose were a walking billboard for Inktastic. "You smell good."

I chuckled. "Thanks."

"Who was he?" she asked with a knowing smile.

My good mood faded. "What're you talking about? I went for pizza. Must be the tomato sauce."

Her brows shot up. "Honey, I work at Sephora. I know my men's cologne. You never wear any, yet now you are." She sniffed. "I'm thinking Tom Ford. He must be loaded."

"Damn. Am I really getting the third degree 'cause I stood on line next to someone who wears that shit?"

Ambrose gave me a glass filled to the top, and I downed half of it and almost coughed up a lung. Ambrose cackled, and I glared at him. "Jesus. Warn a guy before you hand him a glass filled with almost straight tequila."

"Busy today?" Ambrose sipped his drink.

"Yeah. Nonstop. I'm gonna sleep well tonight. This girl wanted a peacock with every fucking color on her back. Took hours."

"You need this drink, then."

I raised my glass in thanks. "What about you?"

"Visited Lucas. Have you talked to your brother about looking at his case again?"

No, and I wasn't about to, but I couldn't tell Ambrose that. "Not yet."

Ambrose grew agitated. "You talk to him all the time. I thought you'd say something."

"Babe, if Keston said he'd ask, he will," Carly attempted to intervene. "You've got to give him some time."

"All I want is for someone to pay attention. The Innocence Project rejected him. Probably not high profile enough for them," Ambrose chafed and finished the rest of his drink. "I hate seeing him like that, locked up on bogus charges. It's so damn unfair. His lawyer was fucking incompetent. You know how it goes, Keston. We're not rich or connected, so we get the shaft."

Over his bowed head, I met Carly's eyes, and she shook her head. We both knew the score. Lucas could commit murder and be caught holding the smoking gun, and Ambrose would still say he was innocent and the cops had framed him.

I had another drink and managed a taco. "Thanks for dinner. I'm gonna peace out. See you on Monday." After my farewells, I headed toward the train station and figured I'd send Bailey a text.

Everything okay?

Yeah, sure.

Feel like picking up where we left off?

It was late, and I was tired, plus a little buzzed, but I wouldn't mind seeing him again.

Sorry. Can't make it.

Fine. Whatever. Stupid of me to even try. There was always a new guy to take care of what I needed, and much as I had an itch I knew Bailey could scratch, it was better not to get too involved.

CHAPTER EIGHT
BAILEY

"Okay, Lindee, tell me what happened."

In her tiny apartment, I sat facing my scared half sister. Unfortunately, it was a scene played on repeat for years, but as big brother Bailey, I was determined to keep the promise I'd made to my father before he died. *"Take care of your sister. You know your mother won't."*

"I told you. I was out on a date, and afterward Jonas came by. First, he buzzed my apartment, but I didn't let him in. Of course, some idiot in the building opened the door for him. You know he can be charming if he wants."

Debatable. Jonas Thomas was many things—a bully, a fast talker, and a rude son of a bitch. Charming wasn't on my list of adjectives to describe my sister's ex.

"Go on," I prodded.

She played with the ends of her hair. "Uh, well, he banged on the door, insisting I let him come inside and work on our problems. You should be proud of me. I didn't. I listened to you."

First time for everything.

"I am. Very proud. But I thought you were going to try and be alone for a little while. Figure things out, like getting a job."

Jennifer had shown up to lay claim to my father's World Trade Center disability payment, bringing little Belinda with her. When I'd discovered I had a younger half sister, I shouldn't have been as surprised as I was that she had attachment issues. Ten years younger, Belinda had spent her childhood watching our mother move from boyfriend to boyfriend. It was no wonder she'd ended up with a skewed vision of a healthy relationship. I tried to watch out for her, but it was hard enough looking after myself, going to school while my father grew weaker.

"I'm trying to find work, but it's not easy." Tears glittered in her eyes. "I answer ads every day. I just wanted to have a little fun, so I thought I'd join a dating app. This guy was nice—real nice. He didn't try and get in my pants or anything. Just walked me home and gave me a kiss on the cheek."

Unfortunately, she followed her mother's tradition of falling for any man who'd pay attention to her, and at twenty-eight, with a slew of disreputable lovers, she was heading down that same failed road, unless big brother Bailey stepped in to save the day. Which meant filing orders of protection to make sure she was safe. Frustrated as I was, I understood her behavior.

Before Jennifer had returned to my father, there had been little to no stability for poor Belinda. Coupled with a mother who cared only about herself, it wasn't hard to understand why Belinda searched for someone who'd give her the love and attention she'd craved and never had. She'd confided to me that she never knew who her father was—whenever she asked, Jennifer refused to tell her anything other than he was a bastard.

"And Jonas came right after?"

"Uh-huh. Calling me all kinds of names." She tucked her hair behind her ears. "I know you're probably sick of me, and I don't blame you, but please don't leave me, Bailey. You're all I have." Sobbing, she launched herself into my arms.

"*Shh*, I'm not going anywhere." I stroked her back to calm her. "You know I love you. I just want you to be the strong woman I know you're capable of being, and have healthy relationships."

Belinda sniffled into my neck. "Is that even possible for us? You've never had a boyfriend, either. Are you dating anyone?"

I thought of Keston but immediately dismissed him. No matter how gorgeous or incredible he was as a lover, I refused to follow him around, hoping for a sliver of affection. Of one thing I was certain: Keston was not boyfriend material. "No. Nobody."

Her laughter was muffled against my chest. "Our mother—and I use the term loosely—really did a number on us. You're afraid to commit, and I fall for the same kind of jerk over and over." Her wet laughter was anything but humorous. "We all need therapy."

"No kidding," I said lightly. "My doctor is a monthly expense."

"What are you gonna do now?" Belinda wiped her eyes and went to the mirror to fix her makeup.

"First I'll notify the police that Jonas violated his order of protection."

Finished with repairing her face, she hugged me again. "I don't know what I'd do without you, Bailey. Thanks."

"Of course." I couldn't help but hold her tight. No matter what, she was all I had. "I'd better get going."

Shifting her gaze from side to side, Belinda clasped and reclasped her hands, then bowed her head. "I, uh, hate to ask, but..."

I knew. "You're short? How much do you need?"

Cheeks red, she bit her lip. "Whatever you can spare. It's just that I wanted to look pretty for my date, so I got new makeup and had my hair and nails done..."

And spent the last of the money I'd given her for the month.

She tried and failed at so many jobs—sales clerk, receptionist, customer service representative. Every month brought a new career, when the reality was, I helped Belinda stay afloat.

"I'll send it to your bank directly." A few taps on my phone, and I gave her a reassuring smile. "All done."

"I really am gonna try harder to get a job. I promise." Belinda walked me to the door. "Did you see her today?" Her lips pursed as if she'd tasted something bitter.

"Yes. She was getting ready for a date."

"Why do you bother? I bet she didn't ask anything about you, or me. She's only interested in herself." She put a hand on my arm. "You're keeping your promise to your father, aren't you? You're such a good person."

I chucked her under the chin. "I'm the best, don't you know?"

Belinda held me fast. "You are. And I want you to know that it's true, not something I'm sayin' just 'cause you're my brother. You deserve a man who loves you with his whole heart. As much as you always tell me you want me to have a healthy relationship, I worry about you too."

Surprised by her fierceness, I made my usual attempt to brush her off. "No need. I'm a big boy, and I can take care of myself."

But Belinda was as stubborn as she was beautiful and wouldn't let me go. "Everyone needs someone to lean on sometimes. It's not a sign of weakness."

Unwanted tears burned my eyes. "I know. Thanks. I'm doing okay. Promise." I opened the door.

She kissed my cheek. "Thank you, Bailey. I'm gonna make you proud one day. You'll see."

Once outside, I was depressed and worn out. Seeing Belinda and hearing her stories of woe always put me in a lousy mood. On the car ride home, a text from Keston popped up to see if I was interested in finishing what we'd started. I was in no frame of mind to see anyone and told him no, figuring that would be that with him. It was for the best. I had enough on my plate dealing with my family.

And I didn't need anyone. That was the lie I'd keep repeating until I believed it.

**

"Good morning, Bailey," Lincoln, my receptionist, chirped at me when I walked into the office. I rented a small suite in a building on Broadway near the courts, occupied mainly by other lawyers. Maybe if I didn't have unexpected expenses and joined a firm, I could afford better. Every few months, I'd field calls from headhunters looking to see if I'd be interested in merging with boutique firms, but I spurned them all. I liked being my own boss. "How was the weekend?"

Eternally cheerful, Lincoln was a gem of a worker and person. He put up with me and my inability to function until I poured a gallon of coffee down my throat. "Great," I grunted, then remembered to ask about him. "And yours?"

"Terrific. Thanks. Alan and I decided we were going to experience everything the city has to offer. We went to three museums, then walked through the park. Yesterday we had brunch, walked the High Line and the Brooklyn Bridge. My feet are killing me."

I winced. "I'm tired just listening to you."

Lincoln chuckled. "I know it's a lot, but I've been living here for more than a year, and I feel like I barely know the city."

"Well, news flash. I've lived here my whole life, still haven't done it all, and I probably won't."

"Oh, don't say that." Lincoln waved me off. "Did you do anything fun?"

I did. Keston. And sadly, our third time was probably the charm and that was it for us.

"Yeah, it was fine."

"Come on. No date or hot sexy times?"

"I didn't say that." I winked. "I have to take care of something, and then we'll go over the calendar for the week."

In my office, I drank the rest of my coffee, picked up the phone, and contacted Belinda's precinct.

"Hello, this is Bailey Marks. Belinda Rayburn's attorney. I believe she reported her ex-boyfriend, Jonas Thomas, violated the order of protection against her. Am I correct?"

"Hold, please."

It took two full minutes before someone came on again. "Hello? This is Sergeant Mulligan."

"Yes, hello. I'm waiting for confirmation that an order of protection was violated. I'd like to know what steps have been taken."

"Lemme see. It says that the report came in around six thirty p.m. We tried to visit the ex, but he wasn't home."

"And? What about yesterday? Today?"

"Nothing yet."

It took all my strength not to raise my voice and instead play nice. "Jonas Thomas is probably at the piers in downtown Brooklyn. He's a longshoreman. He verbally threatened his ex-girlfriend Saturday night and pounded on her door in an attempt to get inside."

"But he didn't hurt her."

"No, is that supposed to happen for you to do anything?"

I must've come off a little too sarcastic, because Mulligan snapped right back at me.

"No, Counselor. I said we'll look into it, and we will. Is there anything else?"

"No, thanks."

"Okay. We'll be in touch."

With that phone call done, I was about to buzz Lincoln, when my cell phone rang.

"Bailey Marks."

"Bailey, it's Grady. How are you?"

Was Grady calling to find out about me and Keston? This could prove interesting, so I reclined in my chair and waited for the questions.

"I'm well, thanks. And you?"

"Good, good. I'm having a little get-together at my new place this coming Saturday and wanted to invite you. Weston and Brenner will be there as well."

My lips twitched. "And your brother? Will he be there?"

A deep chuckle filled my ear. "Was I being that obvious?"

"Like a brick to the face. Since when are you a *schadkin*? That's Yiddish for matchmaker."

"Well...yeah. Keston will be there. I might've heard the two of you saw each other after that night in the club. You took my advice and went to his shop?"

No need for Grady to know that his brother and I had hooked up more than once. Especially since it wouldn't be happening again.

"Yeah. He has a nice business going there. And as for us seeing each other, I never pictured Weston and Brenner as bigger *yentas* than my grandmother and her cronies used to be. What happened? You all had a Monday morning coffee klatch about how Bailey got lucky? Here I thought big firms like yours were all work and no play."

I wasn't annoyed, but I didn't exactly appreciate being the subject of gossip among my friends.

After a moment of awkward silence, Grady cleared his throat. "I'm sorry. I didn't mean to make you uncomfortable. We weren't talking specifically about you. It simply happened to come up in conversation. Look. I'm a little overprotective of Keston. He's still working through the trauma of a rough childhood, and he internalizes everything and doesn't show his emotions well."

Sound familiar? He could be talking about you.

"He seems to have ended up in a good place—a stable job, a condo, and you two are close."

Grady's sigh filled my ear. "Only recently. I'm not sure Keston really knows how to open up to anyone. It took years before I could say with certainty he trusted me."

"Then I don't think we should be talking about him behind his back."

Whoa. Who was this person defending Keston's right to privacy? He and I had a casual hookup, nothing more. If Grady wanted to talk, it shouldn't matter to me.

"I see."

Dammit. I could easily visualize Grady's smirk.

"Uh, so about that invitation. Yeah. Sure. I'd love to see your new apartment. Where is it?"

"Downtown Brooklyn. I'll give you directions. I know how you city people don't like to cross the bridge."

He should only know. "I'm good, thanks. I'll find it."

"Great." He hesitated. "Okay, listen. Maybe I *am* meddling, but I think the two of you could be good for each other. Keston needs someone stable and secure, and he could bring a little bit of the unexpected to your life. I know how boring it can get staring at documents and filings all day."

I wasn't ready or able to step onto that minefield, and so I chose to ignore it. "I'll see you Saturday night. Bye, Grady."

I got started on my work for the day—setting up a trust for Helen Gottlieb's darling grandchildren—but I couldn't keep my thoughts from straying to my conversation with Grady.

Stable and secure.

Maybe instead of law, I should've gone into acting because I sure as hell must be playing the part of a lifetime by fooling everyone.

CHAPTER NINE
KESTON

I opened the shop on Friday, still smiling from Grady's early morning text.

> *It's almost the fucking weekend. Smile and get ready to party.*

"You are such a dork, brother." I snickered to myself and flicked on the lights.

I didn't plan to stay long at Grady's little get-together—cutesy parties weren't my vibe. But for Grady, I'd suffer through it. With Carlos gone, he was the only constant in my life, the only one I could truly count on.

I checked the computer and was satisfied to see a fully booked workday ahead. And not only today—we were booked into the next month. The social media accounts Bailey had suggested were bringing positive results, and along with the new-client special, now prominently displayed on our sidewalk sign every day, the demand had doubled relative to the previous week. Ambrose had hinted that if things kept up, we could even expand, but I shut that down real quick. Carlos had wanted one spot only, and I agreed with him. I wanted to be confident that every design we placed on someone's body met my exacting standards, and I couldn't do that without seeing the art in person.

Ambrose strolled in. "Morning."

"Hey." I sipped my coffee. "How's it going?"

"Good." He set his backpack on the table. "I am so ready for the weekend."

"Sounds like someone has plans." When Ambrose didn't answer me, I crossed my arms. "What's goin' on?"

"Carly and I have appointments to look at houses."

"Cool. Where?"

His gaze shifted to the floor, and I knew something was up. I set my cup on the counter and waited.

"Uh, Florida."

Shock, anger, and betrayal traveled through me like a live electrical wire, but I refused to let him see it.

"Long commute," was all I said, and picked up my coffee.

"Look, it's not what you think," Ambrose started to explain. "Carly has family there, and she wants to see what's available. That's all."

"Yeah, sure. Of course. I know you love it here."

"I do. You know that. I'm not movin', Keston. I'm doin' it for Carly. I told you we're looking for a house, and that means gettin' married, buying a place... You know how it is."

"Not really. That's why I make my own rules. Nobody's gonna tell me what to do." I paused. "Or where I can live."

Red-faced, Ambrose grew agitated. "And I said I'm not movin'. Dammit, Keston. You know you're my best friend. I'm not goin' anywhere."

I didn't mean to piss him off, but if he was going to bounce on me, I'd like to have a little notice. After everything we'd been through together, was Ambrose gonna leave?

"Chill, dude. If you say you're not, I gotta believe you."

"And yet you don't. I see it in your eyes."

He stomped across the store to his space, and I moved to mine. Usually we talked as we set up, a routine we'd honed over so many years of working together, but today we remained silent. I couldn't stop thinking that Ambrose's days here were numbered and he had one foot out the door.

I took out the disinfectant wipes and turned on the auto-clave to sterilize the equipment. When I'd first come to work for Carlos, I'd never thought about the business side of tattoo-ing. All I'd been interested in was creating designs. My first had trended dark—I'd specialized in the reaper—but once Carlos and I got together, I was able to work past the ugliness and fear of the life I'd left behind. I gave myself permission to expe-rience beauty and happiness in my creations. All that I was, I credited to Carlos and the love and faith he'd had in me. His death had killed that joy, and I refused to let any light in.

"What're you doin' this weekend?" Having worked out his anger on cleaning his chair, Ambrose decided to speak to me again.

"Nothing much. Grady's having a housewarming party—he bought an apartment in Brooklyn—so I'll stop by, then work as usual."

"Man, you gotta get a life. All work and no play and all that jazz."

"*Mmm*," was my only response. I wouldn't mind some playtime, and I debated texting Bailey but held off. If he wasn't invited, I'd feel weird, but I wasn't about to ask Grady and give him the wrong idea that I was interested in Bailey and wanted to see him. Even though I did. I'd play it by ear—if he was at the party, maybe I wouldn't be going home alone.

My first client was a newbie, a woman around thirty who flashed me a nervous smile. "I saw your new-client special on Instagram. I've never had a tattoo."

I put on my caring face. "Don't worry. It's probably best to start with something small so you can see if you're okay with it. Do you have an idea of what you want?"

She nodded and tucked her hair behind her ear. "I want to get something representing my dog. She's my best friend. I was thinking a heart with her face inside."

"That might be a little too intense for a first tattoo. Maybe something simple?" I thought for a moment. "What about a paw print with her name underneath?"

"Ooh, I like that."

"All right. Where do you want it?"

She bit her lip. "Where do most people get them?"

I shrugged. "It depends. On the shoulder, the wrist, or ankle is always a popular choice. But the skin on the ankle is thinner, so you might feel it more than say, on your shoulder."

"Uh, okay. I still think the ankle is best. Her name is Maggie."

"All right, then. Have a seat, and I'll work up the stencil."

A steady stream of clients kept us busy past lunchtime. We finally took a break and ordered in sushi. Of course, Ambrose started in again about his brother.

"Listen, dude. Maybe you can ask your brother to take another look at Lucas's case."

"I dunno, man. It's a party—"

"There's always some excuse," Ambrose snapped, and I quirked a brow at his anger.

"I already told you I would, but we really haven't been in a conducive setting."

"Conducive setting? What the fuck kind of lawyer double-speak is that?" Ambrose sputtered. "You been hanging out with the college boys too much, I'm thinkin'."

The door opened, and fuck if Bailey didn't walk in. In a sleek gray suit and those black-rimmed glasses, he had an undeniably corporate vibe, and the truth was, I liked it. The guy was hot as fuck.

I got to my feet. "What're you doing here?"

"Hello to you too. I had a client in the neighborhood and thought I'd stop by." He waited to be introduced to Ambrose, who remained stiff, eyes narrowed with mistrust.

"Uh, this is my coworker, Ambrose. Ambrose, this is Bailey Marks. He's a friend of Grady's."

Bailey arched a brow as if to say, *Oh, so that's how we're going to handle it?*

"Nice to meet you, Ambrose."

"Yeah." Ambrose hopped off his chair. "I got stuff to do." Without saying good-bye, he gave us his back and left us alone.

"What's his problem?" Bailey asked.

"Nothing. You never answered my question. Why're you here?" I could see Ambrose shooting me disbelieving looks that I was talking to "a suit."

"Are you going to Grady's party?"

I fought against a grin. "Yeah. Are you?" Why did I hope he'd say yes?

Because you want him again. You'd do him right now if Ambrose wasn't here.

Heat rose in his big blue eyes behind those frames, as if he'd read my dirty thoughts.

"I was invited but wasn't sure. Now it's a definite yes." He adjusted his glasses. "Maybe we can get together after?" he murmured.

The door opened, and my next client walked in.

"I gotta go. But yeah."

"See you then." He left, and I couldn't help sneaking a peek at that fabulous ass. Damn, he looked as good in a suit as he did naked.

My next job was for a long-standing client, and this time he wanted the constellation of his birth sign. "I'm a Libra. That's balance." He handed me a picture. "Something that looks like this."

"I know. I'll work something up and be right back."

Ambrose was at his desk, putting the finishing touches on a complicated stencil, but he lifted his head to pierce me with a beady eyeball.

"What did that guy want?"

I took a piece of transfer paper for my design and pretended not to understand. "Who?"

"That fucking lawyer. What did he want?"

I raised a shoulder. "Nothing. He's a friend of Grady's, was passing by the shop, and stopped in to say hello." No way could I tell Ambrose I'd hooked up with Bailey. Not that I needed his approval, but I didn't want to hurt him either. He had such blind hatred of lawyers and the legal system, so it was better this way. In the long run, Ambrose was my friend, and Bailey was just another guy.

******

I walked into Grady's new apartment and whistled low. "Dude, you leveled up. This is a nice spot."

His face bright, Grady hugged me. "I wasn't sure you were gonna make it. Busy at work?" He handed me a beer.

"Yeah. Nonstop." I held out my hand and wiggled my fingers. "They hurt like a bitch."

Grady's lips curved over the bottle top. "I bet I know someone who'll be happy to give you a massage. Anywhere you want, I'm thinking—if you ask him nicely."

My cheeks grew hot, and I rolled my eyes. "Shut up." But that didn't stop me from sneaking a look around the apartment, spotting Bailey talking to a group of Grady's friends.

"Jesus, is there anyone here besides me who isn't a damn lawyer?" I grumbled. "It's giving me hives."

"Maybe stop boxing people into versions of who you think they are and learn to get to know them as human beings instead of judging them by their professions. You might find you have more in common with them than you think."

With those brotherly words of wisdom, he left me standing by myself, and it reminded me of the rare high school parties I'd been invited to, where I'd stood alone in the corner, resentment building as I'd watched all the kids talking and laughing together, excluding me. I finished my beer and decided the hell with it. I'd shown my face, and now I was done. Grady was the only one I owed anything to. I set my bottle down and was halfway to the door when a hot breath hit my neck.

"Leaving so soon?"

With a half smile tugging my lips, I turned to face Bailey, whose blue eyes sparkled with laughter.

"You looked busy."

He leaned against the wall, and I liked what I saw—a thin black sweater stretched across his muscular chest and faded jeans hugging powerful thighs. I couldn't decide whether I liked him more in a suit or casual, like this.

"And you look like you're sneaking out without even bothering to say hello. And I *was* busy. Busy waiting for you to come over. So why didn't you? You're exiting stage left, when you've only been here less than fifteen minutes."

"Does it matter?"

If I didn't know better, I'd have sworn he looked hurt. "I mean...kind of, yeah. Not so much for me, but how about your brother? Why wouldn't you want to be here for him? He's having this party for his new place, and you barely show your face before you slip out without a good-bye? That's kind of shitty."

Chastened, the hot flush of embarrassment made me defensive as hell, and I wanted to snap at him to mind his own damn business about Grady and me. But I didn't because he was right. *Bastard.*

"All right, it's just...I'm in a room full of lawyers, and that always makes me antsy."

"Why?"

I huffed and raked a hand through my hair. "Maybe because I've never had a good experience with them. I told you I didn't have the best childhood."

Bailey's face softened. "I know it was rough. But not everyone here comes from wealth and privilege." He slipped his arm through mine. "Come on and say hi. You've met Weston and Brenner at least once or twice. And there're some other folks too."

I could hardly pull away from him without drawing attention to myself, so I allowed him to lead me to the small group. Weston Lively, the son of a senator-slash-failed-presidential-candidate, and Brenner Fleming, both partners at the same law firm as Grady. Definitely not people I had anything in common with, so I had no clue what the hell Bailey was talking about. Also in this group were two other men, wearing matching wedding bands.

Bailey's hold on my arm tightened. "Hey, guys, this is Keston, Grady's brother. West and Bren, you know, but you haven't met Manny and his husband, John. Manny's a partner at the firm, and John is a doctor."

"Finally. Someone who's not a lawyer," I muttered—quietly, I'd thought, but everyone heard me and laughed.

"Yeah, we're a pretty sickening bunch, aren't we?" Bailey snickered. "For those who don't know, Keston owns a thriving tattoo shop that's pretty awesome."

"Oh, yeah? Where's it located?" John asked. "I was thinking of getting some ink."

"East Village," I answered, and Bailey gave him the address before I could.

"You didn't give me a chance to say it," I grumbled, but Bailey ignored me.

"He's also got a great new-client special. You should check it out."

"Bailey's always a step ahead," Weston remarked. "Get used to it."

I caught Bailey's eye, and he winked at me. "What can I say? I'm a lot to handle."

I knew that from personal experience and was hoping to get a chance to handle him again later.

More people entered the apartment, and I took the time while everyone else was talking to scope it out. The building was a sleek high-rise with windows that gave a view of the harbor and a slice of the Brooklyn Bridge. A far cry from where Grady had grown up, in the projects of Fort Greene, not far from here.

Grady had done damn well for himself. A nice apartment, a great high-paying job, and at his side, a beautiful, sexy lady casting adoring looks up at him.

Surprising me, Bailey took my hand. "Keston's had a long workday, so we're gonna say good night."

"See you soon, guys. Maybe we'll all do dinner," Weston called after us.

I muttered, "Not likely."

Bailey tugged on my hand. "Don't be a dick. Weston's a nice guy, even if he's worth a hundred million, give or take. You can find plenty to talk to him about."

"Oh, sure, he and I can sit and compare bank statements." Weston Lively and I had zero in common aside from both of us having XY chromosomes. "Every time we've met, he's tried to make me feel like we're friends."

"Oh, my God." Bailey put a hand to his chest. "What a horrible, terrible person." He poked me. "How do you walk with that huge chip on your shoulder?"

Why couldn't anyone understand what I meant?

We made our way toward Grady and Lauren.

"Dude, you're leaving already?" Hazy-eyed, he waved his glass at me, and despite my annoyance, I couldn't help grinning. I'd never seen Grady this buzzed and not being his serious psychologist and lawyer self. "Did you meet Lauren yet?"

"Dude." I cackled. "I've met her a bunch of times. How trashed are you?"

He continued babbling as if he didn't hear me. "She's an ADA in Manhattan. Gonna make Bureau Chief one day. Lauren, this is my brother, Keston. He's a tattoo artist and does the best work."

Lauren was sweet-faced with big brown eyes, high cheek-bones, and a banging body that promised passionate nights for my brother. With a roll of her eyes, she got up on her tiptoes and kissed my cheek.

"Hi, honey. Yes, baby, I know Keston and his work. I've seen it up close." She winked at us with a saucy smile. "I may have to visit your place and get one myself."

Grady's eyes brightened, and he traced her collarbone with his fingertip.

"Yeah. Right here." He bent to kiss her, but she held him off.

"Okay, lover boy. This is a PG party. Save it for later."

"Give her the family discount, bro," Grady slurred, and Lauren plucked the glass out of his hand.

"That's it. You're getting cut off. It's water for the rest of the night."

"Baby," he protested.

I had to admit it was fun watching them. "I'll talk to you next week, Grady."

He slung a heavy arm around me. "Yeah. Go home with Bailey and have a good night."

Not that I needed his permission, but I had every intention of doing that. Bailey's hand in mine, we left the building. Bailey had his phone out.

"Mine or yours?" He leaned in and bit my ear, sending my dick into overdrive. Then he kissed me, and I had the crazy idea of dragging him back upstairs and into Grady's spare bedroom.

"Mine. It's closer." In between him sucking my tongue, I gave him my address.

"I was hoping you'd say that." In the car, he continued to press kisses to my neck, and by the time we reached my place, I was ready to fall apart. I pulled him into the darkened apartment and kicked off my sneakers.

"Get naked."

"You have such a sweet way with words. Be still my heart." Bailey had his sweater off and his feet were bare. "Halfway there."

I tossed the rest of my clothes to the floor and led Bailey into my bedroom. Lying with him, with my nerves dancing on edge, I thought I'd give it to him hard and fast, but having Bailey spread under me, I found myself kissing his lips slowly, with purpose, tracing their fullness with my tongue as if memorizing their shape. Bailey panted, and his dick poked me in the stomach.

"Come on, do it. Do it," Bailey demanded, but I ignored him.

"Nah. I'm gonna take it nice and easy. Wanna hear you scream for me."

"No. I need—"

"Quiet," I ordered and touched my lips to the jumping pulse at his throat. "That's better." I licked a wet path down his chest, pausing at the hard tips of his nipples. Biting them resulted in Bailey writhing and moaning, and my dick ached as I watched the play of emotions on his face. "You like that, huh?" I sucked on them and nibbled at the tips.

"Oh, fuck me," Bailey cried out, his dick dripping precome on his stomach. "Come on already." His face flushed bright red, he slapped the bed.

"*Mmm*, not yet." I licked the sticky mess, then swallowed his cock whole. I loved giving head, tasting the bitterness. It was a turn-on, all that control and power over someone. "I might keep you like this all night." I held Bailey's thighs as I rose and fell on his shaft, tonguing the slit, getting off on his groans and whines. Bailey was such a mouthy fuck that seeing him reduced to a puddle of pleasure was hot as hell.

"Bastard," he gasped, hips thrusting. "Keston, please."

"Nuh-uh," I teased, sucking the wide crown, flicking my tongue along the smooth surface. I pushed his legs up, released him from my mouth, and plunged my tongue into his hole.

"Oh God, oh shit," he yelled and grabbed his dick, his hand a blur. My thumbs held him open, and I tongue-fucked him while he fell apart. "Fuck me. I need you. Keston, please. Need you so bad." He was almost crying in his desperation.

I'd been with enough guys who'd said they wanted me, but none had ever said they *needed* me. My dick throbbed, and I couldn't hold out any longer. Rolling the condom on was painful, but I managed and gritted my teeth against the ache. Inch by inch I entered him, trying to move nice and slow, but Bailey wasn't in the mood to wait. He grabbed my waist, locked his ankles behind me, and took me deep.

"Oh God, that's it, that's it. Now move. Fast and hard."

I grinned. "Bossy bastard, aren't you—oh shit," I hissed as he squeezed me tight, sucking me farther into his heat. "You want it fast and hard, you got it." I slammed into him, and he clung to me, nails digging into my skin, but the sting only added to my lust-filled frenzy. Every time I was inside this man, I lost my self-control. Bailey brought me to the edge of wildness, and I wanted to mark him, possess him. Make him mine.

"Right there. Right fucking there." He had one hand on his dick and one clamped on my arm. I slammed into him, and he arched off the bed and came, splattering everywhere. His eyes rolled back in his head, and he collapsed.

I pumped fast and furious, his walls clasping me like a hot velvet glove, milking my dick. I swelled and came, my vision blurring.

"God, you're even more fucking gorgeous when you come." Bailey pulled me down on top of him, and we lay together, hearts pounding, a sweaty, sticky mess.

Eventually I rolled off him, tossed the condom into the garbage, and examined the damage. Sheets half off the bed, pillows on the floor...but I was more interested in the naked, sleepy-eyed man lying in my bed. My bed. Having a guy come home with me wasn't something I did, but from the first, everything about Bailey flipped me in a new direction. That must've been why I picked up the pillows, slid in next to him, and nuzzled his neck.

"Stay."

CHAPTER TEN
BAILEY

Shocked by that one word, I tried to make light of it. "Is that a demand, or are you asking me?" I'd already prepared for his withdrawal.

He wasn't smiling. "Does it matter?" His fingertips played with the ends of my hair and trailed along my jaw. "Stay. Please."

My throat tight, I nodded. "Okay," I whispered.

"Let's take a shower." He left the bed, giving me an eyeful of taut ass and muscled thighs before disappearing into the bathroom. I followed him, and we stood under the spray. A wet and soapy Keston was the stuff of fantasies, and I couldn't stop myself from massaging the suds on his muscled shoulders and arms.

Only moments ago, I'd been nearly comatose from my orgasm, but one touch from Keston and my dick twitched with interest.

"Down, boy," I muttered, and Keston chuckled as he poured more of the cool-scented soap into his palm and rubbed it on my chest and stomach.

"Not the fancy brand you're used to."

I let it pass. In the little time we'd spent together, it was obvious Keston had made major assumptions about me, but I wasn't here for deep, meaningful conversation. He'd made it clear we were fuck buddies, and if I wanted him, I had to be content with that.

And boy, did I want him, so I kept my mouth shut.

"Sorry about the scratches." I ran my fingers over the marks I'd left on his skin, then trailed them to the tattoo on his left biceps. "I recognize the infinity sign, but what's the significance of the two birds?"

"I like birds." Water dripped from his stony face, and I believed him like I believed in Santa Claus.

"And the sun on the other arm? What do they all signify?"

Without giving me an answer, he pushed me against the tiled wall, crushing his lips to mine. I let him use my mouth, giving him whatever he demanded because it was what I desired too.

When he backed off, I touched my puffy lips, managing a grin. "You'll have to try harder. That's not going to stop me from talking."

With a roll of his eyes, Keston turned off the water, took two towels, and handed me one. "Dry off. I don't like wet sheets."

By the time I'd finished, he'd gotten into bed and was staring at the ceiling, hands folded behind his head. I crawled in next to him, and in a night filled with surprises, Keston had another one for me. He wrapped his arm around me and held me close.

"Good night," I whispered.

"Night."

I closed my eyes, letting the solid beat of his heart lull me to sleep.

******

I awoke to the pale light of dawn filtering through the curtains. At some point during the night, Keston had rolled away from me into a tight ball, and he still slept, huddled under the covers. That gave me a chance to check out the room, and color me shocked to find dark wood, expensive furniture, and drawings on the wall I could tell were original.

I slipped out of bed, put on some clothes and padded out of the bedroom to the living area. The whole apartment had obviously been decorated by someone with a creative bent. A comfortable sectional dominated the living room, but I couldn't help but be drawn to the modern, state-of-the-art kitchen with an expensive espresso machine on the white quartz counter. From my days as a barista, I could figure out how to use it, so I made a triple espresso, found milk in the fridge, and poured myself a latte.

"Very impressive."

I turned to face Keston and almost dropped my precious coffee. Messy hair, stubbled cheeks, and naked except for a pair of tight black briefs, Keston could replace coffee as my wake-up in the morning.

Chill, Bailey. He's for now, not forever.

"Want one? Lattes are my specialty, but I can make anything you like."

"I bet you can, but I'm good with regular coffee, Barista Boy."

"Coming right up," I said, ignoring the dig, and made him what he asked for.

"No milk, right? You like it black."

"Nice of you to remember." I handed it to him and watched his throat bob as he swallowed.

I remember everything about you.

"You're working today?" It was hard to concentrate with him standing there in all his delicious, half-naked glory, so I breezed past him to sit on the couch.

"Yeah. Shop opens at noon." He finished and rinsed his cup. "What happened to those glasses you wear?"

"Contacts." Was he trying to change the subject of seeing me again? "I was thinking we could have breakfast. I saw a little diner down Second Avenue." Did I sound desperate? I didn't think so, but I wanted to hold on to him today for as long as I could because like the wind, I couldn't tell when Keston would blow back into my life.

"I don't usually have breakfast."

"Well, I do, so you can watch me eat pancakes. Come on, get dressed and I'll treat you to another cup of coffee. I can't guarantee it'll be as good as mine, but the company will be stellar."

I washed my cup and set it by his in the sink. As I crossed the room, he caught me by the wrist. I waited for him to say something, but he continued to gaze at me with those penetrating blue eyes.

"Don't worry." I patted his cheek. "I'm not the clingy type. I know what we're doing here. I'm not looking for Mr. Right. Just Mr. Right Now."

Damn, I'm a good liar.

We walked to the diner and found a booth. I ordered my pancakes, and Keston made do with coffee.

"Don't you know breakfast is the most important meal of the day?" I poured maple syrup on my stack, cut a chunk, and held it out to him. "Open wide for Bailey."

"You've got to be kidding me. Is this how all you guys on the Upper West Side date?"

"No, only me, you lucky dog," I said lightly, not allowing his disdain to dampen my good mood. I'd had great sex again with the best-looking guy I'd ever met and had spent an unexpected night with him. "I can't eat all these by myself. As it is, I'll have to do a double workout today."

"Or you can just meet me tonight." He raised a brow, and I met it with an answering grin and a happy bounce of my heart.

"In that case, forget the pancakes. They're all mine." I turned the fork around to shove the pancakes into my mouth, but he grabbed my wrist.

"Are you retracting your offer?"

That lazy smile did something to my insides, and my breath caught.

"Are you accepting it? If you say yes, it's a binding contract. Remember? That's the law."

"All this legal talk is making me hard."

That husky rasp made me want to call for a doggie bag and go back to his place for a quickie, and from the gleam in his eye, it seemed Keston had the same idea.

"Keston?"

A woman's voice interrupted my dirty fantasy of a Nutella-and-syrup drizzled Keston.

"Hey, Jodi." Keston released me as if burned and flattened himself against the booth, putting as much distance between us as he could.

A bright face peered down. I recognized her as the tattoo artist I'd seen at Keston's shop. I could pinpoint the moment when she remembered me as her brows shot up.

"Hey, aren't you the guy who came in without an appointment?"

"In the flesh."

Keston cleared his throat and shifted in his seat. "I'll be there in a few, Jodi. We were just finishing here."

Her bright-pink lips curved upward. "Really? It kinda looked like you were about to start something." Pretty brown eyes danced with mischief.

I snickered, and Keston glared at me. "What?" I asked him, pretending innocence. "I can't help it if I'm memorable."

"Oh, for fuck's sake," Keston grumbled as Jodi and I laughed at him.

"I'm Bailey, by the way."

"Jodi, as you already heard. How did you two meet? I know Keston's not on any of those dating apps."

"Jo," Keston warned, his color high, but I was having way too much fun.

"I'm fr—"

"At a club," Keston cut me off, and I narrowed my eyes at him but kept my mouth shut. Obviously, he wanted to keep our connection a secret.

"Cool. Well, I'll leave you two alone to finish, and I'll see ya at the shop, Keston, whenever you get there. Bye, Bailey. Nice to meetcha."

"Same, Jodi."

Keston slid out the booth like his ass was on fire. "Hold up, Jodi. I'll come with you. Bye," he threw over his shoulder, and I had to admit I was a little annoyed at being left so abruptly.

Through the large windows, I watched Jodi and Keston walk down the block, Jodi chattering away. Knowing Keston worked, I hadn't expected to spend the day together, but I was hoping maybe dinner and the promised after-dessert activities would come to fruition.

There you go again. Wishing and hoping for a guy who isn't just scared of commitment, he runs like hell from it.

I called for the check and paid it, then decided to walk around the neighborhood a little. The East Village had sure changed since I went to school. It always had a grungy vibe, but now little upscale indicators had crept in. Gone were the old T-shirt and bong shops. No more beloved CBGB. Trendy little boutiques and chain bubble tea and coffee shops had replaced almost all of them. I took a walk along the "Mosaic Trail"—St. Mark's lampposts were covered with bits of broken tile and pottery, creating a mosaic of street names, punk and rock bands, plus the Museum of the American Gangster, famed East Village mobster Lucky Luciano, and the blackout of 2003.

I stopped on Astor Place at the lamppost dedicated to the 9/11 First Responders and located the NYPD tiles. Their sharp edges had worn smooth over the years, but the colors remained vibrant. Tears stung my eyes, recalling how my father had insisted he'd beat the lung disease he'd contracted while working on the pile after the towers collapsed. We'd always planned to visit the museum and his old precinct, only half a mile from where the towers stood, but his health had declined rapidly and he'd became bedridden, slowly withering away.

"Goddammit. I miss you, Dad." I wiped my eyes and called for a car to take me home. We passed by Keston's shop, and I imagined him at work, those sharp blue eyes intent on creating his designs. I itched to learn more about him, but he was so damn prickly. I'd have to make do with what he was willing to give me, unless I somehow managed to chip away at the wall he hid behind.

At home I changed clothes and went for a long, sweaty run through the park. It cleared my mind and worked off the pancakes. Once I'd showered and had some lunch, I called Belinda to check on her.

"Hi." She sounded cautious and apprehensive, which immediately set my antennae buzzing.

"Everything okay? You're not having any more trouble with Jonas, are you?"

"No, of course not. Jonas isn't a problem." Her cheerful answer made no sense until it hit me.

"Lindee, is he there with you?"

"Everything's fine. I'm good, and me an' Jonas decided we're gonna try and work things out."

Exactly what I'd feared. I ran a hand over my face and blew out several breaths to calm down before I answered her.

"Belinda. You can't do this. You have a restraining order against him."

"Oh, I want you to cancel that."

A deep voice spoke in the background, but I couldn't make out what was being said.

"Is that Jonas?"

"Yes. We had a long talk, and he promised me he's changed."

"He's changed," I repeated with a humorless laugh. "This is classic manipulative behavior, can't you see that? He's done this so many times. Please don't fall for it."

"Jonas told me you'd be mad. You can't keep treating me like a child, Bailey. I'm a grown woman, and I'm free to make my own decisions."

This wasn't the way Belinda spoke. She was simply parroting Jonas's words.

"Honey, I know you're hoping everything works out, and I do want you to be happy. I swear. But don't you remember how he treated you? His lying and cheating, not to mention the terrible names he called you just a week ago, when you went out on that date?"

But Belinda had an answer at the ready. "And he apologized and swore it wouldn't happen again. He's goin' to therapy and anger management. Shouldn't he be able to rehabilitate himself? Don't you have clients who've made mistakes? I've always heard you say people deserve a second chance to prove they've changed."

"Of course people do. That's not what I'm saying." I struggled to keep my cool. In my practice I'd seen too many women fooled by sweet-talking men pay a terrible price, physically as well as emotionally. It didn't matter rich or poor, people wanted to be loved and were willing to put up with a football field of red flags. "I just want you in a healthy place, and I didn't think that was the case after I saw you."

"Well, you're wrong," she snapped. "Just 'cause you're a lawyer and smarter than me don't mean you know anything about relationships. I mean, it's not like you have a boyfriend or anything. I gotta go. Please cancel the restraining order. I'll talk to you."

I was left holding a dead phone. Stung by her outburst, I still couldn't be mad at her. With a mother like ours, how could I ever expect Belinda to recognize the warning signs of problematic men? And as she said, it wasn't as if I were Mr. Healthy in the relationship department. My expertise was in finding and falling for men who were determined to remain unattainable. Case in point, the man who'd left fingertip-shaped bruises on my hips. I touched one and relished its slight ache.

I couldn't do anything about the restraining order—courts were closed on Sunday for nonemergency motions. But I made notes for the following morning, then worked on upcoming cases. By the time I powered off my computer, it was after six and my stomach growled. I itched to text Keston to see if he wanted to come by but held off. I was tired of doing the chasing.

"He knows where I live. If he wanted to see me, he would. See, Dr. Sharpe?" I raised my beer bottle. "I'm trying." Instead of mooning over the man, I ordered a burger and fries and turned on the television, searching for a rom-com to cheer me up.

The movie was good, and my hunger had been sated, but my heart was empty. It was almost nine p.m., and I knew

Keston wouldn't be coming. I decided to drown my sorrows with ice cream, but my freezer held no joy, so I needed to make an emergency run to the bodega down the block. On my return, I stopped dead on the sidewalk at the sight of Keston sitting on my stoop.

"It's late," I said, trying to act casual, but my heart pounded madly.

"What flavor?" he asked, ignoring my statement.

"Coffee Heath Bar." Pulling myself together, I mounted the steps, walking past him. Trying to be strong but failing miserably. He stood behind me, his body heat overwhelming. If he touched me, I knew I'd bring him upstairs and let him fuck me senseless.

"My favorite."

I unlocked the front door, but instead of walking inside, I faced him. God, he was beautiful. I wanted to lick every inch of his skin. I ached for him with every throbbing cell of my being, yet I didn't want him to think he could show up, screw me, and leave. I pulled together the shreds of my dignity.

"You should've let me know you were coming."

For the first time, he appeared disconcerted, as if no one had ever said no to him. Which probably was the case.

"Oh. You have someone upstairs?" He shrugged. "I can go."

Without bothering to wait for an answer, he turned and walked away.

I might have been strong, and I should have been proud, but as I sat in my lonely apartment, eating my pint of ice cream, I wasn't sure it was worth it when I could've had Keston with me.

CHAPTER ELEVEN
KESTON

Who the hell did he have up there?

On my way to the shop the following morning, I was still wondering about Bailey's mystery visitor. True, it was late, and I should've let him know I was coming by, but we did talk about it and…well, dammit. Whatever. If he wanted to hook up with other people, it was a free country. I didn't care.

My morning didn't get much better when Ambrose came it, all hepped up about a house he and Carly had gone to see.

"It has a fucking pool in the backyard. Can you believe it?" He and Jodi chatted as they prepared their stations. I remained silent, and Ambrose glanced my way several times.

"How was the weekend, Keston? Busy?"

"Oh, Keston was busy all right," Jodi chimed in with a giggle, and I glared at her.

Ambrose's brows rose, and his gaze shifted from me to Jodi, then to me again. "What? Am I missing something?"

"Not something. Some*one*. As in a really cute guy."

A smile broke across Ambrose's face even as I scowled. "Yeah? You had a date?"

"It wasn't a date. We just hooked up. No big deal."

"Come on," Jodi said, "the guy was so into you. I could tell." Finished with setting out her instruments, Jodi was ready to gossip. And Ambrose was right there with her.

"Oh, yeah? You got a boyfriend? How come you never said nothin'?"

"Because like I just told you, it wasn't anything."

"Don't let him kid you, Ambrose. This guy was totally into Keston. And he was freaking hot as hell, with the most gorgeous blue eyes..." She sighed.

"Enough," I snapped.

The door opened, and my first client, a firefighter named Mike Flynn, walked in. He'd been coming since 9/11 and had tattoos covering his body.

"Hey, how's it going, Mike?" I gave the two chattering fools a stone-faced grimace and went to take care of my client. "I've been working on what you told me when you made the appointment. Where do you want it? You're running outta skin."

Mike, a big, stocky guy with iron-gray hair and bright-blue eyes in his weathered, freckled face, looked like he'd been through hell and back. I couldn't imagine what he'd lived through, seeing so many people die. I'd been a teenager dealing with my own shit when the towers were hit, and I didn't remember much about it aside from feeling like the city was on fire. Mike had told me that no one he worked with had ever fully recovered. For him personally, life had gone south afterward. His wife left him, and he'd told me about the buddies he'd lost as they slowly sickened and died. His stories were a kind of therapy for me, and I didn't say much as I worked on him, just listened—which was a hell of a lot more important anyway.

"It's gotta be special. The cop who helped me and my buddies on the pile died of the same disease killing my buddies." He scanned his biceps and forearm. "Find me a good spot on here somewhere."

"That's cool, man. Take a look at this."

I showed him the sketch I'd made—an eagle holding the NYPD crest, and underneath, the name and shield number, the date he died, and *Never Forget.*

His eyes widened. "That's pretty fucking awesome. Exactly like what I thought about. Not too much, is it?"

"No. I think it'll be cool. Give me some time to work it up, and I'll be right back."

I'd done plenty of work on the FDNY, NYPD, and Corrections officers. Through his work with city youth and art programs, Carlos had connections, and I'd kept them up. Ambrose, on the other hand, because of his ridiculous bias against the cops, had no desire to work on them, so I took all the uniforms.

It took me about forty minutes to make the stencil, and when I showed it to Mike, his eyes lit up.

"Yeah, that's perfect."

"Awesome." I prepped the area, put my gloves on, and began to work. Mike had a spot on his forearm that was perfect for this. "How's it going?" I asked him. "Busy?" I knew that would segue into a conversation where I could listen and not say much. Just the way I liked it.

"Not too bad. Coupla e-bike fires—these dumbasses still don't realize they're dangerous."

"Uh-huh." I placed the stencil on his skin and peeled it off, then began the inking process. "I see that on the news all the time."

"Anyway, I've been thinking about getting this for a while. Bruce was a good guy—had it rough."

"Yeah? How so?" I carefully outlined the eagle feathers.

"He was a beat cop. Coulda made detective, I'm sure, but he wanted regular shift 'cause he had a kid."

"Uh-huh. Makes sense."

"Yeah. Especially since his wife walked out on him and the boy. He told me she just up and left the kid. He was like four. What kinda mother does that?"

My fingers tightened over the handle of my needle. "I dunno." Mike didn't know how I grew up. "At least he had his father."

"Yeah. Everything he did was for his kid—even though he'd make money from overtime, he felt guilty 'cause it was less time with his boy."

Despite myself, I became interested in the story. "He never remarried?"

Mike shook his head. "Nah. Crazy thing is, he never got divorced. Of course the bitch shows up as he's dyin'."

"Damn, that's cold."

"Right? But Bruce was already too weak to do nothin' about it."

I began to carefully draw in a script font for the dates he'd given me. "At least his kid gets his mother back."

"Pfft," Mike scoffed. "Kid's no fool. He knows what she is. Can you believe she's even living in Bruce's house 'cause she got no place else to go?"

"No shit. Sounds like one of those soap operas on television."

"You know it. She'd been running around all that time with different guys and even had another kid. And of course, Bruce, being a good guy, sick as he was, took them both in and treated them good."

"Nice you kept in touch."

"We'd send Christmas cards and stuff like that and ran into each other at the yearly memorial. But I saw how sick he looked the last time, so I kinda knew which way the wind was blowin'... He didn't wanna talk about it, so I left it alone. Eventually the cards stopped comin'."

But I could see the guilt and sadness in his eyes. "It wasn't your fault, Mike. There wasn't anything you could do."

With his free hand, he wiped his eyes. " 'Cept be a better friend. I shoulda pushed harder to see him. He gave his all for us."

Finished with outlining the design, I set the instrument down. "Listen. You did all you could. Maybe he didn't want you to see him like that. And he had his son. They were close?"

Mike cleared his throat. "Yeah, very. I only met him once, the last time Bruce was able to make it to the memorial. Seemed like a nice kid—he'd just started college."

"You wanna finish it all today, or take a break and come back to color the eagle in?"

Mike checked out my work, which I had to admit was pretty damn good. "I like it. Let's finish it up today. I got time."

"Okay." I had the colors all set up, and a little more than two hours later, his arm was done and wrapped for protection.

"Looks great, Keston. Thanks again."

"I agree. Came out nice. Cool tribute to your friend." Even though he'd been to the shop numerous times, I handed him the aftercare instruction sheet. He paid me and left.

Ambrose had finished with his client and strolled over to me. I folded my arms. "So when are you moving to Florida?"

He made a face. "I told you, man. I'm not leaving. Yeah, the house was awesome, but we can't afford it, number one, and number two, it's too damn hot there. Plus, fucking alligators. Did you know they have a highway named Alligator Alley?" He grinned, and despite myself, I returned his smile.

"No shit."

"I'd never fuck you like that, dude."

Relieved that we'd cleared the air, I checked my watch. "Wanna order lunch? My treat."

"Yeah, sure, thanks."

"Tacos?" At his nod, I called out to Jodi. "Hey, Jo, want some lunch? We're ordering tacos."

"You bet. I'll never turn down a taco."

The food came and we dug in, but my appetite had waned. I couldn't get the conversation with Mike out of my head. Everyone had a story in this city, and these walls had heard plenty. I remembered when Carlos was killed. Shellshocked, I'd walked around the shop for hours, unseeing, hearing but not listening to all the people who came in to pay their respects.

At the nudge to my side, I jerked to awareness and saw Jodi's sparkling eyes.

"Thinking about someone special?" she teased.

I knew whom she was referring to, but she needed to cut that shit out.

"Yeah. Carlos." Maybe my answer was harsh, but I didn't want to talk and figured that would shut it down. I crumpled my wrappings and tossed them into the garbage.

Her face fell and her lips trembled. "I-I'm sorry, Keston."

"Not your problem." I checked the schedule. "Gonna take a walk. Be back in a few."

The shop and its ghosts were haunting me today, and I had to break out of there before I lost it. My steps took me to Tompkins Square Park, where I found a bench away from people.

During our years together, Carlos and I would come here on many mornings—him with a sketch pad in hand, and me watching him, forever amazed that a guy like me somehow found a man like him in this crazy city. A man who, knowing the mess I was, loved me despite everything.

With the heel of my hand, I wiped at the wetness in my eyes and held my head. Fuck, I missed him. I missed our life together.

I missed being happy.

Someone sat next to me, and I shifted to put more space between us, resisting the urge to curse at them. Twenty damn benches in the park, and they had to plant their ass on mine. I glanced over with a ferocious scowl, only to see Grady by my side.

Shit. The last thing I needed was for my brother to see me emotional. I pasted a smile on my face.

"Hey, what're you doing here in the middle of the day?"

"What's wrong?" The problem with having a brother who was a psychologist as well as a lawyer was that your every word and mood was analyzed. I had to watch myself.

"Nothing. It's lunchtime. I'm taking a break in the park."

"Didn't look like it to me. We hardly had a chance to talk at my party."

My smile turned into a smirk. "In case you don't remember, you were kinda wasted."

A pained expression crossed his face. "Oh, yeah. Took me all Sunday to recover. No more tequila shots for me. And I had to hear about it from Lauren. She was not pleased."

I cackled. "Not even married and already getting lectured. Man, you are in trouble," I singsonged.

"Speaking of being in trouble, I saw you left with Bailey. You guys dating now?"

I rolled my eyes. "I don't date. You know that."

"What I know is that you were having fun with him." The normally harsh lines of his face softened. "I haven't seen you like that in a long time." He put a hand on my arm, and despite him being my brother, I tensed, but he held on. "Not since Carlos. I didn't have the chance to see you two together for long before—"

"He's *nothing* like Carlos. What the hell, Grady?" Panic welled up inside me, and all the hurt and anger threatened to burst out of me. "I gotta go. I've got clients soon."

"I didn't say he was like Carlos. He doesn't have to be. But I watched you at my party. Your face...your smile was genuine, you looked alive."

What the hell was I supposed to say in response? Not the truth, for sure. Bailey scared the hell out of me because it was all so damn easy with him. The laughter and jokes. The teasing and banter. I didn't have to worry about being myself—if Bailey didn't like something I said, he challenged me. And if I told him to lay off, he didn't badger me.

"Bro, you were trashed at the party, who're you kidding?"

Of course my brush-off didn't work. "Maybe so, but it wasn't too hard to see. And Lauren barely had one drink. She mentioned it to me as well."

"Well, she's a smart lady. You're a lucky guy."

"I know it. She's the one."

"Damn. That's...that's great, Grady."

"I'm tired of the scene. I'm ready to settle down, make a family. I'm in a great place in life. I've got my brother, and now I want it all. Wife, kids, even a damn dog."

Shit, why were my eyes tearing up? I didn't get emotional about stuff like this. "You deserve it."

He put a hand on my shoulder. "So do you, baby brother."

Unwilling to accept that, I shook him off and got to my feet. "As I said, I got a client in a few."

Dogging my steps, Grady came along into the shop, where, as I feared, Ambrose jumped on him.

"Grady. I'm glad to see you. What do you think?"

Grady's brow furrowed. "About what?"

"My brother."

Ignoring Ambrose's death glare in my direction, I fixed Grady with a plea in my eyes. Thanks to his intuitiveness, he picked up on my signal and took out his phone as if it buzzed with a message, which I knew, standing beside him, it hadn't.

"Damn, I have an emergency at the office. I'll talk to you about it soon, Ambrose. But, Keston, can you come here for a sec?"

He pulled me to the front of the shop, and believing it was about Ambrose jumping at him about Lucas, I apologized.

"Bro, I'm sorry. He never lets up about his brother, but I don't want to bother you with it."

"Not a problem. Maybe next week, but I did come by for a reason."

"Oh, yeah? What's up?"

For the first time, Grady seemed nervous, and he ran a hand through his thick waves. "I've...I'm gonna propose to Lauren, and I want to throw a party."

My jaw dropped. "Whoa. That's...congratulations." We hugged. I truly was glad for him.

"I'm gonna do it Thursday night, and I've taken Friday off and rented a place up in the mountains. I want you to come—you have to, as my brother." He paused. "And best man."

Something twisted in my chest. Since we'd discovered each other, Grady had made every effort to include me in his life, yet I still didn't quite believe I measured up to him. Grady was a college man, a PhD, and a partner in a law firm. Soon to be married to the perfect woman and starting a family. He'd managed to move beyond our troubled beginnings.

Then there was me. Problem teen, barely made it through high school, with the only person who'd ever known the real me gone forever.

"Me? Best man?" The words squeezed through the tight achiness of my throat.

"Yeah." He smiled at me. "Who else but my only family and best friend? Please? We're having Lauren's close friends and mine. It's spur-of-the-moment, and her sisters can't make it, so they're coming next week. I need you there, or it just won't be right. I know you work weekends, but can you take the time off?"

"Yeah, of course." My lips formed the words without a second thought. "I'm happy for you, Grady. And Lauren."

"She loves you." He checked his watch. "And now I really do have to go." His voice dropped low so only I could hear, although I saw Ambrose eyeing us. "Ambrose is still convinced his brother is innocent?"

No way was I going to bug Grady now about Ambrose's loser brother. He had important things to think about.

"Yeah. Don't worry about it."

"Okay. I'll text you the address."

He walked out the door, and my client came in. The afternoon kept me busy as hell, and it wasn't until I was at home and lying on my couch, sucking down some drunken noodles, that I checked my phone.

As promised, Grady had texted the address of the cabin. Somewhere up in buttfuck New York. I'd have to check train schedules, since I wasn't about to rent a car. I hadn't driven in years—thank you, New York City MTA—and it looked far enough away that I had no desire to get behind the wheel and get stuck in traffic. And taking the Harley wasn't even a question.

No other messages from anyone else.

Anyone meaning Bailey.

I didn't know whether to be disappointed or relieved.

"You're a fool. He's probably banging whomever he had waiting in his apartment. You were a walk on the wild side for Mr. Suit and Tie."

CHAPTER TWELVE
BAILEY

"You're such a fool," I muttered to myself. "He probably forgot all about you."

I'd already had a hell of a week, and it was only Tuesday. The day before had been taken up with me pleading with my sister to drop her idea and get into therapy instead, but she refused. Belinda remained adamant about withdrawing her order of protection, and when Tuesday rolled around and she told me she'd never talk to me again if I didn't do what she asked, I had no choice but to comply.

Reluctantly, I agreed, and I made the motion to the judge. I was interrogated as if I were the one who'd made the decision, but finally the motion was granted, and I called Belinda to tell her.

"Great. I can't wait to tell Jonas." She ended the call.

I continued to stare at the black screen of the phone. "You're welcome. No problem at all. I always work for free." Not that I expected payment, but a thank-you would've been nice.

What would have also been nice was a call from Keston. Or another surprise visit. This time I wouldn't push him away. I'd rather be weak-willed and well-fucked than strong and solitary.

Unfortunately, my wishes didn't come true, and I went to bed alone and woke up the same way. I decided to drown my sorrows in a spin class. If I couldn't get screwed, I might as well get sweaty and sore another way. The class was crowded, and I used the opportunity to check out the guys. Skimpy, tight shorts made the hour go by quickly, and there was one guy in particular who'd always caught my eye. He was no Keston, but I was so damn lonely.

The music stopped, and the class was over. I got off the bike and headed to the showers. I'd just finished drying my hair when the guy I'd ogled stopped behind me and ran a finger across my nape. He was still in his tight bike shorts, which showcased an impressive package.

"You missed a spot." He smirked. "Want me to get it for you?"

I met his eyes in the mirror and handed him the blow dryer. "Sure."

Hot air hit my neck, followed by his lips. "I've been watching you for a while."

"Have you now?" I murmured, doing the dance, though my heart wasn't in it.

"Wanna get together later?"

"Sure. Call me." I reached into my wallet and handed him my card.

"My name's Dallas. But in case you forget, lemme make sure you remember me." Giving me no chance to take a breath, he kissed me, sticking his tongue down my throat while grabbing my ass. My instinct was immediate, and I pushed him away.

"Whoa. Slow your roll." Huge cock or not, I didn't like to be mauled. Plus, sloppy, wet kisses weren't my thing.

Dallas rolled his eyes. "Don't tell me you're one of those date-me-before-I-screw-you types. We both got an itch. Let's scratch it."

Maybe I was getting old. In the past, I might've been into a little bump and tickle with a random hottie, but somehow the prospect of being merely one more in line with this guy left me depressed.

Besides, I didn't want him. I wanted Keston. *Dammit.*

"I hope you have something else going for you besides being hung like a horse, but I'm not interested in finding out. Lose my number."

I walked away.

My day didn't get any better in the afternoon. In the middle of preparing a complicated estate plan for a new client, I heard a loud, demanding voice outside my door. I tried to ignore it, but when I recognized who it was, I clicked out of the file.

Son of a bitch. Just what I didn't need today. Keeping calm because I didn't want to lose my cool, I opened my office door. In all my years of practice, she'd never come to my office. Why now?

"Jennifer, what do you want?" I put a hand on Lincoln's shoulder to reassure him. "Don't worry. She's my mother."

Lincoln gaped at me. "Mother? I–I'm sorry, Bailey. I didn't know. She just came in and started demanding to see you and wouldn't give me her name. I thought she was your new client at two o'clock, Mrs. Fishbein. The eldercare-abuse client."

Without a word, Jennifer sailed past me in a cloud of cologne. Coughing, I waved a hand in front of my face. "Don't worry, Linc. She might be my mother, but I'd barely call her that." I squeezed his shoulder. "It's okay."

I returned to my office and shut the door. "To what do I owe this greatest of pleasures, Jennifer?"

My mother wasn't done. "That sad excuse for a receptionist should be fired."

I sat at my desk and clasped my hands. "Lincoln is the best. Why would I do that?"

She arranged her hair and smoothed her skirt. "I don't think I look old enough to have an almost forty-year-old son, and he calls me elderly. How dare he?"

"Why are you here?" It could only be one thing. Money. That was the only reason my mother ever initiated contact with me, but I tried to keep an open mind and waited.

"I'm here to talk to you about selling the house. Every time I mention it, you ignore me. Here you can't. I hate it, and I don't belong there."

So I wasn't too far off. But instead of asking me for the cash outright, she went with the sentimental punch to the gut, and it worked. My stomach cramped. She was correct—I avoided talking about the subject. "Sell?" I repeated.

"It's a hassle living in the middle of nowhere. If I sell, I'll take the money and buy a little apartment in the city, where I belong." She wrinkled her nose. "Not buried somewhere in Brooklyn to wither away."

"Dad loved the house. He always told me he was the first one in his family to own property. Grandma and Grandpa were so proud of him." Every holiday, my grandmother would cook a huge meal, as if ten people were joining us, instead of it being only the four of us. I'd sit on the counter and help—whether it was stirring her matzo-ball soup, helping mix the potatoes for her latkes, or making *Hamantaschen*. It was one of my core memories, and when they died within a year of each other after being married for over sixty years, I cried buckets. All the people who'd ever truly loved me were gone.

"That's a nice story, but it has nothing to do with me. Your grandparents never liked me."

With good reason, I wanted to snap at her, but I restrained myself because it would only result in a shouting match, and this was my place of business.

"I'm not sure I want to sell."

My father never bothered to change his will that left everything fifty-fifty to Jennifer and me. He probably never thought he'd die so soon. I was only in college, too young to say or do anything about it, even if I'd known.

A hot-red flush rose to her rouged cheeks. "You can't be serious. Why would you want to stay attached to that dump?"

I struggled to maintain my composure. "It's not a dump. It's my childhood home, all I have left of my father. Dad loved that house—planting vegetables in the garden, playing catch with me in the yard, decorating it for Halloween. You don't give a damn because you don't care about anything but yourself."

Ignoring my heartfelt words and how emotional I'd become, she curled her fingers into the palms of her hands. "I need that money, Bailey."

"Maybe get a job."

Her eyes narrowed, and her lips thinned. "You're enjoying this, aren't you? Seeing me desperate, making me beg. I bet you think I deserve this."

"Sorry, Jennifer. I know you might not believe it, but I don't. As a matter of fact, most days, I don't think about you at all. Now please excuse me, but I have work to get to." I got to my feet, walked to the door, and opened it. Alone in my apartment, I could imagine a time my mother and I might have a relationship like my father had hoped for. Face-to-face, we were oil and water, destined never to mix.

Fuming, she stomped by me and stood seething by the elevator. I waited until she disappeared to speak to Lincoln, who sat wide-eyed and openmouthed. I put up a hand.

"Don't even ask. It's a very long story I've got no desire to relate. Ever."

As my mother exited, the second elevator opened and my next client stepped out.

The meeting with Mrs. Fishbein proved as long and complicated as I'd expected, and I'd never been happier to see my couch when I entered my apartment that evening. With a beer in hand, I sank into the pillows and groaned. A night of Netflix and chill, just me, myself, and I, didn't seem like a bad thing. Although I did wonder what Keston was up to.

Probably up inside someone else. I sighed, fighting the itch to text him.

My phone rang, and seeing it was Grady, I picked up, curious. We were friendly but not close like he was with Weston and Brenner. Still, I liked the guy, apart from his connection to his sexy-as-fuck brother.

"Hey, Grady, what's up?"

"I've got some news. I'm getting engaged."

"No shit? *Mazel tov!* Lauren is beautiful and smart—I've had some dealings with her at the DA's office. Looks like you hit the jackpot." As happy as I was for him, I wondered why Grady was calling to tell me this news.

"Thanks. I know I'm the lucky one. Still trying to figure out what she sees in me, but I'm not gonna look too deep. Anyway, I'm having a little get-together this weekend to celebrate. I'm doing the deed on Thursday, just Lauren and me, and then we're having some people up to this cabin I rented for Friday and Saturday night for a celebration. I'd love it if you could make it."

"Wow, uh, that's really nice of you to include me, but—"

"You're wondering why?"

I set my beer on the coffee table. "Well, yeah. Not that I don't think you're cool and a great lawyer. I just thought this would be something reserved for close friends and relatives."

"Growing up in foster care, I didn't have much of either. I've learned to be cautious, but I recognize good people I'd like to be around."

"Thanks, Grady. I'm honored you want me at your special occasion. I'd love to come."

"I have another reason," he said, his gruff voice turning teasing. "Keston will be there."

"Still trying for that *shiddach*?"

He laughed. "You wouldn't know this, but my mentor in law school was a religious man with a beard. He was the one who helped me find Keston."

I'd never heard the story, and Keston sure as hell wasn't one to open up about it. "How *did* that happen? Didn't you get to see each other growing up?"

"No. I didn't even know I had a brother. The story I was able to piece together from my file was that my mother had me first and gave me up. Four years later, she had Keston. They lived in a shelter for a few years. One day she left and never returned. She abandoned him, and I don't know how a child ever recovers from that trauma."

My eyes smarted with unshed tears. "I'm not sure you can."

"I agree," Grady said, his voice rough with restrained emotion. "He was put in foster care after she disappeared. I was born in Brooklyn, and he was left in Manhattan. You know how the city works—no coordination all those years ago. In college I worked at ACS for a while as a summer job and they fingerprinted me. Keston, because he'd been arrested a few times, was already in the system. Our names popped up as related from our mother's prints from her record."

Fascinated, I listened, sadly aware of how many kids fell through the cracks.

"I got in my share of scrapes as a teenager—I didn't straighten myself out until I got my GED, went to college, and discovered I wasn't just another dumbass kid."

This was a fascinating insight into not only the two brothers' relationship, but why Keston might be so emotionally unavailable. Abandonment, especially as a young child, did a terrible number on a child's psyche. That scenario was one I knew only too well.

"Yeah, you're the furthest thing from that. And now I see why you became a psychologist, and also a lawyer who specializes in foster care and adoption. It must've been incredibly hard for the two of you when you finally reunited."

"That's a story for another day," Grady laughed, but I didn't miss the tension in his voice and knew this unexpected soul-baring conversation was finished. "So you'll come?"

"Yeah, of course. But please. Don't plan for Keston and me to become a thing. He's not interested."

"Are you?"

Aha. I was so not falling into that trap. "I'm not into puppy-dogging anyone. Keston and I had fun, and now that it's over, I'm sure we can both act like adults and move on."

"*Mmm,* maybe."

I didn't comment on his noncommittal remark. "Text me the address. And congratulations again, man. I'm happy for you."

"Thanks. See you Friday."

No longer interested in what was on television, I picked up my beer and wandered to the picture window with its view of 85st Street. Fall was upon us, and I stared up into the trees, memories rustling like the crispy-edged leaves silhouetted against the night sky. I missed my dad. Sick as he was, he'd still gather the strength to encourage me. He'd tell me I was special, and loved, and that one day I'd find someone who'd give me everything I'd ever wanted.

But all I wanted was my father, and he'd died, and I knew love and the stupid happily ever after in those rom-coms weren't real. Life was hard, and it sucked.

Aren't you a merry fucking ball of sunshine...

I took another long swallow of my beer, watching a few leaves left on the tree branches drift down and blow away.

The streetlights glowed, highlighting a happy couple walking hand in hand up the block. Times like this, I hated being by myself. I could change clothes, head out to a club, and find someone who'd chase away the loneliness...but maybe I'd matured, because after I finished my beer, I took a shower and went to bed.

******

Friday afternoon I rented a car and debated texting Keston to see if he needed a ride, but as fast as that thought entered my mind, I squashed it. "Jesus, you're an ass. His brother is throwing the party. You think he's not there? He doesn't need your help."

It took the better part of two hours, and the sun had set by the time I found the godforsaken place in the woods. I parked my car next to the others and followed the sound of laughter.

"Grady, where the hell are you?" I called out, hefting my travel bag on my shoulder. "My people already wandered the desert for forty years. That's why we stay in civilization with great bagel places."

A tall figure appeared in the moonlight, and my heart tripped and began to beat like mad. I took a step back.

"What's the matter, Uptown Boy? You don't like communing with nature?" Keston's husky voice rasped against my tight-as-a-violin-bow nerves. He moved closer, and I drank in the sight of him in a bulky fisherman-knit gray sweater and faded jeans. All that dark hair lay in messy waves over his brow, and his cheeks were rough with several days' stubble.

I'd like to commune with your nature...

"Hi. Where's your brother? I have a gift for him and his beautiful bride-to-be."

Maybe Keston expected me to flirt with him or be friendlier, but during the drive upstate I'd promised myself this weekend I'd keep my distance and not give in to my desire. A whole weekend of temptation would be a battle for sure, but I could be strong. Even if the object of my lust looked like an advertisement for the great outdoors.

"Everyone's out by the firepit. I just got here about half an hour ago. Grady's got drinks set up. Follow me."

I trailed behind him, carrying my bag and the gift I'd picked out—a beautiful sterling picture frame I'd found in an antique store near my apartment. The owner, Presley Dawson, had assured me it was the perfect gift for a newly engaged couple. I left my bag in the front hall and continued after Keston.

The backyard of the rustic cabin was expansive, and I stopped to take in the view. A heavy line of trees rose in the distance, while thick bushes surrounded the perimeter of the grounds. It was hard to see anything else but shapes in the darkness. A firepit was in the center of the outdoor furniture, the flames dancing. Grady and Lauren sat holding hands, and as expected, Weston and Brenner, along with Manny and John, were also present. Two women I hadn't seen before sat sipping their drinks.

"Bailey, you made it." Grady jumped up, pulling Lauren with him, and, still holding her hand, came to greet me. I hugged him and Lauren and handed her the gift.

"Just a little token. *Mazel tov* and congratulations."

Lauren hugged me back. "Aren't you the sweetest. Thank you." She opened the gift bag right there and took out the frame. "Oh, Bailey, this is beautiful. Thank you. We'll treasure it."

"I'm told it's from the early 1900s, so I hope you like that antique art-deco look."

She kissed me. "I love it, and I'm definitely going to put one of our wedding photos in it." Her ring flashed in the firelight.

"Let me see the goodies." I caught her hand. "A beautiful ring for a beautiful woman. Grady, you're a lucky man."

He slipped an arm around her waist and hugged her close. "Don't I know it. I'm the luckiest man in the world."

"Kiss, kiss, kiss!" Weston shouted, and we all clapped until they locked lips.

"That was a nice gift," Keston murmured from behind me. "Thank you."

We were doing an awkward dance, as if we were strangers and not two people who'd already lost themselves in each other.

A drink was thrust into my hand, and I sat beside Weston and Brenner. "How are the lovebirds?" In law school, I'd had many fantasies about each of these men, never dreaming that one day they'd be a couple. Their mutual dislike had been legendary, and for them to have fallen in love was almost like a Hallmark movie come to life.

Brenner's expression was a mixture of tenderness and laughter. "We're good. More interestingly, what's with you and Keston? You two still a thing?"

I sipped my drink, my gaze finding Keston, who sat apart from everyone else with a beer in hand. "No. Not a thing. More like a thing of the past."

CHAPTER THIRTEEN
KESTON

It shouldn't matter that he was here.

I didn't care.

Really.

I'd figured Grady would invite him and had steeled myself for his appearance, but when I'd seen him, it had hit me like a punch to my gut. Those piercing blue eyes. The perpetual quirk of his lips as if he knew a secret and wasn't letting the rest of us in on it. His quick, smartass comebacks. That tight, round ass.

I chugged my beer, keeping my butt planted firmly in my seat on the opposite side of the firepit. Where I belonged. On the outside, looking in.

Lauren sat beside me. "Why do I get the feeling you're here under duress?" Her pretty brown eyes searched mine. "Are you having fun yet?"

I managed a smile. "Of course. I think you and my brother are perfect for each other. I'm happy for you."

She shook her head, dark waves tumbling around her shoulders. "I know, but that's not what I mean. Is it that painful being here with everyone?"

My grin was sheepish. "Is it that obvious?" I lifted a shoulder, doing my best to ignore Bailey across the fire from me. In his usual animated way, he was telling a story, his hands and mouth moving in tandem, keeping everyone laughing. "I'm okay. I'm just used to being alone."

"In your head, right?" Startled by her observations, I nodded.

"Uh, yeah. After Carlos died…"

"You figured you'd be by yourself forever. I understand more than you know." She put a gentle hand on my arm. "Let me tell you a story. In my early twenties, I was engaged. We were high school sweethearts, and he went off to Afghanistan and didn't come home."

Instantly protective, I had to ask. "Does Grady know?"

"Of course. It took more than ten years to find a man who set my heart on fire, and I pushed away a lot of people. I'm happy Grady pushed back."

I looked at Grady, who sat with his friends, his face light and filled with joy. So different from when we first met. "He is persistent, I'll give him that."

"I know. Because when he wants something, nothing and no one will stop him."

I grinned. "And he wanted you."

Her gaze found me, and there was nothing but tenderness and compassion. "You as well. He'll never give up loving you."

I ducked my head. "I know I make it hard. Sometimes I can't help the anger."

She put her arm around me. "Jack was an important part of my life. My past. Grady is my future, and I know everything about him, the ugly and the beautiful. Like he knows about me. And it only makes me love him more."

I shouldn't have been surprised, yet I was. Maybe because I still believed if people knew my truth, they'd walk away.

She gave me a comforting squeeze. "Sometimes we don't take people's inherent goodness into account. We're busy looking for the negative instead of concentrating on the positive." I remained silent, and she shocked me by pressing a kiss to my cheek. "Try it."

I watched her walk away and join Grady, who whispered something in her ear and kissed her. I was genuinely happy for my brother. He deserved love. I'd had mine and didn't expect another. I could live my life, content with memories.

Another burst of laughter rose from the group of Grady's friends. Deciding I'd had enough of the cutesy coupledom, I grabbed another beer and took off down a path toward the woods. I didn't mind being alone. I'd spent my whole childhood living in my head.

The clear night sky spread out above me, a velvet tapestry for the sparkle of stars not often visible in the city. I picked out Orion's Belt and snapped a few pictures. It would make a cool tattoo. I leaned against the rough bark of a towering tree and breathed deeply of the cool night air infused with the scent of pine and fresh earth.

"Beautiful, isn't it?"

Bailey stood off to the side, eyes watchful and wary.

"Yeah. Not something we see every day in the city, for damn sure." I took a hit from my beer bottle.

"Grady called for dinner. I thought you might want to come inside."

"Thanks."

He stared at me and opened his mouth, then shut it, shook his head, and walked away. I caught up to him and blocked his path.

"What? You act like you have something you want to say to me."

His eyes flashed. "Why would I?"

Dammit, he was the most frustrating, annoying man I'd ever met. "Stop lawyer-speaking me."

"What the hell does that even mean?"

Bailey stomped through the crackling leaves, and I strode after him. Everyone had left the backyard area, and through the windows I saw them gathering in the kitchen. I brushed past Bailey and mounted the steps, entering the kitchen to some delicious smells.

"There you are," Grady called out. "Grab a plate and serve yourself. Lauren made lasagna, meatballs, and eggplant cutlets. There's salad over there and garlic bread."

"Beauty, brains, and she cooks? Damn, bro, you hit the jackpot."

"Keston, that's the nicest thing you've ever said to me." Lauren kissed my cheek.

"Probably the nicest thing he's ever said to anyone," Bailey muttered under his breath.

"Screw you," I mumbled.

"You had your chance and blew it," he sniped back.

About to answer, I saw all the half smiles and shut my mouth. With my plate full, I went into the living room and sat in a club chair. The others joined me, and we dug in.

"Lauren, this is as good as Gigante's," Weston said around his chewing.

"Oh, wow, thanks, Weston. That's incredible praise. I ate there once, and it was the best dinner I ever had."

"It's true," Manny agreed. "Johnny and I ate at Rao's and Carbone, and we both thought Gigante's topped them. And this is better."

Having neither the money nor the inclination to eat at places where the bill cost as much as I took in as profit for a day, I stayed silent. It was as I feared. Another reminder that I didn't fit in with these corporate types. Truth was, if Grady wasn't my brother, I'd have already gone home.

"I don't know about those places, but growing up, I had a neighbor who made the best Italian food, and this tastes just like hers." Bailey popped a meatball into his mouth and licked his lips. "Just like Mrs. Russo's."

Like I believed him. I rolled my eyes, and Bailey's eyes narrowed. "What's wrong, Keston?"

With deliberation, I tore off a piece of garlic bread and chewed. "Nothing."

Tension rose between us, but Lauren interrupted, defusing it. "How about a game? Two truths and a lie. That way we get to know each other better."

God, this was torture. Was this really what rich people did at parties? Grady's horrified face met mine, and I had to duck my head to keep from laughing. Okay, he was as uninterested in participating as me, but for his lady love, he'd do anything. And I went along because corny as it was, I'd do anything for Grady.

"I'll start," Weston said, rising to his feet, as Brenner snorted.

"You just love a chance to talk about yourself."

Weston raised a brow and patted his boyfriend on the head. "You're disqualified from playing, so hush." He rubbed his jaw. "I once let out all the air in the tires of my college president's car. I wore the same underwear for a week as a fraternity hazing, and I've never seen a single episode of *Law and Order*."

Bailey bounced in his seat. "The underwear is a lie. And everyone has seen at least one episode of *Law and Order*."

"I haven't," I volunteered.

Bailey rolled his eyes. "Okay, I take it back. I'm not surprised you haven't."

"What's that supposed to mean?" I challenged him.

"Nothing." Ignoring me, he turned to Weston. "Was I right?"

Weston gazed around the room. "Anyone else?"

"No way would you wear the same pair of underwear for a week." Manny made a face. "That's disgusting."

Grady and I shared a look. "Sometimes people have no choice," Grady said softly, and my stomach clenched.

"Well, Manny was right." Weston pointed a finger at him. "All pledges were supposed to wear the same briefs, but I cheated and changed. So, Bailey, you were wrong. I've never watched *Law and Order*. You and me, Keston. Birds of a feather."

My smile was faint. *Oh, yeah.* Weston Lively and Keston Harris. Destined to be best buddies.

Lauren clapped her hands. "That was fun. Okay, Bailey, since you were wrong, you're next."

Bailey, who'd left his seat to put his plate in the dishwasher, paced the room for a bit. He stood in the center with a mischievous grin. My lips twitched. He did have a flair for the dramatic.

"I won barista of the year at the coffee shop I worked at during college. I kissed my first boy at my high school prom. I'd never been away from home until I went away to law school."

"Ooh. These are good ones." Lauren's brows scrunched together. "I think the lie is you were never away from home."

"No way," Brenner called out. "The lie has to be that he kissed his first boy at the high school prom. Bailey was a hottie. He had to be getting some early on."

I snorted, and Bailey's gaze rested on me. "You have something to say?"

"The coffee shop. I bet you didn't have to work during school at all."

"Wrong," he shot back, blue eyes blazing. "It was part of my financial-aid package that I work. And I never left home because I didn't want my father to be alone. So Brenner was right. I was kissing boys long before my high school prom."

Since Lauren was first with the wrong answer, she went next, and I grew more and more uncomfortable, knowing my turn would come soon. Thunder rumbled, and through the large picture window, a bright flash of lightning lit up the sky. At a particularly loud *boom*, we all jumped, and the lights flickered.

"Maybe we'd better call it a night." Grady put an arm around Lauren's shoulders. "I'll put the food away, and we'll see everyone in the morning for breakfast. There are some apple orchards up here and country stores in the surrounding towns we thought might be fun to visit."

"I'll help you," I was quick to offer and started collecting plates from the tables.

"We'll all do it so it'll go faster," Manny said, picking up his glass, but Lauren snatched it out of his hands.

"No, you're guests." Lauren shooed everyone away.

"And you're the bride-to-be," I pointed out. "So go upstairs and get ready for Grady." I snickered as they both turned red. She kissed my cheek, a mysterious smile hovering on her lips.

"I put your bag in the bedroom at the end of the hall. For privacy."

Grady and I worked side by side. "Thanks for being here. I know it's not your kind of thing, but I appreciate you showing up for me."

"Yeah, of course. You're my family. That's what we do for each other."

He put a hand on my arm. "I miss Carlos too. I owe him more than I could ever repay. He gave me back my brother."

The first time Grady had contacted me with the shocking news that he was my brother, I'd ignored him for several months. Angry and hurt, I'd invented a whole scenario in my head that I'd been the unwanted one and he'd lived a charmed life. From the start, I'd told Carlos that someone had contacted me, claiming to be my brother, and he'd urged me to see Grady, but I'd been a stubborn ass with a chip on my shoulder. It'd come to a head one day when Grady had shown up at the tattoo shop and demanded we talk it out. Carlos had taken me aside and insisted I listen to Grady. Pretty sure without Carlos's intervention, I would've continued to push Grady away.

Shocking tears burned my eyes, and I couldn't trust my voice to answer. Grady, though, wasn't finished.

"But it's been almost five years."

"Yeah? And?" I finished loading the dishwasher and started putting the trays of food in the refrigerator.

"And there's nothing wrong with finding someone. Falling in love again."

A harsh laugh burst from me. "Love? Where the hell is that coming from?" I shoved the last tray of pasta onto the shelf and slammed the door.

Grady stepped into my path of escape. "I told you this before–from the way you look at Bailey."

I so did not want to have this conversation, considering I was more than a little confused myself about my feelings.

I shrugged. "All I know is, the guy annoys the shit out of me half the time."

Grady's eyes twinkled. "And what about the other fifty percent?"

I could feel my face turn red. "Has anyone ever told you how much of a pain in the ass you are?"

"Yeah. You. All the time. Give yourself a chance to get to know him. You might be surprised at what you find."

Only with Grady could I talk so openly. "I-I did. Last weekend I showed up at his place, but he had someone else in his apartment. So did you ever think I might've been willing, but he was the one who wasn't?" I scanned the cleared kitchen island. "I think we're finished. I'm gonna head up to bed."

"I'm right behind you."

We separated at the top of the stairs. "Try not to be too loud." I smirked, and Grady punched me in the shoulder.

"Ass." He laughed, and I walked away with a smile on my face.

I opened the last door at the end of the hallway, and my good mood vanished seeing Bailey standing there, stark naked. "What the fuck?" I snapped as he turned away, which didn't help, as I got an eyeful of his firm ass.

"What're you doing in my room?" he snapped, jumping into the king-sized bed.

"Lauren said this was my room. Forget it. I'll sleep on the couch downstairs."

Bailey huffed. "Don't be an idiot. We can share the bed. Don't worry. I won't attack you. You're safe with me. Besides, that couch is too short, and it's lumpy as shit."

I hated that he was right.

"Fine."

I carried my bag into the bathroom, brushed my teeth, and changed into a T-shirt and briefs. Good thing I'd brought them, because I usually slept naked. When I returned, Bailey had also put clothes on, and I gingerly climbed into bed, making sure I kept a wide space between us.

"It's okay," Bailey sneered. You've made it pretty fucking obvious you're not interested anymore. I don't go where I'm not wanted." He shut the light.

Unable to sleep, I lay staring at the ceiling, listening to Bailey breathing next to me.

"Just curious," he said, and I couldn't help my lips kicking up in a grin. I knew he wasn't asleep. The man wasn't wired to sit still and let things lie.

"About?" I asked.

"What did I do that turned you off? And don't worry about my feelings. I won't be insulted."

Was he serious? For this conversation, I had to turn the light on and see his face.

"Ow, why'd you do that?" He rubbed his eyes and glared at me.

"You're kidding me, right? You know why."

"If I did, I wouldn't ask," he sniped, looking grumpy and...-dammit...cute. What the hell? I'd never thought like that about any guy. Hot, yeah. Fuckable, definitely. But cute? No way. Yet there he sat with his hair all messy, and all I could think was... *I'd like to kiss that frowning mouth.*

"I'll refresh your memory, then. I showed up at your place last Sunday, and you had someone else upstairs. So I bailed. It's fine. We're not a couple. But the least you can do is be honest."

Bailey threw back the duvet and stormed out of bed to my side. "Honest?" he sputtered. "Yeah. I remember. You basically treated me like shit with your coworker when she spotted us having breakfast. You showed up without letting me know ahead of time and started talking about ice cream. You didn't even say hello. You just assumed you'd come in, fuck me, and leave."

I winced at his crass words, but also because...yeah, it was true. Although I wasn't so sure about the leaving part. I kind of liked waking up with him. But I had to defend myself. "We had plans. I asked if you had someone up there, and you didn't answer me."

"You didn't text or call. You just came over, and when I didn't jump, you walked away," he hissed, leaning in, nose to nose with me. "What was I supposed to do?"

Having him so close and riled up excited me. I grabbed his waist and pulled him close. "We're here now, and I don't give a damn about any other guy."

"There is no other guy. Only you." Bailey's hot breath hit my cheek, and my lips covered his in a hard, possessive kiss.

CHAPTER FOURTEEN
BAILEY

I was strong. Really. And I could resist Keston if I wanted to. But I didn't want to.

Firm lips fit perfectly to my own. A velvety tongue slid inside and caressed with soft yet demanding strokes. Those strong hands gently drew my T-shirt over my head and tugged my briefs off, releasing my rigid cock, which had been half-hard since Keston had slipped under the covers beside me.

Questioning eyes met mine, and I nodded, knees trembling as his wet mouth engulfed the length of my aching dick. My fingers dug into his muscular shoulders, holding on as he sucked me to oblivion. Thunder and lightning boomed and crackled as rain lashed against the window.

"Keston," I moaned, trying not to cry out, but failing miserably at the touch of his flickering tongue licking and teasing me. My hips rocked, but he held me firmly, his blunt nails scraping along the cleft of my ass before he entered my hole. "Fuck, what're you doing to me?"

He continued to tease, keeping me on the edge, the thrust of his thumb matching the pull of my passage until I couldn't keep the wildness from blowing me apart and I came, a red haze bursting behind my eyes, blinding me. When I came to, Keston was watching me, and I jumped him, noting the delicious-looking bulge in his briefs.

"Come to papa," I crooned and peeled the briefs away, revealing his gorgeous, thick cock. "*Mmm*," I sighed, taking him fully, drowning in his scent. Who the hell was I kidding? I craved this man as if I were lost in the desert and he were my oasis. But Keston was no mirage. He was a living, breathing man, and at the moment, all mine.

I sucked him hard, drawing him deep to the back of my throat. I grasped him and used my hands and lips on him, loving how he tore at the sheets and fell apart underneath me. Warm come filled my mouth, and I swallowed it all. I joined him in the bed, lying next to him. Keston's chest rose and fell rapidly, his eyes were closed, but I knew he was still awake, and I had something to say.

"There was never anyone else upstairs in my apartment. Not then. Not now. Not after my first time with you."

His eyes opened, and he rolled on his side. "Really?"

"Really. I didn't—I don't want anyone else."

A mix of confusion and longing filled his eyes, and I wondered how long it had been since he'd been loved.

A bolt of lightning cracked nearby, shaking the house on its foundation, brightening the room in a flash. "Shit," I screeched and jumped up. Keston grabbed me, and I held on to him, maybe a bit tighter than necessary, but hey. No one had ever called me a fool. I kissed his neck.

"Are you scared or just using this as an excuse to maul me?"

"Be quiet." I snickered. "Let me have my moment." Keston stayed silent but tightened his arm around me, and I settled into his arms with a contented sigh. "Are we okay now? How about we agree to no more making assumptions? If we have a question about anything, we ask."

"Okay. I have one." Keston's nose ran down my cheek. "What're we doing here?"

I opened my mouth to give a flippant answer but decided to hell with it. Maybe it was time for me to lay my heart on the line.

"I don't want to be with anyone else but you. I'd like to know you better. And I hope you might feel the same." Never having been so open and forthright with a man, I held my breath, my hopes sinking as each second passed without a response.

"I–I don't know how to date. I never have."

And my heart broke for him. "But you were in a relationship."

He grew stiff and withdrew. "I don't want to talk about him."

"You were younger and happier."

"Yeah. I was." In profile, his mouth was a harsh line.

I covered his hand with mine. "We don't have to call it dating. We can say we're figuring it out. What do you think?" My heart thumping, I left the question hanging, and relief washed over me when he nodded.

I snuggled under the duvet and curled into Keston. He stretched out and closed his eyes. I fell asleep to the sound of the steady rain pattering against the roof.

**

Saturday morning, we all sat at the long wooden table with our plates. Lauren and Grady had platters of bacon, sausage, and hash browns ready and waiting. We could make eggs as we liked—the stove had six burners and frying pans on each. There were piles of bagels and a plate of lox, cream cheese, red onions, and tomatoes set on the table. Keston and I had separated at the stairs, with him heading to the stove for eggs. I took an everything bagel on my plate and proceeded to build my breakfast.

"Wild storm last night, huh?" Weston crunched a piece of bacon.

"Yeah. The lightning freaked me out." I spread my cream cheese and placed onions and tomatoes on one side, lox on the other.

At the island, pouring himself coffee, Grady chuckled. "I was dead asleep. I didn't hear a thing."

One of Lauren's friends, a coworker named Faith, shuddered. "I thought the house would fall down. It took me forever to fall asleep."

"*Mmm*, us too." Weston chewed his bacon, but the devil was in his eyes. "I heard lots of moaning and groaning." With an innocent expression that didn't fool me in the slightest, he said, "It sounded like it came from your room, Bailey."

Instead of answering, I took a big bite of my bagel, lox, and cream cheese, chewed and swallowed. Keston and I might've decided to see where this thing between us was going, but I'd be damned if I was going to clue Weston and the rest of the house in on our personal life without talking to him.

"Gee, West. I wouldn't know. I went to bed early."

"Yeah, but did you go to sleep?" His green-gold eyes twinkled.

Keston surprised me, sitting by my side and pressing his thigh to mine but remaining silent.

"What did you do, Weston? Listen at the door?" I took another bite of my bagel.

"Don't give him ideas." Brenner's lips kicked up. "But we didn't need to."

Enjoying the warmth of Keston's bulk, I nudged my knee to his and took a sip of my coffee. "Don't know what you're talking about. Must've been the wind."

Weston's eyes narrowed. "Spoilsports," he muttered, and Manny snickered.

"Pay attention to your boyfriend, Weston. Leave Bailey alone."

Weston picked up another piece of bacon and waved it in the air. "Listen. Bailey had no issue wanting the juicy details of my relationship with Brenner. I'm just repaying the favor."

I ate the rest of one half of my bagel before wiping my mouth and giving Weston and Brenner a sunny smile. "No comment."

We finished our breakfast, and Grady gave us directions to the apple orchard. Grady and Lauren were taking Lauren's friends in their car, and Weston and Brenner had Manny and John in theirs.

"I'll take Keston," I said.

"I bet you will," I heard Weston murmur behind me.

In the car, Keston put the GPS on. "What's with Weston? He's up your ass about your personal life."

I followed the directions, which had me turning off on a gravel road. "I can't get too mad at him. I was the same about him and Brenner at the time they got together, and even after. The three of us went to school together. It was my first time away from home, and I went a little wild."

"Lots of boyfriends, huh? I can see it." Keston cast an admiring glance my way. "You must've been pretty hot with those big blue eyes and cute ass."

"Oh, yeah. That was me. A real hottie." I tried to temper my sarcasm.

His brow furrowed at my nonanswer, but I kept quiet. Another ten minutes of driving, and we reached the orchard. I pulled up next to Grady's car and cut the engine.

We got out of the car and picked up baskets. I took a small one because unlike everyone else there, I was neither a baker of apple pie nor part of a couple where my partner was.

We separated, and I half expected Keston to spend time with his brother and his fiancée, but he stuck with me, pointing out which apples were the best for pies versus applesauce.

He pulled an apple straight off the tree and crunched it. "Good. Get some of these for sauce."

I blinked. "Sauce? You make apple sauce?"

His tall figure, hair black as a crow's wing against the blue, blue sky, stood in front of me. I imagined the sweet juice of the apple on his lips. Keston's blue eyes darkened, and he took a step toward me, holding out the apple.

"Taste."

I reached out but found myself yanked into his arms, his mouth covering mine. The half-full basket dropped to the ground, sending apples rolling at our feet, but I didn't care. Not when Keston sucked my tongue. My hands tangled in his hair, anchoring him to me. I couldn't get enough of this man—his taste, scent, heat. I was drowning in an ocean of desire, caught under the waves of hunger and need. He clamped a hand on my ass, squeezing while rocking into me, and I wanted to climb him like one of these trees and pick his fruit.

With great reluctance, I disengaged my lips from his. "If you don't stop, I'm gonna come in my pants, and that won't be fun." But he still held me close, and the unexpected tenderness gave me hope that maybe we had a chance to make this work.

"Is this what dating is like?" he murmured. "If so, I think I'm okay with it."

Unable to resist touching him, I skimmed my fingers across the sharp angle of his jaw, then traced his lips. "I think so too."

Our friends' voices filtered through the orchard, and we picked up the apples that had fallen out of the basket. By the time they found us, we'd recovered and didn't look like we'd been ravaging each other.

Grady saw us first and waved. "Ready to go?"

I lifted the basket. "All set."

The country store was everything I'd expected, cute and kitschy, and I couldn't resist buying some little mementos. A picture frame in the shape of an apple, a little box of fudge, and some honey sticks. Weston and Brenner bought pies, fudge, and were busy taking selfies, which of course I had to photobomb.

"Cute, Bailey." Brenner stuck his phone in my face and called out, "Hey, Keston."

He looked up, and Brenner took a picture. "Niiiice," he nodded.

"Show me," I demanded, and he turned the phone for me to see.

It was a great candid shot—me laughing, with Keston at my shoulder, serious as always, but with the hint of a smile playing in his eyes.

"Text that to me, please," I asked.

We had lunch at a charming restaurant by a lake and ate while deer browsed in the woods. Afterward, we split off, and Keston and I walked with Grady and Lauren.

"Have you decided when the wedding will be?" I figured Grady would want to have it soon.

Lauren stared out at the lake. "As soon as possible. My mom isn't well, so I want to make sure she's able to enjoy herself. I just have to coordinate with my sisters. Annabella lives in Connecticut and Dolores in North Carolina. Neither could get away for this weekend—Belle is away on business, and Dolores is sick, so we'll have our own get-together next week. But to answer your question, we were talking about maybe end of January or beginning of February. Not Valentine's Day because that's too gimmicky."

Grady put his arms around her. "I'd marry her tomorrow. It doesn't matter to me. Just tell me when and where, and I'll be there."

It was sweet to see a couple so happy and in love. In the distance, I saw Weston and Brenner by the woods, walking hand in hand. Brenner caught Weston by his neck, and as they kissed, I couldn't help watching and being envious. I'd finally come to the realization that this life—coupledom, familiarity, love—was what I desired. Coming from an irrevocably broken home, I'd had no one to model my behavior on and had spent the past twenty years finding solace and comfort in strangers. No more.

Keston nudged my shoulder. "You okay?"

"Yeah, sure." My automatic answer, but was it the truth? Could someone whose mother had abandoned him because she'd been bored ever be okay?

"You're a pretty bad liar." Keston reached for my fingers and tangled his with mine.

"And you would know, right?"

His lips thinned. "You've heard my story. I have a right to be."

"So do I." The unexpected emotional state I was in caused the words to tumble from my lips, and I instantly regretted it. We were having fun, nothing heavy.

We locked eyes, and he squeezed my hand. "Looks like we have some talking to do." My attempt to pull away was met with a bone-crushing grip. "Nope," he murmured. "No fucking way."

It didn't matter. I'd had a lifetime of hurt that would take more than one night of talking.

"Sure. Whatever you want."

Grady and Lauren finished with their purchases, and as Grady loaded the bags in the car, she posed a question to our group. "How about stopping at a winery? There's a great one only about a ten-minute drive from here. Does that sound good to all of you?"

"You're the bride-to-be, Lauren," I called out. "What you say goes."

She blew me a kiss and elbowed Grady. "You hear Bailey? He's my new BFF. I'll text you all the address."

Laughing, we got into our cars, and I started the engine. Keston remained quiet until we drove into the winery's parking lot. "I meant it, Bailey. You know my backstory. I know nothing about yours. Only what I assumed."

"Which is what? No, let me." I gripped the steering wheel. "Mommy and Daddy loved me, we had plenty of money, and I never wanted for a single thing. Privileged and pampered. Am I right? Well, guess what? *Buzzzzz.* You're wrong." I opened the door and walked away, and he scrambled out to follow me.

"Yeah? How?"

We were a few yards away from the rest of the group, who'd gathered at the entrance. Lauren had a guide waiting for us. "I'm not doing this here, Keston. Not now, in front of everyone, during Lauren and Grady's party. It's their weekend."

"Then later. Or after we leave. Next week. Whenever. Because you're gonna tell me. I can wait."

He walked away, leaving me wondering what I was doing.

CHAPTER FIFTEEN
KESTON

I must be a damn fool.

Bailey had been pretty adept at skipping around any discussion of his personal life, and the more I watched him slip and slide, the more I wanted to know.

I could admit it. I was interested in him. I mean, that was obvious. The sex was off the chain, explosive and intense. And waking up with him next to me was...very nice. Bailey was a snuggler and into touching. I'd never appreciated the clingy type, but he fit perfectly by my side. I liked the way he challenged me with his smartass mouth, and I enjoyed shutting it up with my lips over his even more. Plus, he was a fantastic kisser, and he sucked my dick like it was his favorite fucking flavor of Tootsie Pop.

Shit. If I didn't know any better, I'd think I was crazy about the guy.

We were on our way back to the cabin when the rain and thunder started up again. A quick glance showed Bailey's concentration remained steadfast on the road, which, with its poor drainage, became a swirling mess of mud and gravel. Not pleasant to drive through for him, but good for me to keep my thoughts to myself.

Despite our decision to give this a try, I wasn't sure where we were heading. There was a lot more separating us than bringing us together. Ambrose might be a pain in the ass with his dislike of the legal system, but he had reasons, as did I. On more than one occasion, the cops had hauled me into court, which was how I'd ended up in juvie. Did I deserve it? Yeah. I hadn't been an angel. After my time, like a stray cat, I'd become adept at hiding in the shadows. Staying out at night to do my street art. My foster family hadn't cared where I was as long as I wasn't causing them trouble.

I raked a hand through my hair. Jesus, how the hell would I ever explain someone like Bailey to Ambrose? As my life became more entangled with Bailey's, I had to acknowledge that priorities needed to shift. His concerns had to come into play, and if they conflicted with my friendships, that was something I'd have to figure out. Because I wasn't about to give up what was growing between us.

I liked—okay, loved—having sex with Bailey, and he made me laugh, but beyond that...it was scary as hell to let someone in. To feel again. My life had become a dark void I'd come to terms with, but being with Bailey had allowed some light to peek through the cracks.

We arrived at the cabin, the rain still pouring down.

"Let's leave the bags in the trunk for later," Bailey suggested, and I agreed, having little desire to get everything soaked.

We ran inside and toed off our sneakers at the door. Grady and Lauren were in the kitchen, along with Lauren's friends, Faith and Della. They'd already dipped into the wine, and I stood watching the two women. I didn't realize they were a couple until I saw them share a kiss after Faith poured Della a glass. Grady waved me in.

"Come. I'm hoping the rain'll stop for us to grill, but we can do the steaks indoors if we have to. Plus, the owners of the cabin told me we could have a fire if we wanted, so I'm kinda hoping it stays cool tonight."

"I wouldn't mind a cold night with you under the covers making it hot," Bailey purred in my ear.

"*Mmhmm.* Maybe tone it down at little."

"Ookay." Clearly confused, Bailey walked away, and I let him go. I joined the rest of the group and accepted a glass of wine from Faith.

"Lauren told us you didn't even know Grady existed before you were in your twenties. That's an amazing story."

I shrugged. "Yeah. I'm still getting used to the idea of having family."

"Which is about to grow larger." Lauren raised her glass. "Maybe this time next year, it'll be even bigger."

I choked on the wine. "You're pregnant?"

"No, but I want to start a family sooner rather than later." She gave Grady a loving glance, and he kissed her cheek.

"I do too. I'm almost forty, and I want to be able to play with my kids. And we want Lauren's mom to have the chance to maybe see a grandchild."

"Nice." I nodded and finished my wine. "I think I'm gonna go take a shower before dinner. Let me know if you need any help."

I left them and went upstairs. I stripped out of my damp clothes and stood under the hot spray. Grady was making a new life—wife, kids...a new family. The whole package. Would he still have time for me? The new brother he didn't have such deep emotional ties with? The prickly one who pushed him away as often as he hugged him?

I washed my hair and soaped myself. No more boys' nights hanging out at the club with Grady as my wingman, or him showing up with a pizza and a six-pack to watch a game. He had responsibilities now. Someone else to talk things through to make decisions.

Out of the shower, I dried off and put on sweats. Barefoot, I returned downstairs to find a fire crackling. Rain continued to pelt the roof, and everyone had a glass of wine in front of them. A large board with cheese, fruit, and sliced meats sat in the middle of the coffee table.

"Did I wander onto the set of a Hallmark movie?" I joked, but it wasn't far from the truth. Cozy cabin in the woods, fireplace with a fur rug, and everyone in their comfy wool sweaters. All that was needed was a Christmas tree and someone singing carols.

God forbid.

"We're all pretty cute, aren't we?" Weston joked, but I didn't smile. I walked into the kitchen, poured a full glass of something red, then wandered to the living-room window streaming with raindrops, matching my mood.

"What's wrong?" Bailey's shoulder nudged mine. "You look...sad."

I stayed silent and drank some more wine.

"It's too much, isn't it?"

"Don't pity me," I gritted out.

"Why would I?" There wasn't any teasing in Bailey's voice, and his profile remained unsmiling. "I understand. You might not believe me, but I do." He plucked the glass from my hand and took a sip. "Come back to the group. Grady's ready to start dinner, and I know he'd like your help."

I nodded, left the window, and went into the kitchen. Grady and Lauren were working side by side, joking with each other. A throb of loneliness pulsed inside me. Carlos had given me almost all my best memories, but now he'd become a memory himself.

"Hey, you two, need any help?"

Grady turned around, relief written in his eyes. I knew I was being a bit of a bastard and decided to tone down the pity party. "Sure, that'd be great. Want to make the salad?"

"I'm on it." At the large island, I assembled the vegetables and chopped and sliced, putting everything into a big wooden bowl. I mixed up a salad dressing and poured it over the leaves. As I worked, I watched Bailey, who'd been enlisted to make twice-baked potatoes. He broke up some bacon, grabbed some grated cheese, and piled them on top of the split potatoes. He slid them in the oven, chattering with Lauren as if he'd known her for years. Carlos had possessed that same enviable quality of making friends quick and easy. I listened intently.

"I used to eat these all the time as a kid. When my father would work a night tour and I'd be too tired to make something, I'd microwave a potato and stuff it with cheese and bacon. My three favorite food groups—bacon, carbs, and cheese. Filled me up, and it was nice and cheap."

"Where was your mother?" I blurted out, regretting it immediately, seeing him pale. He bowed his head.

"She didn't live with us." He walked off, and I shrugged when Grady met my eyes and raised his brows.

Past the wide kitchen island, I could see Bailey sitting with Weston and Brenner. I understood I'd touched a nerve, and though I wanted to know more, it would have to wait until later. No way was I venturing into that threesome.

For the rest of the evening, Bailey avoided me. During dinner, he sat with Weston and Brenner and talked about their law-school days, effectively shutting me out. Afterward, he, Faith, and Della decided to play a game of charades, and that was where I drew the line. I took another glass of wine, and as the rain had lessened, walked out onto the deck, sitting under the covered part, staring into the trees.

The door slammed, and I braced myself. Grady sat next to me.

"You okay?"

I lifted a shoulder and sipped my wine. "I needed a break."

"Yeah. I get it. It's hard being 'on' in a group." He raised the bottle he held in his hand. "I brought reinforcements."

"Good man." He topped me off, and we clinked glasses. "I'm really happy for you. You've got it all."

"It wasn't easy. I made a lot of mistakes along the way."

I snorted. "Yeah, but you managed to turn them into wins."

"And you think you haven't? You know you're wrong."

"Yeah? I'm in my midthirties, and the only reason I have what I do is because Carlos left it to me. Name one thing I accomplished on my own."

"Staying alive."

The reality of his words hit me like a punch to the gut. "That's not what I meant, and you know it."

Grady set his glass on the railing. "Listen. You make the life you choose to live. But you also have to open your eyes and see what's in front of you. Not let opportunities slip by." He rose to his feet. "How about coming back inside?"

Could he be any more obvious? "In a minute." My smile was faint. "I promise."

"Okay." He rested a hand on my head. "I love you, Keston. I'm not pressuring you to get into another relationship. I just want you to see that there are still chances for you to be happy."

I didn't answer because I couldn't. My throat closed up, and my eyes burned with tears. All I could do was nod, but that proved enough for Grady to leave me alone. It took several minutes and another glass of wine to get the damn emotions under control and return to the party.

I took a seat where I could observe the others. Faith and Della were sharing toasted marshmallows, and Weston and Brenner were still busy talking to Bailey, who sat with shoulders slumped and his head hung low.

Damn, I hadn't realized I would hit a nerve by mentioning his mother. He must've had a bad relationship with her, but at least he knew who his parents were. Despite Grady's words, I'd had enough of the warm and fuzzy atmosphere and decided to go to bed. Hopefully I'd fall asleep fast, and when I woke up, it would be Sunday and I could leave for my real life.

I prepared for my exit and half rose from my chair, but Bailey's phone rang, and from his expression, it wasn't good news. He crossed the room for privacy, and while everyone else continued their conversations, I zeroed in on him. I couldn't make out what he was saying, but his words came rapidly and he grew flushed. When he ended the call, he didn't bother to say anything, instead running upstairs. I gave him a minute, then followed.

The door to our room was open, and I stopped outside the threshold, watching him. Unlike the neat piles he'd unpacked, Bailey threw his clothes randomly in his overnight bag and tossed his travel kit on top.

"What's wrong?"

"Nothing," he answered as he continued to push everything inside.

"Oh yeah, sure. Now try the truth."

"I have to leave."

"Obviously. But why? What's wrong?"

"I said, nothing."

I finally entered the room. "And I call bullshit."

He zipped up his duffel. "It's personal."

I folded my arms and planted myself between him and the door, barring his escape. "We said we were going to try this thing between us. I'm no expert, but me supporting you fits that bill. I think we've moved beyond shutting me out with that bullshit *it's personal*."

His face burned red. "I have an emergency, and I need to return to the city."

My brows shot up. "Tonight? It's past ten o'clock. You won't get there until well after midnight."

"Doesn't matter. I have to go. So if you'll excuse me…"

"I'll go with you." The words came naturally without me even realizing I'd said them, and Bailey froze for a second, then snorted.

"Are you kidding me? Please move so I can leave."

"Not until you tell me what's going on."

"It's none of your business. You're delaying me, and I need to leave." His voice rose, and I could see he was upset, but there was something else I'd never encountered with him.

Fear.

"It'll take me two minutes to pack."

"I don't need you to come with me."

Ignoring him, I grabbed my bag from the bench and stuffed in it the few clothes I'd brought, then followed him downstairs, where he was making his apologies.

"I'm sorry, but I've got to leave. I have a family emergency, and I need to get to the city."

Everyone crowded around him, but I hung back. Grady approached me. "What's going on?"

"I don't know, but I'm going with him. It's late. He shouldn't be driving alone."

Grady nodded. "Good idea."

"It's not what you're thinking," I muttered.

"Oh, yeah? What am I thinking?" Grady arched a brow, and dammit, I could feel my face heating up.

"I'll talk to you tomorrow."

Bailey walked out of the house, paying no attention to me, and I hefted my bag over my shoulder and followed him. When I slid into the car, next to him, he glared at me.

"I said I didn't need you to come with me."

"I have a bad habit. I don't listen to people."

Mumbling to himself, Bailey started the car, and we took off. After twenty minutes of silence, he finally spoke.

"Why are you really here?"

"It's dark, and the roads are dangerous."

"Who are you, Triple A? Try again." He signaled to get on the Thruway.

We drove for a bit before I figured out an answer.

"I don't know. Maybe you'll need someone. You just looked like you shouldn't be alone."

CHAPTER SIXTEEN
BAILEY

Shouldn't be alone? I'm always alone.

Why the hell had Keston come with me? I kept my eyes on the taillights in front of me, my hands gripping the steering wheel. The roads up here were pitch-black, and my concentration was on the unfamiliar highway.

"I said I'd be fine."

"You say a lot of things, half of which I don't pay attention to."

"Asshole," I grumbled, and he chuckled.

"That's me. Come on. Tell me what happened. Who called you?"

I wasn't about to open the Pandora's box of my messy family life. "A client."

"You leave a party two hours away on a Saturday night for a client? Are you kidding me?"

Technically, my sister was a client—a nonpaying one, but still. "Yes. I'm a very dedicated attorney, what can I say?"

"What's the problem?"

"Sorry. Can't say. Attorney-client privilege." I increased my speed, flirting with eighty on the Thruway, then slowed to seventy-five. Much as I needed to get to the city in a hurry, getting a speeding ticket wouldn't help me or Belinda.

"I'm not digging for details. But it must be serious. He get arrested for murder? Drugs?"

I pressed my lips together. "Can you please stop?"

He shut his mouth until we reached the city and I drove to the Kensington area of Brooklyn. "Where the hell are we?" he asked, craning his neck.

My lip curled. "Welcome to the real Brooklyn." About a block from Belinda's apartment building, I found a parking spot and got out of the car. "Stay in the car. I'll be back soon."

Of course Keston didn't listen and trailed after me. The beginning of a headache throbbed behind my eyes, and before I entered her building, I stopped and poked a finger in his chest.

"Say nothing. Please. This is a delicate situation."

His eyes grew wide. "Does this have something to do with the call you got that time we were interrupted?"

My stomach sank, but I didn't have the time for a long, involved story. "Yeah. Belinda. She's had a very up-and-down relationship with her ex-boyfriend, which included orders of protection."

"Sounds like a real prick."

"He is. Last week she asked me to withdraw the restraining order, which—against my better judgment—I did. She claimed Jonas had changed, but I had my doubts." I pinched my eyes shut for a second. "Tonight she called, semi-hysterical about something. She couldn't get out what the problem was but said she needed to see me. I just know it wasn't good. So here I am. Now I have to find out what's wrong."

I didn't wait for Keston to respond, using my key to open the entrance, then waiting for the elevator. Surprised but relieved that Keston seemed to accept my explanation, I danced on my toes with impatience on the way up and burst through the doors when they opened, racing to Belinda's apartment. I knocked, my heart pounding. It wasn't Belinda but Jonas who answered, bare-chested and in a pair of sweats that left nothing to the imagination.

He smirked at me. "Bailey, buddy. Long time no see."

Keston stood behind me, silent, but at the moment, I was grateful for his presence.

"Where's Lindee?" I trembled, almost afraid of the answer. "She called me."

"I know. I was right next to her." He waved a hand. "Baby, come. Bailey's here."

Baby? My mind windmilled in a million different directions. What the fuck was going on?

"I'm not standing out in the hallway like some delivery person." I shouldered my way inside, and my gaze found Belinda, hair twisted up in a messy bun, wearing a little T-shirt and short shorts. Like Jonas, she wasn't wearing anything underneath, and I averted my eyes. "Lindee, what's going on? Are you all right?"

Arms outstretched, she ran to me. "Bailey, I can't believe you came. Look." She held out her hand, and I saw a large diamond on her finger. "Jonas gave it to me tonight. We're gonna get married. He got a big promotion at work." She admired the ring. "I couldn't wait to share the news with you."

Stunned, I stepped away from her. "Wait. So you...you're okay? You were crying so hard, and when you asked me to come, I thought..."

"The worst of me, as usual," Jonas finished my sentence. "She was crying with happiness because of the ring. Beautiful, ain't it? Three fucking carats." He put a muscular arm around her.

"I've had reason to think that, haven't I?"

Jonas's lips thinned. "Lindee don't need you bailin' her out no more. I take care of what's mine."

It was an effort to keep my voice from shaking. "My sister isn't your possession. And I haven't forgotten how you *took care* of her in the past."

"No, Bailey, Jonas never did nothin'. I swear." She pulled on my arm. "He treats me real good now." She let go of me. "Who's this?" She transferred her attention to Keston, and her lips curved in a bright smile. "Hi, I'm Belinda, Bailey's sister."

Fuck. The last thing I needed was Belinda to give Keston the third degree. She'd be all over him with a thousand questions, and I had no desire to give any explanation.

"I'm Keston. A friend of Bailey's."

"A close friend?" She giggled. "Are you his boyfriend?"

"No," the two of us responded in unison.

Shutting this down, I took her by the elbow. "Can we talk for a minute? Alone?"

She darted a glance at Jonas, who grunted, "Fine."

"I wasn't asking you for permission." I walked her to the tiny kitchen. "Lindee, what the hell is happening?" I hissed in a furious whisper. "Are you telling me the truth? Please. You can be honest with me. Jonas won't know."

"Yes, I am." Blue eyes flashed fire. "I told you. Jonas was promoted to foreman, and he's makin' top money. He knows he's made mistakes, and I told you he's goin' to therapy for anger." She played with the ring. "He says he loves me and wants us to be together and have a baby."

I didn't trust Jonas. I couldn't forget the sight of Belinda crying in her trashed apartment because of him screaming and cursing her. But I also couldn't live her life. This had been going on for too many years with no conclusion.

"I worry about you. I don't want to see you hurt."

"I swear I'm not. I love Jonas. I hated bein' without him, and we're gonna make it work this time. We're both gonna go to counseling." A mischievous grin kicked up her lips. "And I don't believe for a second that Keston ain't your boyfriend. He's gorgeous. Go home and have fun with him insteada being all wrapped up in my life."

"He's not…" I raised my eyes to the ceiling and shook my head. *Fuck it. Why am I trying to explain?* "I came because you were crying and I was worried."

"I was crying 'cause I was happy and wanted to tell you. Please don't start anything. Go home." Her jaw set firmly, and she folded her arms.

There was nothing left here for me. Belinda had made her choice, and I had to accept it and be ready to pick up the pieces if it all fell apart.

"Did you tell *her*?"

For the first time that night, she lost the sparkle in her eyes. "Are you kidding? She's not a normal mother. She wouldn't give a damn. She'd probably try 'n make me sell the ring."

Apparently, I'd had enough time with my sister, because Jonas rejoined us. "The less Lindee has to do with that bitch the better. All she does whenever we see her is ask for money."

Well, that appeared to be the one thing we agreed on. I met Jonas's eyes. "Keep it that way."

He jerked his head. "Not a problem. I'm movin' Lindee outta this dump. Got a lead on a house in Dyker Heights." He puffed out his chest. "She ain't gonna need your money no more."

"I don't care about that. Keep her safe. I don't want any late-night calls from the police."

His jaw tightened. "Yeah. Ain't gonna happen." Again, he slid his arm around Belinda. "You mind if we cut this short? It's late, and I gotta get up early tomorrow for work. I know you don't trust me, but you'll see. I ain't gonna screw it up this time."

I gave him a curt nod and kissed Belinda on the cheek. "Call me if you need anything."

"Nice to meet you, Keston," Belinda called out as I opened the door. "Hope to see you soon."

I shut the door behind us.

"Mother of God," I muttered, striding down the hall to the elevator, and then to the car. Keston remained silent, matching me step for step. I waited until we were on the BQE to talk. "It's late, and I'm in no mood to discuss anything. I'll drop you off at your place."

He didn't answer right away. Once we were on the Williamsburg Bridge, heading toward the city, he stated, "I don't think so. I'm coming home with you."

As much as my body screamed *Hell to the yeah* at his words, my head wasn't on board. "Look, Keston, I can't right now."

He put a hand over mine on the steering wheel. "I know. But I can."

There wasn't much traffic on Delancey Street, which was a good thing as a rush of tears blurred my vision. I sniffled. "Dammit. I would've taken the West Side highway if I'd known. The Lower East Side is such a bitch to drive through."

I caught the edge of Keston's smile and turned the car in the right direction. It took half an hour to find parking a few blocks from my place.

"I'll return the car tomorrow," I explained, slipping the keys into my pocket. "I'm fine, you know."

"Yeah, sure." Keston put a hand to my back. "Let's go."

At that hour, relatively few people walked the streets in my neighborhood, yet cabs still whizzed past. I could've insisted Keston go home and put him in a car—I was crashing and emotional and might say things I'd later regret. But all the fight drained out of me, and the adrenaline that had kept me in forward motion seeped away. I put my head down and walked to my block.

Keston kept the pace easily, and my shaky fingers dropped the keys on the stoop. He picked them up and unlocked the heavy entrance door and the one to my apartment.

"It's late," I protested again, weakly, as he put his arms around me, but I didn't resist when he tucked me into his chest. We might be the same size, but at that moment I felt as helpless as a kitten.

"I can tell time. And I'm still staying. Nothing's happening except us sleeping in the same bed. I remember every time bad things would happen to me as a kid, all I wanted was for someone to be there for me."

"And you want to be that person for me?"

"I think that's obvious."

I couldn't object even if I wanted to. I'd spent hours driving, worrying about Belinda, afraid I'd show up and find her hurt and hysterical. Instead, she was excited and celebrating her engagement, warning me off her and her new life. I felt stupid, used, and wanted to curl up in a ball and hide.

Keston, sensing my submission, steered me to the bedroom, where he undressed me and put me into bed. He shed his clothes and climbed in. True to his word, he didn't put the moves on me, not even a kiss. I scooted closer, needing his strength, and sighed. Contentment spread through me, warm as the Mediterranean sun, and peace filled my fractured soul.

"Good night, Bailey."

I closed my eyes.

**

I awoke to the smell of coffee and an empty bed. I heard sounds in the kitchen. I ran to the bathroom, put on briefs, and when I entered the living room, seeing Keston in my kitchen, drinking coffee, had my stupid emotions in overdrive creating hopes and dreams of us living here and mornings like this being a daily occurrence.

"Hey," he said, glancing up from the mug in his hands. "I figured you'd want coffee, so I made some. Nothing fancy, but it does the trick."

"Thanks." I joined him at the island and took the cup he handed me. "It's good."

"You really were a barista?"

I sipped my coffee. "Yeah. Three years. It helped me through college. Money was tight, and my dad didn't make a hell of a lot as a patrol cop."

"I didn't know."

"What, you thought I was too cute to be serving coffee drinks?" I teased. "And why would you know anything about me other than I'm great in bed?"

"And that you're modest?" But he gave me one of those rare, beautiful smiles, and I couldn't help grinning back.

"One of my better qualities." My humor faded. "Thanks for being there last night."

He sipped his coffee. "You're welcome. It must be hard watching your sister make mistake after mistake."

"For years I tried to protect her the best way I knew how—money, legal advice. And I didn't mind because I knew she'd had it rough. Now?" I shrugged. "Maybe I'm ready to let go. I think my promise to my father was fulfilled."

"I agree. At some point she has to own up to her responsibilities. And if she's marrying that guy, they'll have to deal with each other."

While I understood Keston's logic and agreed with him on principle, I knew it'd be hard to walk away completely. Some part of me would always be watching over Belinda. I also wanted to change the subject.

"What're you doing today, now that we're home early in the city? I know you don't have any clients scheduled, so we could have one of those brunches you're so intent on avoiding."

Keston's brow furrowed. "I'm not avoiding them. It's just not my scene."

"Well, I love them. How about we compromise?" I set my cup aside and circled the island to hug him. "We go out for brunch, then you can decide what we get to do for the rest of the afternoon." I pressed a kiss to his mouth. "I think we both have the same idea for how we'll spend the night."

He groped my ass. "Is this part of the figuring-out-what-we're-doing thing we talked about at the cabin?"

I already knew my feelings, but no way in hell was I going to tell Keston.

"Yeah. I think so. What do you say?"

He kissed me. "Bring on the Bloody Marys."

It was the perfect day, leading to an even better night. After brunch, which he admitted—grudgingly—that he'd enjoyed, we walked past the Dakota, and into Central Park. The weather stayed sunny, and hand in hand, we strolled along the path. Keston bought a pretzel, and I bit almost half of it off. Pretend-outraged, he pulled it away from me.

"What the hell was that?"

"I like a man with a big pretzel, what can I say? Especially yours 'cause it's extra salty."

"There's no stopping you, is there?" he groaned and finished it off. He wrapped his arm around my waist, our lips brushing together. His eyes sparkled in the sunlight, and my heart pounded.

"Nothing could keep me from wanting you."

Keston blinked and kissed me. "Let's go to your place."

Once home, he didn't jump me as I'd thought but led me to the couch. I sat, and he lay with his head in my lap.

"You were right."

My fingers played in his hair. "About what? There are so many possible answers."

"The brunch. It was nice."

"I'm glad you liked it." My fingers trailed the cut of his jawline. "What do you think about sushi for dinner?"

"I'm thinking they better deliver late."

I glanced down at him, and at the familiar glint in his eyes, my body leaped to respond.

"Guess we'll have to find out." I raced to the bedroom. Keston followed me, and I met his lips eagerly as I pulled him to the bed.

**

Monday morning, I awoke with Keston's arm heavy across my waist, and I welcomed its weight. For a few minutes I luxuriated in my fantasy. Keston and me, together. In love. Carefully, I turned to him and studied his face as he slept, something I never got a chance to do when he was awake.

Even in rest, his brow was furrowed, and I wondered about the pain still living inside him. Was he irrevocably broken, too fractured to feel? To love? Was I? My head spinning, I closed my eyes, as if that would settle my jumbled thoughts into some semblance of coherence.

"What the hell are you so serious about this early?" Keston asked, his voice a husky, delicious rasp.

"I thought you were asleep."

"Nope. Just lying here, getting ready to face the day. Again, why are you looking so grim?" He frowned. "Oh. Still thinking about your sister? That's rough. Do you want to talk about it?"

I flipped the sheets and hopped out of bed. "I need to take a shower." I left him and stood under the water, getting my wits together. I dried off and returned to the bedroom, but Keston was gone. I found him in the kitchen, drinking coffee. Seeing me, he poured a cup.

"Here." He pushed it toward me. "You didn't answer me. Do you want to talk about your sister?"

I put up a hand. "I have a miserable week ahead of me, filled with divorce settlements and custody battles, so I'm not in the right headspace to talk about anything."

Keston set his cup on the countertop. "That's fine. Can I take a shower?"

I'd been prepared for his poking and prodding, but I should've known Keston, as private as he was about his life, wasn't about to insert himself into mine. We went through life shouldering our demons alone.

"Yeah, of course."

He rinsed his mug and left me to drink the rest of my coffee. I heard the shower running, then shut off, and I took my second mug into the bedroom, where I watched him rummage through his bag and pull out some clothes. I hated seeing that beautiful body covered, but I had to admit, he looked as good dressed as he did naked.

He zipped up his bag, and I walked him to the door. I undid the locks, and he surprised me by tangling his fingers in my hair and settling his mouth over my willing lips. I sank into that kiss, sucking his tongue, inhaling his scent, his breath, until he broke away, wild-eyed and panting.

"Tonight?" He waited, and stunned by his question, I couldn't find my voice and nodded. "I'll come here."

And he was gone.

"Jesus," I muttered, still on fire from the raw lust and passion of that single kiss. I'd been with plenty of guys, had lots of enjoyable sex, but there was something about Keston that made me nervous and unsure. Like a virgin.

"Get it under control. Your dick doesn't pay the bills."

I laughed to myself and went to finish getting dressed, already anticipating the evening ahead.

CHAPTER SEVENTEEN
KESTON

I couldn't stop thinking about him.

While prepping my clients, sketching out stencils, even listening to one of my longtime customers, bass player Noel Valentine, go on and on about the threesome he'd had the night before, all I could see was Bailey's frightened face illuminated by the dashboard light as we drove to the city.

I'd been so fucking wrong about him. From the bits and pieces I'd picked up, he'd been raised by a single father and had a sister he'd bailed out of trouble numerous times. Not a trust-fund baby like his friend Weston. *Shit.* His story sounded almost as complicated as mine.

"Dude, what'ya say? You interested?"

"In what?" Refocusing on Noel, I stopped filling in his latest ink—a large bass guitar weeping tears and hearts—and set my instrument on the tray. "Sorry, I was concentrating."

"I got this gig tonight, and then a bunch of us are goin' to this club uptown." Noel's green eyes glinted. "Maybe we could hook up. Could be a blast."

My brows shot sky high. It was the first time Noel had put the moves on me, but that life of hard partying wasn't my scene. Listening to his stories made me wonder how long he could keep it up. When he'd been playing with Remi Angel, they'd partied together, but last I'd heard, Remi had settled down, gotten married, and retired from the performing life.

"Sorry. I can't tonight." I continued working on his tattoo. Another forty-five minutes, and it was done. "All right, that's it. You know the drill."

Noel watched me prep and wrap his arm. After I'd finished, he leaped off the chair to follow me to pay. "Yeah. Looks good, bro. And if you change your mind, we'll be at Haven, on West Ninety-eighth."

I smiled and shook my head. "That'll be nine hundred." He tapped his card and tossed me a two-hundred-dollar tip.

"Awesome as usual. Thanks, and see ya later." He winked and strode out, blond hair catching the sun. The man looked like an angel but, from everything he'd told me and what I'd heard, he had the soul of a devil.

"Dude, are you fucking nuts? He's hot and a rocker. Why'd you say no?" Ambrose, whose client had already left, came over to me. Jodi was still working on her customer, a young mother having her baby's name and birthdate inked on her ankle, along with a tiny footprint.

"Not my scene." I returned to my station to sanitize my equipment and wipe the chair.

"What? What the hell is your scene if it's not him?"

I hadn't yet figured out how to fit Bailey into my life. The fact that I was having those thoughts about him still didn't make sense, but fuck it. Something about Bailey was addictive, and seeing him so lost and broken, when I was used to only the flirting, joking, and sensual side, chipped away at my rock-hard heart. Spending the weekend with him opened my eyes to more of the puzzle that made up Bailey Marks. I'd never been into games, but I itched to fit his pieces together.

"Maybe I'm not looking."

In a rare bout of gentleness, Ambrose patted my arm. "I know it's been hard since you lost Carlos. But it sucks to be alone. Since I met Carly, I've been less angry."

Not that I'd seen, but if he believed it, more power to him.

"It's not that." I didn't want to talk about it, and luckily the phone rang with a new appointment to distract me. But Ambrose waited until I ended the call and put the customer in the computer.

"I meant to ask. How was the weekend with your brother? You were in a cabin upstate?"

My smile was true. "It was cool. I really like Lauren, his fiancée. She's pretty awesome. It was fun, actually. Grady had a bunch of his friends there, and Lauren had some of hers. We all hung out, went apple-picking. It was...nice."

Ambrose rolled his eyes. "Sounds like a commercial for one of those cheesy holiday movies Carly loves to watch."

I snickered. "Yeah. I said that too. A bunch of lawyers and me."

"So did you have a chance to talk to Grady about Lucas? You had the whole weekend. Could you find a couple of minutes?"

I hesitated. "He wasn't too hopeful. I've told you that before. Remember, he's not a criminal attorney. He does family law—adoptions, child custody, that kind of stuff."

Ambrose's shoulders slumped. "I know, I know. It's just... Lucas didn't get a fair trial, I'm positive. His lawyers sucked. No offense to your brother, but they all suck. Money-grubbers makin' a living off people's suffering."

While I could agree with him on some of that, it didn't apply to all of them, and definitely not to the people I'd met this weekend, like Faith and Della, who prosecuted scumbags preying on kids and vulnerable people.

"I never asked, but what does Lauren do? Don't tell me she's a lawyer too?"

The last thing I'd reveal to Ambrose was that Lauren worked for the office that put his brother away.

"Yeah. But nothing that could help Lucas."

His hand formed a fist. "Dammit. How can you surround yourself with all these sharks?"

"Maybe I'm learning not to judge a person's character by their profession. I mean, how many times have we bitched to each other that people think we're criminals or in a gang because of our tattoos?"

But arguing with Ambrose was like spitting into the wind— he just flew right back at me with my own words.

"Yeah, but lots of different people have tats now. You gotta be a certain kind of person to be a lawyer."

Tired of his complaining, I brushed him off. "Yeah. Grady's got ink, and he's a lawyer. He's also my brother, so knock it off already with the lawyer crap."

His face turned hard. "Damn, they sucked you in too."

"Enough," I snapped. The door opened, and my next client appeared. "I've got work, and you have someone in about fifteen minutes."

"I know my schedule. Thanks."

The rest of the day was spent mostly in silence, and I hated it. Ambrose had been with me from the start, and I'd seen how his blind loyalty to Lucas was beginning to destroy his relationships with the people who cared most about him.

At six o'clock, as I was cleaning up, I got a text from Bailey. I'd thought about him all day but had refrained from getting in touch. He'd seemed upset when I left that morning, and when his name popped up, I immediately wondered if he was canceling.

Still on for tonight?

I could feel happiness tugging at my lips, and darted a glance over to where Jodi and Ambrose were putting away their instruments. I didn't need them in my business, for different reasons. Jodi would go next level with ooey-gooey giggles, and Ambrose would either take a swing at me or accuse me of fraternizing with the enemy.

Yeah. Just finishing up. Be by around 8.

I'll be waiting.

He tacked on several flame emojis. I chuckled to myself and stuck the phone into my jeans pocket.

"Care to share with the class what's so funny?" Jodi asked in wide-eyed innocence.

I put on a stern face and narrowed my eyes. "Nothing." Judging by her saucy smile and eye roll, she knew I was a damn liar, but I refused to take her bait.

"Looked like something to me," Ambrose chimed in. "You got a hot date?"

I kept my face neutral. "No. I have things to do."

"Things to do," Ambrose repeated. "Why so secretive?"

"I'm not. I have errands...shit to take care of. I was away all weekend. Enough with the third, fourth, and fifth degree." I picked up my jacket and zipped it up. "Ready to close up?"

"Damn. So touchy." Ambrose put on his coat, and Jodi did the same and grabbed her purse.

"All set."

I shut off the lights, locked the door, and set the alarm. "See you tomorrow." I bumped fists with Ambrose and gave Jodi a nod, then walked to my place. It took me less than half an hour to shower, change, and pack a bag because yeah, I was spending the night uptown with Bailey.

But first we were going to talk.

**

Bailey had changed from Mr. Suit and Tie into athletic pants and a T-shirt, and he was freshly showered, his dark hair lying in wet curls, his skin glowing. His eyes lit up when he saw my overnight bag.

"I take it you're staying?"

"That's the plan."

"Come on." I stepped inside and Bailey hummed. "You smell amazing." He drew in an audible breath. "*Mmm-mmm.*"

I hesitated only a second and kissed him. Hard. Soft, yielding lips moved over mine, and I yanked him close...closer. He opened to the pressure of my mouth, and at his moan, I realized I couldn't let him go. Not tonight. Or tomorrow.

Maybe never.

Whoa. Where the fuck did that come from?

"Come with me." Bailey tugged my hand, and all my good intentions to talk first flew out the window. My body demanded his, and I tangled our fingers together as we walked to the bedroom. He stripped, I tossed my clothes, and we fell on the bed in a hot, hard tangle of limbs. I loved that his thighs were scratchy with hair and his chest wasn't bare—too many pretty boys shaved themselves sleek as a seal, and it was like kissing a teenager. Not my thing.

Bailey, with his toned legs, firm ass, and hard six-pack, was all man. And tonight? Mine. But as usual, he wasn't a silent partner.

"I need it bad, Keston. Just give it to me hard and fast. I've been thinking about it all day, and I can't wait."

He was telling me the truth. He had the condoms and lube out on the bed, ready for us. His dick was rock-hard, flushed and thick. He got on all fours and grasped himself. I mapped the globes of his perfect ass with my hands and dove in for a snack.

"Oh fuck, please, God. Keston. I want..." His words garbled as I plunged my tongue in deep and worked on him. I wet my fingers and thrust them in and out of his twitching body, loving his hoarse, broken cries. He squeezed me, and my dick ached, needing him. Wanting him.

I flipped him to gaze into his hazy eyes. "Bailey," I whispered and nudged his cheek, kissing him. I'd had plenty of sex, but this was something more. Something intensely intimate. My skin prickled with awareness. I wanted to run, to hide from what was happening, but I couldn't move. I didn't want to.

"I know." He caught my shoulder and slid his arm around my neck, anchoring me to him. "I know."

I used the lube and rolled on a condom, and with one smooth push, entered him. He sucked me into his heat with a grip so tight, I couldn't imagine him ever letting me go.

Or wanting him to.

Wishing I could hold on to these breath-stealing moments forever, I raised his legs to my shoulders, willing myself to become one with him. He writhed as I pumped, his hand moving on his shaft, faster and faster. Being inside Bailey took me apart to the very blood rushing through my veins, and I exploded. Beneath me, Bailey quivered and shook as he came, spilling across our bellies.

Chests heaving, we clung together, bodies slick and sticky with sweat and come. Bailey slid his hands past my waist to knead my ass. "Absolutely fucking perfect."

"No one's perfect." I nuzzled beneath his ear, sucking the lobe. "Especially me."

"You are perfect. To me." He traced the tattoos on my arm with his fingertips, then his tongue. I slipped out of him, rolled off to get rid of the condom, and returned to him in bed, where he picked up where he left off, skimming the outline of the infinity symbol.

"That was for Carlos," I blurted out, shocking myself. Bailey stopped, his finger resting on my skin. "That date is the day he died." My head hung low. "It was as if I died too."

I didn't know what I expected Bailey's reaction to be. I'd never explained it to anyone, not even to Grady, but I knew my brother had understood. Everyone who knew me accepted it without question.

"I'm glad you didn't die. But you're lucky you had someone to love you."

"Come on, you've never been in love before?" I teased.

His smile was devastating in its sadness. "If you're not loved in return, it's not true love because that requires sharing. I was in lust and make-believe fantasies about guys who only wanted sex. None of it was real." He sat up, his mood shifting like the wind. "But enough about me." He swung his legs off the side of the bed. "Let's have something to eat to get ready for round two." He put his pants on.

I stopped him before he could leave the room. "Enough about you? Are you kidding? You haven't said jack shit about yourself."

He laughed. "What? I'm a boring guy. Nothing to see here." He spread his arms wide, but I folded mine and refused to move.

"I disagree. So yeah, let's have dinner, but we're gonna talk." I caught him by the arm as he pushed past me. "I want to know."

He kept his head down, and the despair in his voice was haunting. "Don't say I didn't warn you."

CHAPTER EIGHTEEN
BAILEY

I slurped my pho. "This is the best. I could have it every day."

Keston had finished his and was crunching on a spring roll. "We have some good places down by me. But this is good too."

"Maybe we'll try them sometime. Do a comparison."

He didn't agree or even respond, and I wondered again why he was so intent on keeping me away from where he lived. I'd only been there one time, and even when I visited him at the shop, I felt he couldn't wait for me to leave. I knew he liked his privacy, but nonetheless, it didn't make sense.

"You finished?" He shoved his takeout containers in a bag. "I'll take your stuff."

"Yeah, thanks. The recycling goes in the blue bag. I'll take it out later." Yawning, I stretched my arms over my head.

"What a day. I could go for a beer and just vegging on the couch."

Finished with his cleanup, Keston returned to the table. "Fine. Get your beer, and you can tell me what the hell happened the other night, because I still can't figure it out."

Dammit. I should've known he wouldn't give up. But I kept my cool. "Yeah, no problem. You want one?" I opened the refrigerator.

"No, I'm good." He sat on the couch. Waiting. Hard eyes pinned to mine as I approached.

"Yeah, you are," I teased, but he didn't smile.

"You don't need to make a joke about everything, you know."

Sure I did, but he didn't need to know that. "I'm not. It was amazing before." I sat next to him, but he shifted away.

"Bailey. Saturday night you almost had a breakdown because you thought your sister was in trouble. Then she talked about your mother."

"You heard all that?"

The harsh lines of his face softened. "What's going on? You can talk to me."

I wasn't used to this...this intimacy. No one I'd been with previously had been interested in knowing me beyond which drawer held my condoms and lube. Their interest never extended past what happened between the sheets. Yet now I had Keston asking me to open up, and I hesitated.

"Why?" I gulped down my beer. "It's not like anything's going to change."

"That's what I used to think. When I was a kid, I was angry. All the time. I kept everything bottled up—my mother dumping me, no father, kids teasing me 'cause I didn't have money to go places or wear cool clothes. And all that rage built and built until I exploded. Hitting people, tagging, stealing, anything to stop the—"

"Pain," I finished for him. "Yeah. I understand." I pinched my eyes.

"Because...?" Keston urged. "Listen, if you're worried I'm gonna tell anyone, don't be. I know what it's like to live inside your head with too much stuff floating around. Thinking you're not good enough, that you'll never be, because of who you are and where you came from."

Going to a commuter college, and with my father dying, I'd come and gone and hadn't socialized much. In law school, I'd broken free and decided to be the fun one. The gay friend always up for a good time. No one in my fraternity had pushed to talk about ourselves—we'd all known Weston was rich and a senator's son and that Brenner was quiet and brilliant. The other guys were legacies, with girlfriends. And then there was me.

No one cared about the real Bailey Marks. I was the one with a joke and a smile, and that was what I'd let everyone see. There'd never been a need for me to shed my skin. But there'd never been anyone like Keston in my life before.

"My mother left when I was four. Just walked out on us one day and never came home. My father was a cop, but she wanted him to become a detective, a chief in the department, up, up, and away on the ladder of the NYPD, but he liked being on the street with the people. A patrol cop. So she bailed, to find better, richer prospects. He was the best dad and worked so damn hard. Our neighbor would watch me after school, or if I was sick, my dad would stay home. Money was always tight." I twisted my hands in my lap and shifted in my seat. "Then 9/11 happened."

Keston's eyes grew wide. "He was there? Jesus..."

"No. But his precinct was close by, and they all went to help, you know? With the rescue at first, then the recovery. He worked on the pile, breathing in those fumes." I wiped at my eyes. "He contracted a lung disease that eventually killed him." A laugh escaped. "That's when my mother decided to reappear, with Belinda in tow. She'd heard—no idea how—that my father had a 9/11 illness and was eligible for a nice, fat payout from the fund set up."

"Damn, that's cold."

"The saddest thing is that they never officially divorced. My father couldn't bring himself to do it. So he died, and she got half his pension, the house, and the 9/11 settlement. I was in college, impotent to do anything. And my dad asked me to take care of Belinda. I couldn't say no."

"So you help her out?"

"Yeah. 'Cause as you can imagine with a mother like ours, she's had a ton of her own problems."

"And your mother? She still in your life?"

Merely talking about my mother gave me cramps and heart palpitations. "*Pfft*, barely. She lives rent free in the house —my father's house. But now she wants to sell it."

"And you don't." Keston nodded. "Can't say I blame you."

Funny how it felt good to bare my soul, like a bloodletting releasing the poisons.

"It's the last memory I've got of my father and me. My mother forgot about us, but I never did." I pushed my shaky hands through my hair. "Look, that's enough of my sob story."

Unable to sit still any longer, I ran away from Keston's sympathy and pity. I couldn't bear either one. I had my hand on the doorknob when Keston grabbed me around the waist and hauled me away.

"You have no socks or sneakers on. Where the hell are you going?"

Feeling like a complete fool, I returned to the couch, Keston following.

"What's the deal with your sister? Aside from giving her money, I take it you watch over her?"

"Yeah. Belinda's still suffering the effects of being an unwanted child. She keeps falling for every guy's line, no matter how fake. She so desperately wants to be loved by someone that she'll do almost anything. Including staying with some jerk whose mouth is bigger than his brains."

"You mean that guy who was at her apartment."

"Jonas. Her ex. They've been on and off for years. I could never prove that he actually touched her because she refused to say, but he's scared her with his temper so badly that she finally got a restraining order against him—which as I told you, she insisted I have the court lift. Now this engagement. Color me suspicious, but she told me to butt out."

"And you've been giving her money?"

A valid question, and the answer would make me sound like a sucker. "She's had trouble keeping jobs. I couldn't let her live in a shelter, and she and our mother can barely be in the same room without screaming their heads off. I found her that place after I got her out of Jonas's apartment. I pay for it and give her money." I attempted to lighten the mood. "And there you have the whole sad story of Bailey Marks."

"I don't see it like that. You're a nice guy, and your sister is lucky to have someone like you."

"I think so," I joked, but Keston frowned.

"Don't downplay it. If I'd known Grady when I was a teenager, who knows? I might not've gotten into all the trouble I did."

"But you found someone else to help you." It was time for Keston to spill his guts like I had. "Carlos."

Keston's eyes flickered. "Yeah, but…"

"No buts, Keston. I had no one. Carlos taught you not only how to love him, but how to love yourself. My dad was the best, but I couldn't really talk to him about personal stuff. He got sick and I never told him I was gay."

At some point while I was talking, Keston rested his hand on my nape and began a slow massage. This touch was different from the others, warmth flowing from his skin to mine, but without anything sexual. He was letting me know he understood and was there for me. I couldn't explain how his simple gesture altered everything between us. Keston was fast becoming my compass in the wandering roads of my life, leading me to a safe place.

"Carlos saved me. More than the job, he gave me a way forward, out of the bitterness and anger that had become the parameters of my world. He showed me another path. And when I was older, he gave me his heart."

"You're very lucky," I said. "I've never had that."

"I know I am. But why do you think that? You've got good friends."

"Friends, yes. But good friends?" I huffed out a fake-ass laugh and shook my head. "If you're talking about Weston and Brenner, nah. We were friendly during law school, but with West and Brenner too intent on one-upping each other and me being gay, I always felt a little on the outside, looking in. We reconnected once Weston moved to New York, and yeah, we've definitely become better friends, but I've never told anyone any of this. Only you."

Keston stopped the gentle movement of his fingers. "Why?"

It would be so damn easy to make a joke of it. Like I always did when it came to things I didn't want to talk about. But dammit, I was tired of holding it all inside. So what if I told him how I felt?

"Because." I shifted away to look him in the eye. "I knew you'd understand. I have feelings for you. More than just sex."

Keston didn't break our stare-down. "Is this part of that dating thing we said we were trying?"

"Yeah. I think it is. But maybe it's too much for you, or not what you expected. If you don't feel the same, I'll back off. I know I'm not the kind of guy you're used to." For years I'd been content with scraps from random men I'd slept with, but if I was going to try this with Keston, I needed the entire meal, not simply a bone he wanted to throw to placate me. I'd learned so much about him, yet I knew there was more.

"No, you're not. You wear suits, live uptown. Pay your bills in full on time. Hell, half the time I forget a guy's name right after he tells me." He returned to stroking me, and I had to refrain from purring. "But I can't forget your name. Or you."

He went from stroking my neck to cupping my cheek, and I knew all I had to do was meet him halfway and we'd be naked again. My body was all for it, but I'd learned I was worth more than what my body had to give. Time to let my brain lead the way.

"I like hearing that." I moved out of reach and watched his expression grow wary, tense. I went for a change of subject. "Do you think I should sell the house?"

"Do you ever plan to live there?"

"No, probably not."

"Is the upkeep expensive?"

"Not really. Just taxes, insurance, and the monthly bills." I shrugged. "Of course my mother contributes nothing."

"I gathered that," he answered dryly. "I guess the main question is, why? Why hold on to it? Is it to keep the memory of your father alive, or to spite your mother?"

I appreciated Keston not dismissing me and instead asking informative questions, though they made me dig deep–uncomfortably so–and I might not like what I'd uncover.

"I-I don't know." Lies, all lies. I knew, but I wasn't ready to face the truth out loud. "How about we stop talking about me for a while? Tell me more about Carlos."

Keston grew pale under his scruff. His hands clenched over his thighs. "You already know."

"Yeah, but not much. You met him when you were a teenager, right? In your arts program? He taught you how to tattoo?"

"Yeah." He snorted with the laughter of painful remembrance. "I graduated from pen-ink designs on my skin to learning the true art of skin ink. I was fourteen when we met at the school program, and I worked in the shop until I was eighteen, when we first kissed. A kiss I instigated. I had a huge crush on him. And no, in case you were wondering, we didn't have sex right away. Carlos wanted me to see other guys my age. I was crazy about him. I didn't need anyone else, but I went out with other guys to please him. We waited two years, and he was my first."

"He sounds very smart and caring."

"The best. Even though we were so far apart in age, we were in sync. When he died, I fell into a cold, dark depression. If I didn't have Grady..." He rubbed his face and took off, heading for the window. I let him go, giving him the space he needed. Several minutes passed before he returned. "Sorry about that."

"Never apologize for your emotions. I learned that in therapy." Keston's brows rose high, and I laughed. "Yeah, I've been in therapy for years. You're not the only one. You used art to channel your pain; I used sex. When my mother came back, waltzing into our lives like she'd gone for a night out with the girls instead of years of nothing, it fucked me up." My smile was frozen. "She didn't apologize or try and get to know me. She just showed up with Belinda in tow and said, 'This is your little sister.' Belinda is ten years younger. From that moment on, I tried to watch out for her because no one else was. Soon after their return, my father's health declined rapidly, and he died while I was in college."

"I can't imagine the shock."

"As much as when you discovered you had a brother," I pointed out.

His lashes lowered. "Yeah."

I persisted. "But see, neither of you knew of the other's existence. As soon as Grady learned he had a brother, he started looking for you. My *mother* deliberately left me behind and only reappeared when she somehow found out my father was sick. It meant she would eventually come into money. It was never about me. It never is."

This time when Keston put his arms around me, I didn't push him away. "I'm not going anywhere."

I should continue to be strong, but I didn't want to let him go. My mother's abandonment had left a hole in my heart, but the caring Keston showed me filled a little of that aching emptiness.

"I don't need you staying because you feel sorry for me."

"What is there to feel sorry for?" He kissed my hair. "You've got a great job, a roof over your head, money in the bank, and people who care about you. You had a father who loved you."

"I should be happy because so many people don't have what I do. You didn't."

"No, I didn't, but I had Carlos." He tangled his fingers in my hair and met my eyes. "Maybe we can figure the rest of it out together."

CHAPTER NINETEEN
KESTON

Before Bailey got the wrong idea, I wanted to explain what I meant, but when I opened my mouth to speak, his tongue pushed inside and I forgot what I was about to say.

"Come to the bedroom with me." He rocked the bulge of his thick cock against mine, and I held his face, continuing to press kisses on his throat. As it happened every time, my brain switched off, and all I could do was feel.

We shed our clothes, leaving them scattered on the shining floor, and jumped on the bed. Bailey took my dick fully while sliding his fingers over my balls. I trembled from head to toe, caught between wanting to melt into his now-familiar scent and being afraid to give in because in doing so, I'd be moving on from my safe life to something I never thought to have again.

Having no idea how my mind spun in multiple directions, Bailey continued his assault on my body. "I need you tonight," he whispered and sucked my cock. Broken, desperate sounds fell from my lips, and I lost myself in his hot, wet mouth.

"Bailey, Bailey," I moaned, consumed by the fire bursting through me, and I came, shouting his name. His throat convulsed and he swallowed my release, his fingers digging into my thighs.

"I'm so caught up in you." He rested his head on my shoulder, and I rolled him to his back. Our eyes met, and his expression was hesitant. "You're still staying with me tonight, aren't you?"

I didn't like seeing him so uncertain. Bailey was a bright light...my personal sun who chased away the darkness.

"Yeah. And you're making me coffee in the morning, Barista Boy."

His laugh turned into a sigh of pleasure as I worked his stiff length with my hand from root to sticky tip while licking the sensitive head. His hips rolled, and our gazes held as he panted. I wanted to see him fall apart. From me. For me.

"Don't stop. Oh God," he cried out. His eyes turned hazy and his body shuddered, but I held on while he bucked and came. A lazy smile warmed his face, and my heart thumped in double time as the realization struck me that I didn't want anyone else to ever see him so open and free. He was mine.

"What's the matter?" he asked, concern twisting his brows. "You have a funny look on your face. Is something wrong?"

I bent and kissed him. "Nothing. Let's shower."

On the way to the bathroom, he took my hand and tugged. "Hey. You know I'll never repeat what you told me. But I'm glad you shared that part of yourself. I know it's not easy."

I nodded, and we cleaned up and returned to bed. Bailey fell asleep with ease, but I remained awake, staring into...nothing. I might not be that forgotten kid from years ago, but the past had a way of handcuffing itself to you and throwing away the key. I still wasn't sure I belonged here. Or deserved to be happy.

Bailey shifted closer, and I scooped him to me. "What's wrong?" he murmured sleepily.

"Nothing. Go back to sleep."

He sighed, and his lashes fluttered closed against my chest. I played with the curling edges of his silky hair, my mind unable to settle.

Shouldn't it only be once that your stars aligned? I'd never believed in destiny, but it had brought me Carlos, so I'd accepted it. Now here came Bailey, smashing through every damn brick in the wall, and on the other side, fate awaited again with an outstretched hand. All I had to do was take it, and I'd be free.

I finally closed my eyes...and awoke to a kiss. I blinked to awareness to see Bailey standing by my side with a steaming mug in his hand.

"Good morning, Sleeping Beauty. It's eight. Time to wake up."

"Fuck." I groaned and flung my arms out to stretch. "What time did we get to sleep last night? Feels like I just closed my eyes."

The bed dipped, and I scooted over to make room for him. "Well, I conked out right away, but I know you were up because each time I opened my eyes, I saw you were awake. It wasn't until around four a.m. that I saw you asleep." He handed me the cup. "Your barista is here with your coffee order. As sinful as you. Black with a kick of cinnamon."

I drank. "Damn, that's good. Thanks." I yawned. "Yeah, I guess it was sleeping in an unfamiliar bed."

Bailey smirked. "Nice try, but come up with a better lie. You slept fine the first time you were here and up in the cabin." Concern filled his eyes. "Is everything okay? Is something bothering you from last night?"

My stomach cramped but not from the coffee. I couldn't let Bailey think it was him. "No." I held his gaze. "Nothing's wrong. That's just it. Everything is good. Really, really good."

Those big blue eyes lit up. "Yeah, I think so." He got to his feet. "I showered already, so it's all yours. And I have bagels if you want me to toast one for you."

I made a face. "I don't toast. What kind?"

"Oh, you're one of *those*. I have plain, everything, and sesame."

"I'll take an everything with cream cheese, please."

"Got it. And I brought your bag in." He shifted on his feet, suddenly nervous. "Uh...if you want, you can leave your tooth-brush and stuff here for tonight. You know, if you come back."

Damn, he was cute. I rose and could see Bailey eyeing my morning wood, but I had no time to take care of it, or him. I grinned. "I'd like that. I'll be out in a few."

Giving one final, lingering look at my dick, he nodded. "Okay. I'll get on that."

I couldn't resist giving him a kiss. "You'd like to get on this, wouldn't you?" I rubbed up on him, and he groaned.

"Don't tease me unless you mean business." Bailey took me in his hand. "And this is to keep you thinking about me all day."

He sank to his knees, and using his tongue on my shaft and his fingers playing with my ass, had me coming hot and heavy down his throat in a minute flat. When he stood and kissed me, I could taste myself on his gleaming lips, and I held him close.

"You think I could forget you?" I cupped his ass and played with his rim, teasing and pushing inside him until I felt a warm, sticky wetness spread over my stomach. "And that's so you understand. No one gets to touch you like I do."

He kissed me. "No one ever has."

I went to shower, and when I came out, dressed in my jeans and a sweater, Bailey had put on his slacks and a shirt and had a tie slung around his neck. I sat across from him but didn't start eating.

"Do you ever dress casually for the office?"

Bailey glanced at his shirt and frowned. "No, I always wear a suit. Why?"

I picked up my bagel and took a bite to stall. "I don't know. I guess to be more comfortable?"

"I'm fine wearing this. I can't exactly go before a judge in jeans and sneakers."

"Why not? Do they have a dress code?"

In the middle of eating his bagel, Bailey set it on the plate and directed a hard stare at me. "Why all the questions? Does it bother you that I wear a suit and tie?"

"No, I don't care. Just curious." I took another big bite out of my bagel.

It was true. Bailey in a suit was fucking hot. Guess I was as guilty of judging Bailey as Ambrose, and I'd better change that mindset in a hurry if Bailey and I were going to have a chance. Time for me to stop worrying about what Ambrose might think about my life.

While we cleaned up together, I couldn't help comparing Bailey's apartment to mine. I liked my apartment, but I hadn't changed a thing since Carlos died. It was his books on the shelves, his art on the walls. The furniture wasn't my style, but I couldn't muster the nerve to redecorate. Why should the kind of chair I sit on matter? Hell, I hadn't even gotten rid of his razor and cologne on the bathroom shelf. Even now, I still found myself referring to it as "Carlos's place."

Bailey's co-op was the opposite of him—low key and neutral. I'd expected it to reflect his personality, with loud colors and cheerful, bright art and a touch of chaos. Instead, it was furnished with a beige couch and a club chair. White cabinets and pale-green and white tile in the kitchen. Light oak furniture and several pieces of pottery and sculptures.

"What is it?" Bailey stood in front of me. "You've been looking around like you've forgotten something."

"No, I'm just thinking. Who decorated your place? It's nice."

Bailey's lips twitched. "Me."

"Really?"

He snickered. "My taste in decorating is only surpassed by my taste in men." He ran his tongue across his lips, and my face heated.

"Idiot," I murmured. "I just figured you'd have more ultra-modern stuff. Single guy and all that."

"Well, I must confess my secretary's boyfriend works for an interior designer, and he helped me get some good deals and gave me advice. I was already living here when it went co-op, so I got it as an insider for a great price." He scanned the rooms. "I love it."

"So why keep your old house? Sell it, and use the money for something else." As soon as I spoke, Bailey's eyes dimmed.

"I don't want to talk about this right now. I have to get to the office. Ready to go?"

I swung my bag to my shoulder. "Yeah, sure."

On our way to the subway, I got a text from Ambrose.

Gonna be in a little late.

Everything ok?

Yeah, just gotta stop by the bank. Lucas needs money for the commissary.

I grunted and shoved my phone into my jacket pocket.

"Problems?" Bailey side-eyed me.

About to shrug it off, I thought, *What the hell.* "Listen, I have a favor to ask. My coworker, Ambrose, has a brother in jail. Got arrested for drugs. Ambrose is convinced Lucas is innocent."

"And you're not? Why?"

" 'Cause the guy's a piece of shit. From what I was told, he also slaps around his girlfriend."

Bailey frowned. "So why do you want to help him?"

"Not Lucas. Ambrose. He's the little brother and always looked up to Lucas. I've met the guy, and he's slick, you know? Doesn't have a job, yet always has money."

"That's a red flag for sure. So what can I do?" We stopped at a red light.

"Most likely nothing, because I'm positive the guy is guilty. He was arrested for possession—cops found coke and fentanyl in his apartment."

Bailey winced. "Ouch. Yeah, that's a pretty major felony." He shrugged. "If you want me to take a look at his case, I'm happy to."

"I'm sure you're busy."

"Yeah, I am, but this is your friend. Send me the info, and I'll see if there's anything there. Did he have his own lawyer, or was it Legal Aid?"

"Legal Aid, and that's also part of the problem. Ambrose thinks the guy just skimmed the file because they have so many cases."

"It is a problem."

We approached the 86th Street train station and went through the turnstiles. Waiting for the 1 train, Bailey took out his phone. "Give me the guy's full name, and if you know it, the date of his arrest. I'll start when I get to the office."

I recited what I knew, and we got on the local and transferred to the express at 72nd Street, but not before Bailey gave me a kiss on the platform. We crowded into the subway car. I now appreciated I could walk to work.

"Damn, I haven't taken a train during rush hour in years. This sucks."

"Spoiled," Bailey murmured. "Guess you won't like it if I get squashed up against you, *hmmm*?" I had no chance to answer, and he put his hand on my ass, and my eyes widened.

"What're you doing?" I hissed.

With a face as innocent as a baby's, Bailey replied, "Giving you something to think about during the day. You know, so you don't forget me."

From 72nd Street to 42nd, Bailey teased me with his hands, and it was an effort to control myself. When the train slowed into Times Square, I faced him, attempting a glare but failing because I was too damn worked up from having Bailey's hands on me. "I'll see you later. You're gonna pay for this."

"I'll be waiting. See you tonight." He winked, and I couldn't help myself. I grabbed him and planted a kiss on his laughing mouth, then escaped with the crowd onto the platform. The walk through the tunnel to take the shuttle to the East Side gave me a chance to cool off, yet I continued to think about Bailey.

Why him and not any other guy I'd been with throughout the years? Yeah, the sex was incredible, but from that first night I spotted him at the club, with those laughing eyes and smart-aleck mouth, he'd planted himself in my head and I couldn't stop thinking about him. My phone buzzed again, and it was Grady.

> *Call me later. You still haven't told me the whole story of what happened between you and Bailey.*

I hesitated, still cringing at the thought of revealing my innermost emotions, but I'd learned to trust Grady and he'd yet to let me down.

K

Seeing the shuttle pull in, I hustled to the platform. Maybe it would be a good thing to talk to Grady about what I had going on with Bailey. He'd understand. Hopefully.

Because I sure as hell didn't.

CHAPTER TWENTY
BAILEY

I was whistling when I walked into the office, and Lincoln raised his immaculately groomed brows.

"Well, well, someone had a good night."

I waggled my brows but said nothing and set my coffee on the desk. "Any calls?"

Lincoln followed me. "Your mother. Twice. Dr. Engle wants to talk to you as soon as possible. Madeline Abruzzi has a question about her workers'-comp claim." He checked his pad. "And Patrick Reilly got arrested early this morning for trying to hold up a bodega."

"Jesus. Is that all?" I'd hoped to have a few minutes to sit and savor what was growing between Keston and me.

Plus, I wanted to look into the case of his coworker's brother. While the guy sounded like pond scum, if he didn't get a fair trial, that wasn't right either. But he'd have to take his place in line, which was in front of my mother but behind my paying clients.

"The city never sleeps." Lincoln cackled and handed me the messages. "I sent the files to you for all the callers so you can go through them before returning their calls."

God, I'd be up shit creek without Lincoln. "Thank you, my savior. Lunch is on me today."

"Ooh. I was feeling like sushi. Maybe Nobu?"

"More like No-you. But Sugar Fish is good too."

Lincoln gave me the thumbs-up, and I answered my ringing phone. "Bailey Marks."

"It's Grady."

"Oh, hey. Sorry I didn't get a chance to call you yet. How'd the rest of the weekend go?" Multitasking, I tucked the phone under my ear, reached for my coffee with one hand, and clicked to open the first file Lincoln had sent. "I'm really sorry I had to run out on you all. I felt terrible. Please give Lauren my apologies."

It was the truth. I liked Grady—the times we'd spent talking, he'd listened. He was smart as hell, fun to be with, and a little more open than his brother.

"We had a great time, but you were missed." He paused. "As was my brother. Everything okay with you? We were all concerned, and when I didn't hear from you, I almost came by your office yesterday. The last thing Lauren said to me as I left this morning was to check up on you and make sure you're okay."

"I'm good." I chewed my lip. "I received a call from my sister—half sister, actually—and I thought she was in trouble. Turns out it was a misunderstanding. She's fine."

"Oh, man. Glad to hear that. I didn't know you had a sister."

"Long story, but yeah, I have a half sister. She's had some problems with an ex, so when she called me crying, I got very worried and left to check up on her. Turns out the ex proposed to her, and she was crying with happiness."

"But you still have reservations," Grady said, proving he was as sharp as I believed.

I sighed. "Let's say I'm cautious. With reasons."

"Look, I've got a mediation in a few minutes, but I have some meetings downtown today. Would you want to have lunch? I'm happy to listen and have you bounce your thoughts off me."

I checked my calendar. "Yeah. That'd be great. When and where?"

"How about Smyth Tavern at twelve thirty?"

"Perfect. I'll see you there."

"Great. Bye."

"Bye."

I entered the lunch on my calendar, then tackled my files. There were days I wished I was part of a firm, like Weston, Brenner, and Grady, but I liked working on my own, without worrying about a senior partner hanging over my shoulder, telling me what to do and how to do it.

I placed a phone call to Patricia Engle. Patty and I had met at a college alumni event and became friendly. She was an orthopedist who'd fixed my broken wrist when I fell on the ice one winter, and throughout the years, I'd helped her with some minor legal issues.

"Patty, good morning. How are you?"

"I'd be better if I hadn't discovered Chase cheating on me with his yoga instructor. Could it be any more clichéd? I need a good divorce lawyer. Could you represent me?"

Hearing that shocked me. I'd met Chase numerous times and had always thought they were a happy couple. "I'm sorry. I'm...stunned to hear that. And yes, of course." Divorce cases always left me a little sad, and if they involved custody issues, it could be even worse.

"It's not the first time, either. I mean, we've only been married ten years, for Christ's sake." Her voice rose, and I gave her a moment to pull it together. "Sorry, Bailey. I didn't mean to take it out on you. It's just, I'm blindsided. He's moved out, said he's sick of being tied down and needs to be free to express himself. Everything about him has changed this year. Worst of all? He doesn't want custody of Juliet. What kind of parent does that?"

I sighed. "I don't know what to say." Though I knew all too well. "How old is your daughter now?"

"She's six and has no idea what's happening. Just that her daddy left. Thank God we have a great live-in nanny. Juliet loves her, and I'm taking some time off to be with her as well."

As Patty spoke, I took notes. "Remind me again what Chase did when you first met?"

"He was a jewelry salesperson at Cartier. I'd gone there to pick out a birthday present for my mother. He was so helpful, and we talked and talked… I asked him out to dinner, and we just clicked."

"And he stopped working after you got married?"

"Yeah. He was busy decorating our apartment, and it seemed silly for him to stand on his feet all day selling jewelry when I could buy anything from the store myself."

"Of course. Do you know who his attorney is?"

"Yeah. Weston Lively. That senator's son? I forgot the name of the firm."

"Don't worry." My lips twitched. "I know it. All right, I'll get in touch with him, and we'll start the ball rolling. I'm sure there will be alimony, and maybe he'll have changed his mind about custody."

"You know what? Screw him. If he could even think of walking out on his child, he doesn't deserve to have her. I want full custody. You tell them that. I'll pay him to get it done quickly. Lump sum, three hundred thousand. No more."

"Okay, okay," I soothed. "I'll be in touch."

"Talk to you soon." Patty ended the call, and I sat staring off into space. Patty had a demanding practice, but I knew she always put her daughter first. She'd rejected the chief-of-department position because she'd thought it would take too much time away from her family.

Contrast that with my mother, who'd disappeared and had never once tried to contact me. Then had walked back in as easily as she'd left. No explanation, no apologies.

That conversation still weighed heavily on my mind when I met Grady for lunch. I arrived first and ordered a sparkling water. The server handed it to me just as I spied Grady entering.

"Sorry I'm late," he apologized. "We got hung up after the mediation."

"No problem. I'm not in a rush."

"Just water for me, thanks," Grady told the server, and turned to me. "How's it going?"

"Had a depressing conference with a client. Her husband walked out on her and their six-year-old. He's having an affair with the yoga instructor. Doesn't want a custody arrangement with the child."

Grady made a face. "I hate those cases. As a kid who never knew his mother or father, I don't get how a parent willingly walks away." Despite myself, I must've reacted because Grady hitched his chair closer. "What's wrong? Are you all right?"

"Yeah, sure." I laughed it off, then decided, fuck it. No reason to lie any longer. "No, actually, I'm not." I gripped the stem of my water glass, but the server returned to take our order, so I waited, nerves jumping, until he was out of earshot.

"I was one of those kids whose mother walked out on them."

As I related my sad tale of woe, Grady's face grew dark with anger.

"Dammit, that's so sad. I'm really sorry about your dad. And I understand why you're protective of your sister, but family is gonna do what they want. We can support them, but we should also be prepared to walk away if it destroys our own peace."

"Thanks," I managed to squeeze out through a throat so tight, I could choke. "It's been hard."

"I'm here if you need to talk." He reached out and covered my hand. "Anytime." His eyes twinkled. "Although I think maybe you and Keston have been chatting it up a little?"

I allowed a smile, and my face grew hot. "Yeah, we've gotten close." My gaze lowered to the white tablecloth for a moment before meeting Grady's. "He's the most interesting man I've ever met, and we've got a lot in common, even though he doesn't seem to think so."

"Keston's like one of those Rubik's Cubes. When you first see him, his pieces are all jumbled into different colors, and you wonder, how the hell can I do this, but if you try hard enough to solve his puzzle, it finally clicks and you've won."

"I never give up if I want something bad enough."

Our food came, and I dug into my burger while Grady waited. "And you want my brother? I think you two would be great together."

"I figured that from the first night you texted me where he worked." I grinned and popped a fry into my mouth. "But I think he's hung up on the fact that I'm an attorney and I live in a different world, so to speak, than he does. He's so worried about what his best friend will think. Why is that?"

"He's torn between wanting to support his best friend and me." Grady chewed his chicken sandwich. "I won't deny he has a stick up his ass about authority, stemming from some problems he got into when he was young, but I think he's gotten past it for the most part. His best friend, Ambrose, is another story. The guy hates lawyers and cops."

In the flurry of work that morning, I'd forgotten about Keston's friend. "Yeah, he told me about the brother being in jail and Ambrose believing he was set up, framed…what's your take? Is it possible the arrest is problematic?"

Grady dipped his fries in ketchup. "I doubt it. Nothing I saw led me to think that. Did Keston ask you to look at the file? I did, and nothing jumped out at me." He wiped his mouth.

"Yeah, he did ask, but I don't want you to think I'm second-guessing you. I trust your expertise."

"Nah, feel free. I don't do criminal law. I've got copies of the papers back at the office. Want me to email them to you?"

"Yeah, that'd be easier than me having to request them. Thanks."

We finished our meal, and I took the check. "My treat."

"Thanks. Listen, Bailey, I know what you went through leaves lasting hurt and emotional scars. But you and Keston have more than trauma to bring you together. You give him steadiness and a sense of humor he needs, and I think he can give you a little bit of the wildness you crave. You truly comple-ment each other."

I had to ask, even though I wasn't sure Grady would answer. "I know it might not be any of my business, but what did you think of Carlos?"

Grady's eyes flickered. "Keston told me the whole story of their relationship, and I had concerns, but I wasn't in the picture when they first met. It took Keston a while to agree to meet me, and even longer to learn to trust that my love for him was real." His shoulders slumped. "Years, in fact. I don't have much insight into their life as a couple because I didn't see them together that often. Keston was extremely protective of their relationship, but I know Carlos was the impetus for Keston and me to go to therapy together."

"But he was the real deal?"

Grady nodded. "Yeah. I'll admit the twenty-year age differ-ence worried me, but whenever I did meet him, I could see they were good together." He squeezed my shoulder. "Like you are." His smile broadened. "You really care about him, don't you?"

"Yeah. I do." There was no denying it.

"Good. Carlos complemented Keston. And so do you, albeit in a different way. Don't compare yourself to his past. Make him your future."

We separated on the sidewalk. Grady took the subway uptown, and I walked the few blocks downtown to my office. I prepared the divorce filings for Patty Engle, and put in a call to Weston.

"Bailey, baby, when my client told me you were his soon-to-be-ex's lawyer, I was so happy. Our first case together."

"West, *bubbale*, *your* client might not be so happy after I tell you he can kiss my *tuchus* if he thinks he's going to fleece mine."

His deep chuckle filled my ear. "Listen, I'm not defending the little shit. Any parent who walks out on their kid is garbage in my eyes. There's no prenup, though."

I winced. *Shit*. "My client is happy to do a lump sum payment, but nothing else."

"How much?"

"Two hundred fifty thousand, payable monthly over two years. Full custody to the mother. Fifty-fifty expenses for school and camp, but Patty will pay for the full-time nanny. Chase gets one weekend per month and one holiday per year, to be decided by my client."

"*Hmm*. That's mighty generous of your client."

"She's angry with him, but she doesn't want to punish her daughter by denying her the chance at a relationship with her father. Best and final, West. We know the score here. He used Patty to get into her social circle, and abused her trust. Patty is a totally sympathetic figure and was the one wronged."

"I agree. I'll prettify the language so he sees he's getting a good deal. I'm not happy with this guy."

"Why take him on as a client? You said he's garbage. Jesus, West, come on."

"His girlfriend runs tons of studios all across the city. Her best friend married a son of one of the senior partners, so they bumped it to our division, and lucky me, I was next up." He made an ugly sound. "I'd never represent a dirtbag like that normally, and you know it. I had no choice."

And that was the exact reason I chose to remain my own boss. I might have to scrounge for clients sometimes, but I got to decide whom to represent.

"All right, West. I'll talk to my client, but I don't anticipate a problem. Talk to you soon."

"Hold up. We were sorry you had to leave early. How're you and Keston doing?"

A smile played on my lips. "Wouldn't you like to know?" I teased.

"Well, yeah, that's why I'm asking." Weston snickered. "You two make a hot couple. I could totally see you together."

"Don't tell me you think about Keston and me? Does Brenner know?"

"You know what I mean. All the years we were at school, you never had a serious boyfriend." His voice gentled. "I'm happy for you, Bailey. Really. You're a good person, and you deserve to be loved."

Whoa. That was not what I'd expected. "Uhhh...thanks. But it's not—"

"It is," he cut me off. "He does. I'm not wrong. You'll see."

And in typical Weston Lively fashion, he ended the call and left me hanging.

My email dinged, and I pulled up the files Grady sent me. I read the initial police report, looked at the photos and evidence, and something made me stop and return to the initial write-up from the arresting officers.

"*Hmm...*"

CHAPTER TWENTY-ONE
KESTON

"Starting the morning with a smile?" Ambrose leaned against the front counter, his eyes questioning.

"Yeah, well, I'm still thinking about my brother and his girl getting engaged. She's a pretty awesome lady." I was also thinking about all the time Bailey and I had spent together since then, but wisely, I kept silent on that.

"Nice. Glad it was fun, even if you were stuck with a bunch of lawyers."

Ignoring his dig, I booted up the computer. "We were so busy yesterday, I don't think I thanked you for taking the weekend."

"No problem. And I gotta say I was pretty surprised you didn't check in. I think it was the first weekend you've ever taken off."

It surprised me as well. I couldn't admit it to Ambrose, but I hadn't thought of the shop once the whole weekend. Not Friday night while Bailey was in bed with me, or when I was with him Saturday night and he was so broken up about his sister. And certainly not while we were having sex. Nothing and nobody else had been on my mind except Bailey.

And what the hell was I going to do about it?

"Yeah, well, I trust you and Jodi."

"Yeah? You sure that's all it is?"

In the middle of checking out the day's schedule, I stopped scrolling and peered over the top of the monitor.

"What the fuck is that supposed to mean?"

Ambrose stepped behind the counter. "Look, man. I don't know why you think you gotta keep whomever you're seeing a secret."

My stomach twisted with nerves. "I don't have any secrets."

Ambrose nailed me with a glare. "Carly got off at the Seventy-second Street station this morning for work, and she swears she saw you on the train platform with a guy. And you were pretty cozy with each other."

I snorted. "What're you talking about, cozy?" I left him standing by the front and crossed the shop to get my instruments ready for my first appointment, which was the beginning of a huge project on some football player. Ambrose tailed me.

"Meaning, she saw someone who looks exactly like you with his tongue down the throat of another guy."

"She's mistaken." I arranged the ink colors.

"I don't think so. She said it was you. And a guy in a suit."

I had no desire to discuss my personal life with Ambrose. I knew he'd crawl up my ass about Bailey being a lawyer and so establishment. If he ever found out Bailey's father was a cop, he'd probably force me to make a choice between Bailey as my lover and him as my friend.

And I wasn't so sure whom I'd choose.

I caught Jodi giving me the eye and frowning, but I deliberately ignored her. What I did and with whom was my business. "Well, I do, since I know where I was. Now how about you stop involving yourself in my personal life so we can get to work?"

"You've changed all of a sudden. Must be those richy-riches you've been hanging out with."

"What the fuck is your problem? You don't like money? You wanna work for free?"

"Don't be an ass. I don't give a shit if you're hiding this guy. Go ahead. But Carly knows what she saw, and I believe her."

"And I said leave it alone," I growled and gave him my back. "I gotta get to work."

The day passed without much interaction between the two of us. Jodi, always Miss Sunshine and hating the rift simmering in the air, tried everything to lighten the mood–silly jokes, coffee runs, doughnuts–but Ambrose refused to even look my way. I'd always known he was a stubborn SOB, but this was beyond ridiculous.

At five, I received a text from Bailey:

> *Need to discuss something with you.*

I checked my calendar.

> *Have a client in a few. See you later tonight at your place. We'll talk then?*

The door opened, and my next appointment walked in, so I had no time to wait for his response. Ambrose, unusually silent while working, kept shooting me looks. After we'd finished and were cleaning up, he walked to my chair.

"I'm sorry, man. I was outta line for getting on your case." He held out his hand.

Relieved, I smiled. "It's cool." We bumped fists and gave each other a hug. "But you gotta understand Grady is my blood, and I'm gonna be hanging out with him and whomever else he's close with on the regular. So you need to get used to it. Can you?"

Ambrose shrugged. "I'll have to. You're not gonna get rid of me that easily."

"Get out of here and go home and kiss your girlfriend. I'll see you tomorrow." I gave him a shove, and laughing, he left. Jodi had gone at five. I checked the computer and entered in some new appointments that had popped up. I'd just turned off the light and was pulling my jacket off the coatrack, when Bailey walked in.

"What're you doing here?"

"Nice to see you too. Didn't you read my text? I had a meeting with a client near Astor Place, so I took a chance you'd still be here." He slipped off his trench coat and put his arms around my waist. "I figured we could have dinner somewhere and then..."

"I like the way you think." I cupped that perfect ass. The pull toward him consumed my senses, and I inhaled deeply of his warm scent. "And the way you smell and taste. Maybe I can have you for dinner."

"*Mmm*, yeah? Taste me, now." His tongue met mine and he popped open the button of my jeans. "I like everything about you. A lot."

"You do, huh?"

Bailey's eyes glittered with lust, and he nodded, the pace of his breath kicking up. I pulled him into the office by the tie and bit his bottom lip.

"Come show me how much." No way could I wait until later to be inside him. My body ached to possess his, and I tugged at his slacks and briefs. They fell to his ankles and my business brain shut off. Sex in the shop? Never before Bailey, but he pushed my limits to places I'd never been.

"I wish I could fuck you against this desk and hear you scream for me." As I spoke, I touched the globes of his ass. He moaned and tilted it upward.

"Do it. Fuck me hard. I want you so bad. Need you."

"Can't. No lube or condoms." I sucked two fingers and slid them past the tight rim of his hole, playing with him. Never quiet during sex, Bailey's groans and whimpers echoed off the walls of the small space. My blood grew hot as pleasure spiraled through me. I was a starving man, needing to feast on Bailey. I unzipped and yanked my jeans and briefs down far enough to free my cock. I fisted it for a moment to gain control, then slid it in the crease of his ass. It wasn't perfect, but it would have to do until we were home. Bailey panted and trembled. Fuck, he was made for me. Only me.

Mine.

Bailey was mine, and I was never going to let him go.

"Yeah. Like that. Oh God, Keston."

"You love it, don't you? Love my cock." Blind to everything but this hunger to own Bailey, I squeezed his ass. Passion claimed me, and I leaned forward and bit his neck. "Thought about you all day. Did you miss me? Tell me how much." I needed to hear him say it.

"Yes. Oh God, please, I need you. Need you so bad," he wailed, shivering violently as he hit his climax.

I loved hearing him say he needed me. I gathered him close and moved faster. "You're everything, Bailey." I came so hard, my heart thundered and everything went black for a second. Sweat dripped from my brow, blinding me. I tasted blood on my lips, yet I couldn't stop kissing him, over and over.

"Baby," I whispered, and he held me tight.

He pulled up his slacks, and after wiping us off, I tucked myself in.

"Well, that's one way to brighten up a random Tuesday," Bailey joked, taking some more tissues to dry his hands.

"I have something better than those." I gave him some disinfectant wipes, and we both cleaned up. My senses still teetered on the edge, and I reached out to him. "Come here." He leaned on me, and I rested my cheek against his. "So you need me?"

His lips curved against mine. "Maybe."

I kissed him. "Only a maybe? I'd better up my game."

His shoulders shook as he laughed. "Oh, trust me, if your game was any more *up*, I wouldn't be able to walk."

I tightened my arms, gazing at the taut shadows of his cheekbones. "Challenge accepted. Now tell me what was so important that you came here to talk to me instead of waiting until later?"

He rubbed his face. "Give me a second to recalibrate. You short-circuited my brain." Bailey walked around the office a bit before pulling out his phone. "Whew. Okay. Grady sent me the files on Ambrose's brother."

I winced. "Sorry. I didn't mean for you to waste your time–"

"No. I'm not. I mean, I didn't. There is an issue, I think."

Confused, I put my hands on his shoulders. "Wait a sec. You're telling me you actually found something?"

"There's a possibility the officers violated the Fourth Amendment."

"What's that?"

"In layman's terms, if the police don't have probable cause, they can't arrest you."

"That makes sense."

"Of course it does, but you'd be surprised how easily law enforcement violates it. In Lucas's case, they got a tip he was selling drugs, but I didn't see any notes of surveillance on the premises, shady dudes coming and going, nothing that would justify them going into the apartment. Just some vague comment from a CI, which wouldn't be enough for a warrant. The arresting officers simply went and knocked on his door–

they had no warrant, no probable cause. How did they know he had drugs?"

"Uh, I dunno."

"Me neither." His eyes narrowed. "But I'm sure gonna find out."

My brain exploded. "Son of a bitch, Bailey. But...so...what the hell does all that mean?"

"It means that without probable cause they had no right to even be in the apartment. The fact that they found drugs is secondary to the defendant's right to no unreasonable search and seizure."

"English, please."

Bailey folded his arms. "They had no right to enter the apartment. Lucas said no, but they said they had probable cause and went in anyway."

"But he did have drugs." I scratched my head. "They found a whole bunch of shit he was selling."

Bailey huffed a sigh. "That's the problem. We know he's a bad dude. But the law has to protect bad people as well as good. I know he was selling drugs, and you know it, but the police must follow the rules, like all of us. Their search has to be legal, and from what I'm seeing so far, it wasn't. They didn't have probable cause to go to his apartment in the first place."

"Damn. I can't believe Ambrose was right all along." All his bitching had paid off. "But I don't understand. Grady's a great attorney, and he looked through the same stuff you did. How come he didn't see this?"

"The law has many different specialties, and Grady's is family law. He might've assumed the police did the right thing. I did too at first, but something didn't feel right."

"So you do criminal law?"

He shrugged. "I'm a general practitioner. I do family, real estate closings, estates and trusts—although nothing too complicated—and some criminal. It's how I'm able to stay solo. Anything I can't handle with my resources, I refer to firms and get a fee from that."

"And you don't mind that you gotta suck up to the hot-shot firms?"

Clearly annoyed, he stuck his finger out. "I don't suck up to anyone. It's a symbiotic relationship. I refer cases to them for a fee, and many times they send their smaller matters to me and I get new clients that way. It's business, Keston. Remember the first time I saw you at the club? You should've had your business cards there. Think of it like this. If you're busy and can't fit someone in and they don't wanna wait, wouldn't you refer them to someone else you knew?"

"*Hmm*." I rubbed my chin. "I guess. I just never thought lawyers did that."

"Oh, we lawyers do all kinds of things." A cunning light kindled in Bailey's eyes. "Come home with me, and I'll give you a more intimate lesson in search and seizure." He fisted my sweater and settled his mouth over mine. A hum of pleasure escaped me, and I allowed him to walk me backward toward the desk. I was about to suggest we forget going all the way uptown and instead head to my place, when the lights in the shop came on.

"Keston? You still here? Forgot my phone."

I sprang away from Bailey, who stumbled backward. "Shit. That's Ambrose." I gazed at Bailey—his disheveled shirt and tie and his kiss-swollen lips left no doubt as to what we'd been doing. The scent of sex lingered in the air. "He can't know what's going on."

Red patches slashed across Bailey's cheeks. "Why not?"

A shadow darkened the lights from behind me, and anticipating trouble, I turned to see Ambrose standing there, arms crossed, a tight smile playing on his face.

"Yeah, Keston. That's what I'd like to know. Why not?" He glanced at Bailey, who stood silent. "Wait a second. You're that lawyer." Ambrose's lips thinned to a white line. "I bet he lives on the Upper West Side, right? Were you guys at the Seventy-second Street station this morning?"

My heart sank as Bailey nodded. "Yeah, why?"

" 'Cause Keston swore he wasn't there, kissing a guy on the 2 train platform. But it was you, wasn't it?"

Hurt-filled blue eyes met mine. "Why would you lie to your friend about us?"

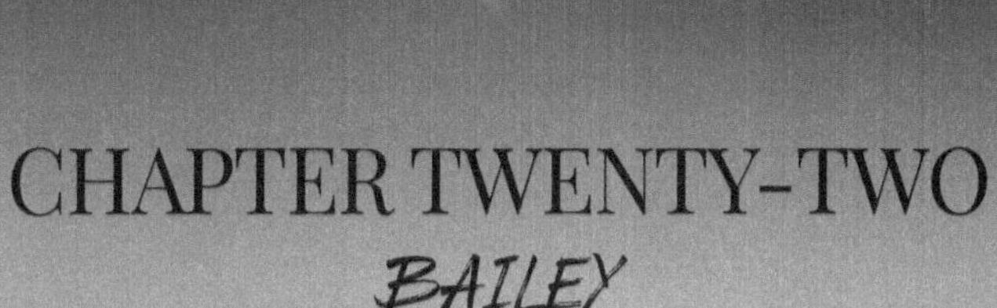

CHAPTER TWENTY-TWO
BAILEY

I'd always heard the phrase, "*The tension in the room was so thick, you could cut it with a knife,*" and now I watched it come to life before me. Keston locked gazes with Ambrose, even as he spoke directly to me.

"I'll explain later, Bailey."

Oh, that so was not going to fly with me. "Nah. I think you'll explain it now. Because if you don't, I'll guarantee there won't be a later."

For the first time Keston looked disconcerted. "Excuse us a second," he said to Ambrose and pulled me into a corner of the office. "Shit...look, I don't talk about my personal life. That shouldn't surprise you."

It didn't, but this went beyond being cagey about dating. "No. But this isn't a casual discussion with acquaintances. This is your best friend. Why don't you want him to know about me? I thought we were trying to make this thing between us work." At the flicker of Keston's eyes, I nodded. "Oh, sure. I'm not your usual type, is that it?" I laughed but not because it was funny. Far from it. "But that's only when it's in the dark, huh? You're ashamed that you're attracted to a guy like me. I'm not part of your cool, hip vibe? I'm one of them—a *lawyer.*" I laughed, but damn, it hurt. "I'm too straight, even for a gay man. Well, fuck you. I thought we had something real. Something special. Goddammit, I was falling in love with you."

Keston paled. "Bailey—"

I put up a hand and stepped away. "No. Don't say anything. I'm fine. I should've known. Wanna hear the funniest thing? Here people were teasing me, joking that I was taking a walk on the wild side with you, when all along, it was you who was afraid to admit to being with me because I'm what? A lawyer? You're embarrassed you like screwing a guy in a suit who sits behind a desk for a living?" I pushed past Keston and Ambrose, virtually running out of the shop. I wasn't sure if Ambrose heard me, and I didn't care if he had. What a god damned fool I was. I had to get out of there and go home to lick my wounds.

The night air hit my overheated face, and I walked down St. Mark's toward Astor Place, blind to my surroundings. At the touch of a hand to my shoulder, I stopped and spun around to tell Keston to fuck off, but instead I met Ambrose's chastened face.

"What do you want, Ambrose? Go back to your friend."

"I'm sorry. I-I shouldn't have acted like that to Keston."

"It doesn't matter to me." I started walking again.

"Wait, Bailey." He came after me.

"I don't need your explanations for Keston's behavior." Then I remembered about Ambrose's brother and stopped. The crowd passed by us, several people shooting us glares, as we were in the middle of the sidewalk, blocking traffic. "I have to tell you something. Let's move over so we can talk a minute." We found a spot by a lamppost, and Ambrose cocked his head.

"What is it?"

"I looked into your brother's case. I think he might have a shot at an appeal."

Ambrose's eyes bugged out, and he grabbed my arm. "Are you shittin' me? Really? I fuckin' knew it. Awesome. When can he get out?"

"Whoa, whoa." I put my hands up. "It's not as simple as that. I'd need to meet with him to get some details straight, and talk to the DA. They're not just gonna unlock the cell and let him stroll out. These things take time."

Excitement drained from Ambrose, and his shoulders slumped. "And lots of money, I bet. Listen, I can pay you a little every week. I swear I'm good for it."

Dammit. I hated the thought of Ambrose putting so much effort into getting his brother out, when the guy was a piece of crap who sold drugs. I took on very few criminal cases because while I believed everyone deserved a fair trial and you were innocent until proven guilty, guys like Lucas turned my stomach, and they deserved a lawyer who would give it their all. But I'd made a promise to Keston to look into it, and knowing Ambrose didn't have much money, I'd suck it up. I wouldn't take my hurt feelings out on Ambrose, even though it was partly because of him that Keston lied about us.

Shit, my brain hurt from those mental gymnastics. How the fuck did I get myself into these things?

"It's fine, don't worry about it. I'll take his case pro bono, but you have to understand there is no guarantee."

"Yeah, yeah, of course. But you're the only one willing to do anything. Even Keston's brother didn't want to help."

I wasn't going to let anyone put Grady down. "This has nothing to do with wanting to help. Grady's a great attorney, but criminal law isn't his specialty, so I understand why he passed. If I'm gonna work with you, there'll be no shitting on him. Got that?"

Ambrose nodded like a bobblehead. "Yeah, okay, sure. So what's your next step?"

"I meet with your brother and see what he has to say. I gotta go to the DA. Give me your number, but like I said, these things don't happen overnight, so don't expect him to be sitting at your dinner table next week or even next month. I'll be in touch." I entered Ambrose's contact information into my phone.

Ambrose stepped in front of me. "Listen, about you and Keston—" he began, but I put a hand up.

"Don't. I'm done talking about it. I'll call you if I have any info." And this time when I walked away, he let me.

I boarded the 6 train at Astor Place and spent the trip in my head, missing my stop to transfer for the West Side. I got off at 68th Street, and cursing my stupidity, decided to cool my anger by walking home across town instead of calling a car. Head bowed, I'd crossed Park Avenue. I heard my name and looked up to see Weston and Brenner waiting. Just what I didn't fucking need. Inwardly I groaned, while on the outside, I pasted a fake-ass smile.

"Hey, guys. What's up?"

"Not much, just going home. What're you doing on this side of town?" Brenner asked.

Not about to reveal my mistake, I shrugged. "Client meeting. I decided to walk home."

Despite his playboy demeanor, West was sharp as hell in reading people. "Yeah? Must've been a hell of a meeting 'cause you look like shit. Why don't you come to our place and have a drink?"

"No, I'm fine."

"Bailey. You've been with us two minutes and haven't made a joke yet. Plus, you ran out of Grady and Lauren's weekend like you had the devil chasing you, with no explanation. Bren and I called to check up on you several times, but you never answered."

Crap. I'd ignored their calls, figuring they only wanted to tease me about Keston. Almost forty, and I still didn't believe people cared about me or for me.

"We spoke, West. In the office."

"That's bullshit. It was about work. Not the important stuff, like what's bothering you."

I rubbed my face. "Sorry. It was a...false alarm. Everything's fine. And I should get home..." Was that my voice sounding so weak and pathetic? Obviously so, as Brenner put an arm around me, and I found myself sandwiched between them, walking toward their apartment.

Weston squeezed my shoulder. "Bailey, come on, we're your friends. What's wrong?"

Damn Weston because when he was caring and nice, he became impossible to resist. I waited until we entered their apartment to answer.

"I doubt you have all night to listen to my tales of woe."

Brenner and Weston exchanged a look. West walked to their bar, picked a bottle of vodka, and set it on the table between us. "We have all night."

I shook my head. "Nothing for me."

"Okay, now I know something's wrong." Brenner leaned forward, the penetrating gaze he was famous for piercing straight through me. "C'mon, Bailey. It's us."

I covered my eyes, and the words spilled out, revealing everything I'd spent the last twenty-odd years hiding. I held nothing back—my mother's abandonment and return, my father's absence while I grew up and his subsequent illness, the guys I slept with in law school to keep the loneliness at bay, hoping someone would love me. And finally, Belinda's poor life choices and her new fiancé with anger issues.

"So that's why I left on Saturday night. I thought she was in trouble, and instead she was celebrating." I forced my shaky lips to smile. "Nothing that horrendous."

"Aw, man, Bailey, I'm sorry. That must've been rough." Weston's green-gold eyes were thoughtful. "You never told us anything."

I snorted. "When would that have happened? At a frat party while we were pounding down beers, or when you came in after a date? I don't think so."

"I understand." Brenner steepled his fingers under his chin. "I'd see everyone laughing and enjoying themselves, but I couldn't. I never belonged."

How well I knew that feeling. I was the kid with his face pressed to the window, watching all his friends at a party he wasn't invited to. I'd thought I'd beaten the inferiority complex, but like a scar, it remained a permanent mark, no matter how determined you were to get rid of it.

"But how does Keston fit into all this? And don't say he doesn't because that man couldn't keep his eyes off you all weekend." Brenner's grin grew wolfish. "I wasn't kidding about the sounds from your bedroom."

I sighed. "All right already. Yeah, we've been hooking up for a while now."

"I knew it," Weston crowed, and Brenner frowned.

"West, it's not a game. Bailey's upset."

"Ah, shit. I'm sorry," Weston apologized, immediately contrite. "I'm just excited for you. I didn't mean to joke about it. So what's the problem, then? From that night at Grady's housewarming to this past weekend's engagement party, you two have been getting close. Is it serious?"

I sidestepped the question. "You want to hear something wild? He's been hiding the fact that we're together from his best friend. He's never mentioned we'd been seeing each other."

"I mean, it's not as if you've been so forthcoming either," Weston pointed out. "Here we are, practically prying it out of you."

"What was I supposed to do, call you up and say guess whom I'm *schtupping*? Those two work together every day. And I didn't lie to you. I just didn't say anything. Keston deliberately lied to Ambrose."

"What're you talking about?" Brenner asked. "How?"

"Tonight I was at his shop. Ambrose's girlfriend had mentioned seeing Keston kissing someone on the subway platform this morning. He denied it, but it was us. He'd stayed over, and we were going to work. When Ambrose confronted him, he tried to wiggle out of it. It's because I'm not part of his cool world. I'm an uptown, suit-and-tie-wearing lawyer." I laughed at the absurdity of it. "People would see Keston—the longer hair, the tattoos—and think, *look at Bailey Marks, nice Jewish boy, taking a walk on the wild side.* Meanwhile, it's Keston who's ashamed of me."

"Ah, that's what had you so upset." Weston laid a comforting hand on my shoulder. "You really like him and wanted to hear him tell Ambrose you two were seeing each other. Instead, he jerked you around."

"Yeah. He's afraid to say we're together because what? I'm a snob? You know I'm not. Or I have some money so that makes me a bad person? Also false." I shook my head. "This is so fucked up."

"I don't see it that way," Brenner stated. "Maybe it's simply his way of trying to figure out how you fit together because you two are so different. And if Ambrose hates lawyers the way Keston says, he could be looking at how to smooth the road for the two of them to have that discussion."

"He didn't have to lie," I repeated, stubborn in my conviction.

"And you walked out, giving him no chance for an explanation," Brenner said pointedly. "That's not the adult way to handle things. Especially if you care about him."

"Do you?" Weston prodded.

That wasn't something I planned to discuss with them before talking to Keston, especially after how this night had exploded. "I should go home."

They accompanied me to the door, and Weston gave me an unexpected hug. "Whatever happens with Keston, any man would be lucky to have you as his boyfriend. I know I am to call you my friend."

Damn. Talk about a one-two punch to the gut. "Thanks," I managed to whisper.

I called for a car to take me home. It let me out in front of my brownstone, and I stopped short. On the steps, waiting for me, was Keston.

CHAPTER TWENTY-THREE
KESTON

I wasn't used to remorse. But seeing Bailey emerge from the car with his shoulders slumped, those normally twinkling eyes vacant, and his always-at-the-ready smile nowhere to be found, my heart turned over and guilt streamed through me, hot and painful.

I'd done that. Taken away his joyful spirit, reducing him to a shadow. A figure in grays and blacks, when usually he'd be filled with every color of the rainbow. This wasn't the Bailey I knew, and I didn't like myself very much at the moment.

Bailey remained on the sidewalk, so I rose to my feet from my seat on the stoop and came down the steps to meet him.

"Can we talk?"

His steady gaze met mine. "I don't know. Can we? You weren't so interested in talking in your shop. All you wanted was to shut me up. So if you're here to give me more excuses why you want to keep hiding me, you can keep walking."

People passed by, giving us curious looks, and I took him by the elbow. "Can't we go inside?"

Without answering, he walked up the steep stairs, and like a puppy, I trailed after him, hopeful because he hadn't yet told me to fuck off and get out of his face. Once in his apartment, he tossed his keys into the dish by the door and kicked off his loafers. He eyed me.

"They're Cole Haan, bought at the outlet store. I may wear designer, but I still buy thrifty."

I held out my hands. "Come on, Bailey. Don't be like that."

Eyes blazing, he pointed at me. "Like what? You lied to Ambrose's face about me...us. And worse even, you thought it was okay for me to shut up and listen to your bullshit explanation. For what? So you could prepare him for me? What the hell—I'm not someone you can fuck in the dark and hide away in the light. Because he doesn't like lawyers? Big deal. I don't like to go to the dentist, but you can be damn sure I wouldn't hide him away if he and I were together. Not that I'd want to be with Dr. Brady because he's sixty and straight with a paunch and a wife..."

My lips twitched, but Bailey was on a roll and wouldn't be denied.

"I deserve more. I am more."

"I...I know. I—" But he cut me off.

"I would never let anyone talk down about or to you because you're a tattoo artist and didn't go to college. I'd build you up, show you off. I'd tell them how talented and creative you are and how you run your own business. If anyone said something negative, I'd challenge them. You know what your problem is? You're too busy judging people on face value, and that's shallow as hell."

"You're right. I was wrong."

"That's it?" He stared at me, and a snort of disbelief escaped him. "You've got to be fucking kidding me. You think that's all you have to say and I should be grateful? That everything between us will be fine and we'll jump into bed?"

"I'm trying to say I'm sorry," I yelled. "Dammit. I don't need this shit." I opened the door.

"Go ahead. Leave. That's what you do best, run away when it gets tough," he shouted back at me. "I didn't ask you to come here. I'm sure you can find someone who'll be okay with your moody, grumpy ass. But it won't be me because I'll have met someone who appreciates me."

At those words, I froze. "The hell you will." I slammed the door shut and faced him. He glared at me.

"You have no say. Remember, you won't even admit you and I are sleeping together."

"That's not true. I-I told Ambrose."

"Wow, I'm so honored." Bailey slow-clapped, and my face flamed.

"Forget about him. What did you mean you'll meet someone else?"

Jaw set, he folded his arms. "It's pretty self-explanatory. I want a lover who's proud to be with me, not someone who pretends I don't exist because I don't fit with his lifestyle. If I try hard enough, I'll find someone else who wants me. So go ahead. Leave. Sit at home and brood about the world instead of living in it."

Bailey had made it easy for me. I could walk away, and that would be it. I'd probably see him occasionally at Grady's, but I could work it out so I didn't have to. But as Bailey spoke so easily of replacing me, I saw red. The thought of another man touching him, kissing him...being inside him? No fucking way. Unthinkable.

"I'm sure you can find someone else. But he's not gonna get the chance. Not as long as I'm around."

Bailey rolled his eyes. "Yeah? What? You're going caveman on me? Talk is cheap, Keston. I need someone whose actions match his words."

"How about this?" I pulled him to me and slammed my mouth over his. He clung to me, pushing his tongue past my lips to play with mine. I tangled my hands in his hair, breathing deep of his smell. "You're mine. No one else's."

He sucked my tongue, then nipped it. "Yeah? You want me? Say it to my face."

"I want you." I licked a wet path up his neck, touching the jumping pulse at the base of his throat. "I'm crazy about you."

"Are you just saying that to get me into bed?"

I gazed into Bailey's lust-drunk eyes, his mouth swollen, face reddened from my stubble. "No. If you want me to leave, I will, but it won't change how I feel. You've gotten under my skin."

"Like a bedbug?" He grinned.

"Only if it's my bed." I cradled his face between my palms. "I am so sorry I didn't stand up for us earlier. I was caught by the shadows of the past instead of living in the sunlight of the future. I promise to try and be better."

"That's very poetic. It would make a great tattoo." Bailey kissed me. "I accept your apology. Were you being honest with me? Did you tell Ambrose about us?"

"Yeah. He was pissed I lied, but he admitted he made it hard for me to tell him the truth with his stupid attitude toward lawyers."

"I told him about his brother. That I'll be looking into his case."

I nodded. "I know. Also that you're doing it for free? Bailey, that's nice of you."

He shrugged. "Don't you know? I'm a nice guy."

"Really nice." I slid my arm around his waist. Bailey fit me, no matter that our pieces came from two different sets. "Hot too."

"Flattery will get you everywhere, you know." He blinked at me. "Where do we go from here?"

"We said we were gonna try out this dating thing." One hand splayed at the small of his back while the other undid his tie.

"We're a little past that phase, don't you think?" His gaze was steady, and I squirmed under his scrutiny.

"I guess...yeah. We are." My phone buzzed, and Grady's name popped up. "Do you mind if I get it?"

"No, of course not."

"Hey, what's up?"

"I know it's a little late and short notice, but Lauren and I were gonna meet for dinner downtown. Want to join us?"

Bailey had put some space between us to give me privacy, but I grabbed his arm and put my hand in his. "Can I bring someone?" He raised a brow, and I grinned.

"Uh, yeah. Sure." A smile softened Grady's normally husky voice. "Do I know them?"

"Kind of."

"Okay. I'll text you the place. She's picking."

"Sounds like a plan."

"Bye."

I slipped the phone into my pocket. "I hope you don't mind, but I invited you to dinner with Grady and Lauren. I figured Grady deserves to know about us. Even though he's probably guessed by now."

"He's smart."

"He is." I pulled him close again. "So are you."

"*Mmm*, tell me more." Bailey's mouth brushed mine.

"Smart, sexy, hot as fuck. With a mouth that won't quit," I teased.

"I'll take that as a compliment." He stroked my cheek, then rubbed it with his own.

"You should. It's a very talented mouth."

"Keston?"

"*Hmm?*" I nuzzled his neck, the pulse beneath my lips jumping, his breath hitching.

"I love you."

My lashes fluttered, and I jerked away to gaze at his face. "What? How can you?"

Eyes soft, he traced the outline of my lips. "How can I not? I know who you are—strong and so hurt by your past. Filled with so much anger at a system that failed you, but also with tremendous love for your brother and friends. You need to accept that love can heal you."

I caught him by the wrist. "What about you? You don't think you're part of that healing process?" Bailey might be great at pumping up others, but he was terrible at recognizing he was special.

Breaking eye contact, he lifted a shoulder. "I don't know. I helped, but—"

"But what?" I silenced him with a rough kiss. "You were the driving force."

"Come on." Bailey pulled away from me. "You don't have to say that to make me feel better because you don't feel the same way."

"Says who?" Seeing the protest rising in his eyes, I put two fingers over his lips and took his hand. "Let's sit." I led him to the couch, where of course, he dominated the conversation.

"I'm not the driving force. You have Grady. He's the one, and I don't blame you because he's your brother. Of course you trust him most of all. And—"

"Dammit, will you shut up for a minute and let me talk for once?" At his outraged face, I pressed my lips together to hide the laughter that threatened.

"Listen. I love Grady. One of the best days of my life was when he showed up and I found out he was my brother. But he's so afraid to say the hard stuff to me, and I always feel like he's waiting for me to...I don't know. Lose my shit, fall apart. I want him to see that I'm not that angry kid he met. I'm capable. I can handle whatever comes my way."

"You don't think he knows that?"

Damn, expressing emotion was fucking hard. But I looked at Bailey, and knowing the life he'd hidden because of his pain, he was the one person I could expose myself to without judgment.

"I don't know. I'm always afraid if I show the real me, he'll walk away because it can get ugly sometimes." I paused. "Maybe you will too."

"Never," he whispered. "I think I fell in love with you the first time we met, and I've been falling ever since."

I wrapped my arms around him. "You tell terrible jokes, and never stop talking, but you're the sexiest bastard I've ever seen. You're kind, caring, and go the extra mile for the people you care about. I might not have gone to college, but I know when I've met the perfect man."

Bailey's eyes glowed, and he put a hand to his ear. "And? Keep talking."

"And I love you too, you annoying little shit."

**

When I walked into Gran Morsi with Bailey a step behind, I spied Grady immediately. The hostess was about to greet us, but I pointed across the restaurant. "It's okay. I see my brother."

Lauren glanced our way, and a satisfied smile tugged up her lips. She leaned in to tell Grady, who stood as we approached.

"Bro. Looking good." He hugged me. "Bailey, I had a feeling I'd be seeing you." They shook hands.

"Glad to make your night," he joked, and Lauren kissed his cheek before hugging me. We sat, me by Grady, Bailey next to Lauren. She couldn't stop beaming.

"You definitely made mine. I said to Grady the night of the housewarming party that you two make a gorgeous couple, and after you left the cabin last weekend, I'd hoped you could work it out because I knew there was something special between the two of you."

I gave Bailey a look. "I think we have."

Grady put a hand to his brow, and I nudged his shoulder. "What's wrong?" I'd never seen Grady get emotional.

He lifted his head, and I met his watery eyes. "I'm just so damn grateful you're finally happy. I know you don't like to talk about your feelings, and you don't have to with me, but now that you have Bailey, I know you'll be okay."

Throat tight, I couldn't speak, but glancing across the table at Bailey, I could see he understood without me saying a word and held out his hand. I took it, and his comforting squeeze was all I needed. The power of touch from someone who loved you could heal even the most wounded heart.

"Well, I have often been referred to as a lifesaver," Bailey announced, and as usual, he brought humor to the situation.

"Funny, that's not what I've called you."

"Keep it PG, Keston." Bailey wagged a finger at me. "There's a lady present." Releasing my hand, he hitched his chair closer to the table and directed the full extent of his attention to Lauren. "Can we talk shop for a minute before the fun starts? I have an issue to discuss with you."

At that moment the server appeared, and Grady beckoned him. "We need a bottle of champagne—Roederer if you have it. We're celebrating."

"Babe"—Lauren blew him a kiss—"that's so sweet and perfect. Now what were you saying, Bailey?"

The two of them got right to it, and I watched Bailey as he recounted the problems he'd discovered while studying

Lucas's file. Lauren listened intently. When he finished, I couldn't help interjecting.

"What do you think, Lauren? Is there a chance the cops screwed up?"

She made a face. "It happens. They might've been overeager to make an arrest, or they knew there were drugs but couldn't prove it, so they hoped an overworked lawyer wouldn't pick up on it." She refocused on Bailey. "Let me poke around a bit and see what I can find. It's not my division, but I know people. Give me your number, and I'll let you know."

Grady leaned closer to me. "You're looking at Bailey like he walks on water. He's a great lawyer, you know. Not everyone has to work for a big firm to be a success."

"Yeah, I know. There's a lot more to him than people see."

"Like you." Grady nudged my shoulder. "I know you think people might look down on you for not going to college, but not the people who count. The road of life is paved with people's broken dreams, and it's not a smooth path. Everyone needs to find their own way to safety. And wherever it leads them, they'll always have to learn to walk it alone the first time. But don't cut yourself off from me because of misconceptions you have about my friends. They don't judge—trust me, you'd be surprised at the similarities you all share. Most importantly, Lauren loves you. She's dying to start her own family traditions of big Sunday family dinners, and you're an integral part of that. My family."

For so many years I'd lived in my own world, sounds muted, colors faded. I'd only allowed Grady to see part of that because he'd climbed so high above me, I figured he'd gotten the brains and I was the brother people would whisper about.

That's Keston. He's gay, you know. Works at a tattoo parlor. One of those types.

"I didn't think I deserved to be happy. That you were putting up with me because you had to, and one day you'd get sick of my shit and move on. And if you did, I wouldn't know how to make it right again."

Grady's brown eyes filled with emotion, and I struggled to keep my own in check, but something shifted inside me, like the unraveling of a tight bandage that had held my broken pieces together until they'd begun to mend. I could breathe, and the air was fresh with promise and hope instead of clogged with bitterness and despair.

"Sorry to disappoint you, little brother, but you're stuck with me. Like a permanent tattoo."

"Maybe we need to add to our collection. Our own personal rebirth day."

Grady squeezed my shoulder. "That would be amazing."

Bailey and Lauren continued to chat about cases they'd had and the judges they'd faced, but I knew my man wasn't whole. Bailey needed to come to grips with his own family issues. And I'd be right by his side to help him.

CHAPTER TWENTY-FOUR
BAILEY

"Your Honor, as you can see from the affidavits and motion I've prepared for the court's inspection, this was a serious violation of the defendant's Fourth Amendment rights, and for that reason, we are asking you to reopen the case of Lucas Charles."

The trial judge, whom I'd never appeared before, peered at me over his reading glasses. "You were not the original attorney on the case, were you, Mr. Marks?"

"No, Your Honor. I've been retained by the defendant within the past month."

"Couldn't the police officers have had a reasonable suspicion that Mr. Charles had drugs in his apartment based on his activity?"

"Yes, that would have been true, had the arresting officers actually seen any criminal activity. Instead, they relied on a CI, a known drug addict, and without any surveillance on Mr. Charles or his apartment or corroborating evidence at all, took it upon themselves to arrest Mr. Charles, only finding the drugs afterward."

"*Hmm.* Mr. Velasquez, what do the People have to say about that?"

Looking uncomfortable, the ADA sitting across from me shuffled some papers on the desk in front of him. "Your Honor, we believe that the information from the CI, with whom the officers had a good relationship, was enough to raise reasonable suspicion."

Perhaps I needed to check my poker face, because the judge's lips twitched. "I see you believe the ADA's excuse as much as I do. But tell me, please, Mr. Marks. Why wouldn't the attorney have brought up this glaring fact at trial? It seems like first-year criminal procedure."

"Ah, well, this is delicate because I don't like speaking ill of my fellow attorneys, but I happen to know that the Legal Aid attorney was brand-new with a caseload the size of a Katz's pastrami sandwich. At the time, I'm afraid he wasn't equipped to handle this. But I'm here now."

We both waited while the judge read and reread our papers. He pushed the wire-rimmed glasses atop his head and folded his hands. "The scourge of drugs in our society has been the downfall of many. I doubt there's a family in this city that hasn't been brushed by its poison. And getting those who act as a pipeline into our men, women, and children is and should be a top priority."

My heart sank. *Fuck.* He was going to rule against me. I wasn't mad that Lucas would remain in jail. I did, however, dislike overreaching law enforcement.

"Nevertheless, the Fourth Amendment is there for a reason. It acts as a protection for citizens from overzealous police officers. However bad a defendant may be, he has the same rights as any other citizen—the right to proper search and seizure. It is apparent from the papers in evidence that the officers didn't have reasonable expectation that drugs would be found in Mr. Charles's apartment—the lone statement of one confidential informant is not enough to establish a *prima facie* case. The proper thing for them to have done was set up surveillance, talk to more people in the neighborhood to establish connection, even send in someone undercover to make a buy. They did none of these things. Instead, they went on assumptions, and though they were proved correct, it is all the fruit of the poisonous tree. Inadmissible." He huffed out a disgruntled sigh. "Therefore, I have no choice but to reopen the case."

"Thank you, Your Honor. And when that occurs"—I pulled out my motion papers—"I move to dismiss the case for lack of evidence and prosecutorial misconduct. The DA's office obviously knew they had no case except for the drugs found in the apartment by their illegal entry, and yet they pushed to have him convicted to save face because they had to hide their police officers' incompetence."

Behind me in the gallery, I heard Ambrose's hiss of approval. This wasn't a case I wanted or was proud of, but I said I'd do my best and I would.

"I'll take it under advisement and make my ruling in the morning. Mr. Velasquez"—he fixed my opponent with a pointed stare—"I hope you have a good enough reason for why I shouldn't vacate this?"

The ADA ducked his head. "I-I'll have to see."

"Which most likely means no. Am I going to be wasting my night, then, reading Mr. Marks's motion, when I could be enjoying my wife's delicious roast beef and mashed potatoes? And I really love her mashed potatoes." At the ADA's silence, he pounded the gavel. "Motion granted. Mr. Charles' case is dismissed without prejudice."

"Thank you, Your Honor." I stuffed my files into my bag and turned to see Ambrose waiting.

"Dude, that was awesome. You're amazing."

My smile was thin. "So now you like lawyers?" I couldn't care less about Ambrose's answer. I did what I said, and I was done. "It'll take a few days for the paper work to get sorted out. I'll let you know."

"Thanks." Tears streaked down Ambrose's face. "Bailey…I don't know what to say. You gave me back my brother."

We walked out to the courthouse hallway, where I turned and pointed my finger in his face. "This was a one and done. If he fucks up and gets himself in trouble again, lose my number. I did this for Keston and no one else." Maybe I was too hard, but Ambrose was about to get a harsh reality check if his brother returned to his old form, and he should be prepared.

"He won't. You'll see."

He took off, and I waited a few minutes so as not to have to ride in the elevator with him. My phone buzzed with a text from Keston.

How'd it go?

I sat on a bench to answer. I didn't have another client until later that day.

I won, but I'm not thrilled about it.

Tell me tonight at dinner.

Yours or mine?

Mine.

I *sure am*. With a smile on my face, I left the courthouse. I had a therapy session scheduled for my lunch hour and could walk to the doctor's office, which was only a few blocks away.

On the street, I ran into Lauren. Dressed in a charcoal-gray pantsuit, pearls in her ears and around her neck, and a belted black-wool coat, she looked every inch the power prosecutor.

"I hear you won and made mincemeat of poor Edwin Velasquez." She pushed up her sunglasses to meet my eyes. "I told him not to worry since it wasn't his case initially."

"Yeah." Curious, I asked, "What's going to happen to the ADA who did such a shitty job?"

Her lips thinned. "Oh, we'll have a meeting. You worked in Legal Aid, Bailey. You know how many cases these people juggle—prosecutors and defense attorneys. Shit happens."

"I know, but it still makes attorneys look bad, and God knows we don't need another excuse for that. I wonder if the police will even do anything."

Her expression grew fierce. "Don't you worry. I had a talk with their lieutenant. They won't be pulling shit like that again."

I could see what drew Grady to Lauren. Off duty, she was fun, flirty, and sweet. But on the job, she was a lioness. And a confident woman was a sexy woman.

"Let's hope not. I gotta get back to the office and make some money. I'll see you soon."

She kissed my cheek. "You know, Grady's always been so worried about Keston. I never met Carlos, but I heard how his death sent Keston into a dark place. But now, seeing you two together settles his fear that Keston will one day disappear. He's a changed man since he met you."

The brothers' separation had caused such damage. Losing those early years together was a wound that even decades later still festered and might never heal.

"I didn't change him. I gave him space to breathe and showed him that he's allowed to be angry, but that doesn't mean he shouldn't let people who care about him help him."

Her phone went off, and she grimaced. "Ugh. I have to go. Hopefully we'll see you soon. Love you, bye."

She kissed my cheek and took off. I watched her, wondering if Belinda could have become a strong, independent woman like Lauren had she been given opportunities. My phone rang, and seeing it was Belinda, my heart started racing. I didn't know what I'd find on the other end of the call.

"Belinda, what's wrong?"

She laughed. "Why does something have to be wrong for me to call you?"

Maybe because that's usually the only time you ever call me.

"Oh, well, no, of course not. I'm glad you called. I always like hearing from you. How's everything between you and Jonas going?" I asked, hoping my question sounded casual and not accusatory.

"Fine. I told you, he's a different guy. He comes home every night and stays, and we haven't had one fight."

I had to admit I was impressed. "Good. I'm glad to hear that. You know all I want is for you to be happy." I stopped on the corner of Broadway and Chambers to wait for the light, thinking of my therapy session with Dr. Sharpe. I was truly happy that Jonas was proving me wrong.

"Yeah. Speaking of not being happy, *she* came to see me the other day."

There went my pleasant afternoon—and the obvious reason for Belinda's call. "What happened?"

"She tried to get me to talk to you about selling the house."

The absolute fucking gall of that woman. "And what did you tell her?"

"I said I don't know anything about it, and that it's got nothing to do with me."

Not exactly the backup I'd hoped for, but at least she hadn't taken Jennifer's side.

"Okay, well, thanks for the heads-up."

"I do have a question, though. How come you don't wanna sell? Jonas said you could probably get like half a million easy for the house. Maybe more. That's a lotta money."

A chill ran through me. "So you think I should sell?"

"I mean, it's not like you'll ever live there again. Why don't you want to?"

"I don't know. I just don't feel like selling it simply because Jennifer wants money. It's all I have left of my father."

"Eh, that's kinda silly. Jonas says you—"

"I'm not exactly interested in what Jonas has to say about my life." I approached Dr. Sharpe's building. "I have an appointment. I have to go."

"I knew you'd get mad at me." She sniffled.

"I'm not mad," I soothed her. "I really do have to see someone. I'll call you soon."

"Okay. I just think your father knew you loved him. Selling a house you haven't lived in for almost twenty years doesn't mean you don't."

"I know. Bye, Lindee." I ended the call, signed in to the building, then took the elevator up to the doctor's suite. Her secretary led me in, and Dr. Sharpe greeted me.

"Bailey, nice to see you again. How's your week going?"

Dr. Sharpe's silver hair in its meticulous bun gleamed in the overhead lights. As always, she wore a knitted suit jacket and skirt, navy blue this time with gold buttons. In the fifteen years she'd been my therapist, I didn't think I'd ever seen her in pants. Around sixty, she exuded a calm, almost cozy presence, something my overactive mind and mouth appreciated, as she always made me stop and think my answers out. Today was no exception.

"I'm not sure."

She cocked her head. "Would you like to explain? Are things still going well with you and Keston?"

A smile pulled up my lips. "Oh, yeah. No problem there."

Her eyes brightened. "Good. I'm glad to hear that. So is something else bothering you?"

Frustrated, I clasped and unclasped my hands. "I feel like it's a rinse and repeat. It's my mother. Again. Right before I came in here, I heard from my sister, who told me Jennifer talked to her about getting me to sell the house. Belinda said she wasn't going to get involved, but she's starting to push me."

"How so?"

"She says she's on my side, and yet she's quoting me what the home is worth and telling me that the house has nothing to do with loving my father."

"And you disagree? You think it does?"

As always when I delved deeper into the subject, my body went into defensive mode and it was fight or flight. "I can't imagine not having the house. He loved it so much. It holds all my memories of us together. When we were happy."

Dr. Sharpe put her pad down. She took notes the old-fashioned way, pen to paper. "Is it really the house that holds the memories, or your heart? When you think of the good times in your life, do you think of the place or is it the person?"

I sat in thought, her words resonating. "I-I know it's all him. But thinking of how we'd play catch in the yard, or when I'd help him plant his vegetable garden...my grandparents baking in the kitchen. I don't want to lose that."

"And you wouldn't even if you sold the house. I'm not telling you what to do, Bailey. But those memories are of the emotional connection with people. You could toss a football in Central Park and think the same. Or put a pot on your windowsill to grow something." Her eyes twinkled. "Even try your hand at baking in your kitchen. All these actions will revive memories that don't require you to be present in the place where they occurred. The only thing required is the love that existed between you and that person."

I wiped my eyes. "I never thought of it that way, but you're right. Whenever I see the 9/11 memorial, I think of my dad and our good times." I blinked to clear the blurriness. "And I know I'm being petty, but I hate the thought of having to give my mother anything from the sale of the house."

"Think of it this way—if and when you decide to sell, once she has her share, I doubt you'll see her anytime soon. That peace of mind could make it worth it. I don't often encourage my patients to cut ties with their families, but in your case, I don't believe you can heal unless you make a clean break."

Later that evening, when Keston and I were on his sofa, after eating dinner, I relayed Dr. Sharpe's analysis and waited for his reaction.

"You know, sometimes I think about finding my mother. I get in these moods where I want to come face-to-face with her and ask why she let us go and never tried to get us back or even contact us."

I stroked his hand. "I'd wondered if you ever had. There are ways you know, similar to how Grady found you."

He laced our fingers together and tugged. I crawled over to him and rested my face on his chest as he held me. "It goes both ways. She could've tried as well. And the more I thought about it, the angrier I became that she never made that effort. So I decided against it. Maybe she had a good reason or maybe not. For me, I'm better off as I am now. With the people who want to be with me." He played with my hair. "If you're interested in my opinion on your situation, I think you should sell."

At his words, I sat up. "Really? Why?"

"Because the doctor is right. It's the person, not the place that makes you happy. I think that's why people get tattoos of their loved ones after they die. To carry the memory of them wherever they go."

I reached out and traced the infinity symbol on his biceps, with the date of Carlos's death underneath. "Like you did."

"Yeah. But there's something else I've been meaning to do since we've gotten together. Something I haven't been able to face until now." Blue eyes dark with sadness, Keston bit his lip. "Would you come with me? I can't do it alone."

"Of course. Anything."

He took my hand in his cold one, and I followed him, mystified as to where we were headed.

CHAPTER TWENTY-FIVE
KESTON

Maybe I was making too much out of it, but sweat poured down my brow as we walked to the bathroom. From his confused face, I knew Bailey had no idea.

"I've kept this apartment exactly the same since Carlos died. I haven't even had the courage to go through his closet or drawers to donate his clothing." I opened the medicine cabinet and took out a razor, a bottle of aftershave, and some other bottles and set them on the vanity. "All this belonged to Carlos, and I felt like if I dumped it, it would be betraying his memory, wiping him clean from my life. And I can't do that."

Bailey wrapped his arm around me. "I wouldn't expect you to. He's been the single most important person in your life. Next to Grady, or course."

"Yeah. But now there's you. And it's not erasing Carlos to make room for you. I don't need all these things to remind me of him when all I have to do is close my eyes. Just like I can think of you when you're not here." I had a crazy thought and spoke without thinking. "Which could be rectified if you moved in with me."

"I-I don't know what to say."

I laughed. "That's gotta be a first."

"Not funny." He glared at me for a second, then said, "I would love to move in with you. But what would you say if I asked you to sell this apartment? I think if we take that step, it should be someplace new for both of us."

It made sense, and I'd be a hypocrite to say no after telling him he should sell his father's house. Still...I ran my finger over the marble top of the vanity. This apartment had been Carlos's, and I was so damn grateful to have been given his love and protection all these years.

But like Bailey's therapist suggested, maybe it was time to hold the memories in my heart and let go.

"All right. I guess...that means you'll have to sell your place as well. Are you okay with that?"

Face soft, his smile was sweet. "Yeah. I love the place, but I kinda love you more." At his words, my heart did a silly flip. "Besides," he continued, "living downtown will make my commute to the office shorter."

I laughed. "A New Yorker answer if I've ever heard one."

His eyes danced. "Excuse me, Mr. I-Can-Walk-To-Work."

This was such a spur-of-the-moment decision, but nothing I'd done in years had felt so right. "You think you can put up with my moody ass twenty-four-seven?"

Bailey leaned in and kissed me. "I've wanted that gorgeous ass and every other part of you from the first time I saw you. And once I learned about the beautiful heart you possess, no way I could let you go."

I held him tight, needing the balance of toughness and humor he gave me. "I can't promise I won't get into a dark place sometimes. Don't give up on me."

"That would mean giving up on myself because loving you has made you part of me."

I kissed him, my desire rising, but with regret, I disengaged my lips from Bailey's. At his protest, I nudged his cheek with my nose. "I have to do this now, while I still have the courage and the mindset." I released him and picked up the razor first, looked at it, and tossed it into the wastebasket. Next, I unscrewed the aftershave and poured it down the drain, then put some other bottles and boxes, all outdated, in the bin with the razor. Bailey remained quiet and watchful as I emptied the rest of the bathroom of Carlos's things.

I left the bathroom and picked up several large bags from the kitchen before entering the bedroom. Bailey trailed behind me.

"Keston, you don't have to do this all tonight."

My head was already in the closet, so I poked it out. "I need to. Not only for me, but for Carlos as well. By keeping all this here, I couldn't let his spirit rest. It wasn't fair to him. He deserves peace, and I think knowing I'm in a happy and healthy relationship, he'll finally be able to."

It took close to an hour to clean out all his clothes, folding them into neat piles and placing them in the bags for donation. Groaning from the strain in my back, I rubbed the base of my spine. "Ouch, it hurts. God, I feel old."

Cackling, Bailey flexed his fingers. "Come on, Grandpa. Stretch out and I'll give you a massage. But lose the pants." He waggled his brows.

The jeans came off, and I lay prone on the bed. The mattress dipped under Bailey's weight, and he began massaging me, pressing hard at my nape.

"I'm starting at the top and will work my way down," he crooned, following each touch with a gentle kiss. "You can do me after." The wicked tease in his voice couldn't hide the edge of exhaustion, and it hit me that I hadn't asked about his day.

"Tell me how the trial went."

"Motion to reopen," he corrected, rubbing each vertebra. "Then another motion to dismiss the charges for lack of evidence."

"*Mmm*, keep talking that sexy lawyer talk. Makes me hard."

"I've heard that before." Bailey peeled off my briefs and massaged each ass cheek. "I think everything makes you hard. You just want me for my body."

Grinning, I rolled over and watched as he got naked. "What's wrong with that?"

"I can't think of one damn thing." Bailey ran his tongue across his lips, and with a sigh, sat back on his heels. "Lucas should be free in a few days. I gather Ambrose was happy when he returned to the shop?"

"*Ecstatic* is a better term. He couldn't stop talking about what a great lawyer you are and how you made the ADA look like an idiot."

Bailey winced, and his eyes blazed. "Jerk."

"The ADA?"

"No," Bailey snapped, and at his tone, I sat up. "Sorry. I meant Ambrose. I didn't make the ADA look foolish. I did my job by reciting the facts. It wasn't the other lawyer's fault—it wasn't even his case."

"But the cops were wrong. You said that." Maybe I was missing the point.

Grumpy now, he swung his legs off the side of the bed to sit. "Yeah. They screwed up, but Lucas is nothing but trouble. Ambrose hero-worships him for no reason other than he's the big brother. I hope he's prepared for more heartbreak when Lucas screws up again, because I have no doubt he'll be on the other end of some handcuffs sooner rather than later. Maybe then Ambrose will get the message that Lucas is no good and doesn't deserve his time. I hate seeing relatives get caught up by family members who don't give a damn about them."

Bailey was a great attorney because he cared about his clients, regardless of the fee. There was so much more to him than he allowed most people to see. The fun and joking personality was his facade, masking the sadness he hid from everyone else. Just like I'd chosen to be hard and closed off, each of us held on to a past we could never revisit, but had chosen to cling to, despite how much it hurt. Now we needed to create a bright new future that, like a tattoo, would be everlasting.

"Come here." I patted the space beside me. "Were you serious about living in this area? I don't want you to think I wouldn't move to live with you."

His cheek rested against my shoulder. "I wouldn't mind a change of scenery. I have no ties to that area, and we work downtown. But I'm not sure about those high-rises where everything is cookie-cutter. I want my place to have personality. Like me."

"I don't know if I can live under such chaos." I ducked away from the pillow he tried to hit me with. I grabbed him, and we kissed until our laughter turned into moans of pleasure.

**

"Can we really afford a two-bedroom?" I asked Bailey.

It was a busy Saturday, but I was on my lunch break. Bailey was at his office, catching up on some files, and we were reading the listings our real estate agent had sent. Almost two weeks had passed since the night we'd decided to sell our apartments and move in together. Our plans were moving full speed ahead, no stop signs in sight. Bailey had put his place up for sale, and it was snapped up in four days, with a bidding war driving the price well above asking. Once he'd accepted the offer, he'd moved in with me as the buyers had asked for a thirty-day closing. The real estate agent assured me she could get the same kind of interest on my apartment, but first we were waiting to see what she'd come up with for us to look at.

"You're kidding, right? Between our places, we'll have plenty of cash for a significant down payment. Remember, I didn't pay much as an insider, and you said Carlos's mortgage is pretty nominal because the apartment was a fixer-upper and he bought it before the East Village took off as a hot spot."

As usual he failed to mention his father's house. It was a ticking time bomb between us, something that had yet to be settled.

"I-I don't know. These prices scare me. Hundreds of thousands, millions. I'm not sure I see myself with that kind of money." For someone who'd grown up without enough change to buy snacks from vending machines, I couldn't catch my breath at those numbers. It all seemed like pie in the sky.

"It's overwhelming. Trust me, I understand." Bailey's warm, soothing voice sought to calm my nerves, and he almost succeeded. Almost. "But you're not that lost kid anymore. You're a business owner, an employer. Plus, you're not alone. You have your family—Grady and Lauren. Friends who care about you. Most importantly, you have me. The one who loves you. So damn much."

My face grew warm, and I wondered if I'd ever get used to hearing someone say they loved me. "I never would've taken this step without you. It still feels surreal."

The door burst open, and Ambrose rushed in. "Where's Bailey? I need to speak with him."

Without answering him directly, I asked, "What's wrong? Are you in trouble? Is Carly?" Of course, I already knew the answer.

"No, it's Lucas. Is that Bailey?" He pointed to the phone.

"Sorry," I hedged, not directly a lie, and when I heard Bailey's whispered, "*Thank you,*" I ended the call. "What happened?"

"He was with his old girlfriend, Tiffany, and they had a fight. Her pain-in-the-ass neighbors called the cops, and Lucas told them they couldn't come in, and they did anyway."

I struggled to keep my temper. "Let me guess. They found drugs."

"And a gun, but it's like last time. Bailey can get him off."

I set my turkey sandwich on the desk. "You've gotta be shitting me."

"No, can you believe they'd fuck up like that again?" Oblivious to my sarcasm, Ambrose danced on his toes. "I need Bailey to represent him."

"Dude, I don't think so."

An ugly flush stained Ambrose's cheeks. "Why not?"

"You forget he did that as a favor. For free. He's not gonna keep doing shit like that every time your brother fucks up."

"Forget it. I'll talk to him myself. I thought you were my friend." Without another word, Ambrose stormed out, and I picked up the phone and called Bailey to fill him in.

"There's no way the cops would make a mistake like that twice, right?" I asked.

Bailey mused, "I mean, it would be a royally dumb move, but I can't say definitely no. I've got some work to finish up, but tomorrow I can make a few calls to see what the real story is, if you want."

"Have I told you lately you're the best boyfriend?"

"*Hmm*," he hummed in my ear. "Let me think. No, it's been a while. Remind me."

"Kind and thoughtful...smart..."

"Keep going."

"Face of an angel, lips of the devil that suck my brains out through my dick."

"*Mmm*, say that again, big boy, and I'll be right over to make your dreams come true."

I busted out laughing just as the door opened. My client Mike Flynn had arrived. "Hold that thought, and I'll see you later."

"I'd rather hold something else."

"You will be, all night long. Bye." Still smiling, I tossed the remnants of my lunch and went to meet Mike, who'd already settled in the chair. "Back so soon, I see," I greeted him. "You really are addicted. And a bouquet of flowers you wrote when you made the appointment?"

His weathered face split in a grin. "Listen, I got a new grandbaby. Gotta put her name with the rest. I got Lily and Jasmine, and now Rose."

"Sweet. You've got a real garden growing. Now let's see if you like what I drew up."

I showed him the sketch, and his eyes lit up.

"Now that's what I'm talkin' about."

"Great. Where do you want it?"

He pulled off his jacket and sweater and turned around. "On my shoulder. There's a nice patch of empty skin. I wanna nice big buncha flowers." He flexed.

"You got it."

I drew the stencil, but my mind was still on Ambrose and how he was allowing his brother to once again dominate his life. I hoped this time he wasn't going to ruin it.

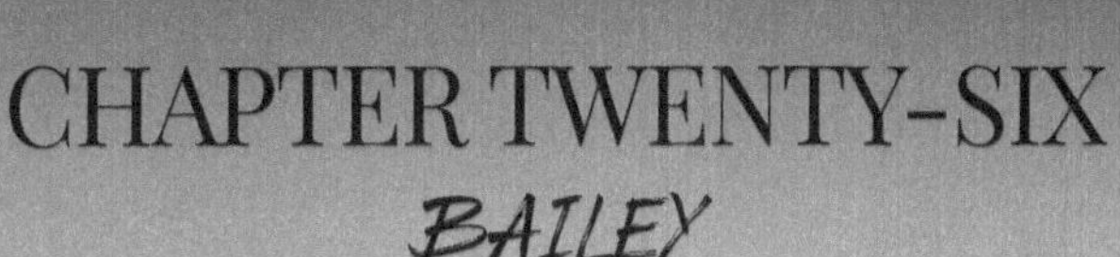

CHAPTER TWENTY-SIX
BAILEY

Working through my files wasn't the most pleasant way to spend a Saturday, but with Keston at the tattoo shop, I figured I might as well get a jump on the week ahead so I could concentrate on finding us a new apartment. For perhaps the fifth time that afternoon, I checked comps in the area of my father's house. Prices had only gone up, and I chewed the inside of my cheek almost raw, paced my office, and downed two cups of coffee before picking up the phone.

"Madison?"

"Hi, Bailey. You just caught me. I'm on my way to a showing. Did you and Keston like any of the apartments in the listings I sent you?"

"We're still going through them. I'll make this quick. I'm going to put my father's house on the market. Can you do the listing?"

"Hold on a sec, my car is here... Yeah, I can. It's outside my normal area, but I don't see why not. What's your asking?"

"I'm thinking five hundred? Maybe five fifty?"

"When you mentioned it, of course I did a comp run. Let's do six fifty, and we'll see where it goes. Listen, I gotta run, but I'll reach out later, okay? I've got a few more great places for you and Keston to check out. I'll email you."

"Sounds good. Talk soon."

That was the easy part. It was the second call I had to make that made me wish I kept a bottle in my desk.

"Hello, Jennifer."

"Bailey? To what do I owe the honor of a call?"

I squeezed my eyes shut. It wasn't that I hated giving her what she wanted. *Dammit.* Yes, it was. I was being petty as shit. But Keston and Dr. Sharpe were both right. There was no reason to hold on to a house when the memories of my father would always live in my heart.

"I'm going to put the house up for sale."

As executor of my father's estate, I was the person to initiate the sale, but since Jennifer was half-owner, she also had rights.

"Thank God you're finally listening to me. How much?"

"Six fifty."

"What?" Her shriek nearly took out my eardrum. "That's not enough. Any apartment where I'm looking to move is much more expensive than that."

"It's what the real estate agent and I feel is appropriate, considering it's not updated. If there are multiple offers, the amount could go higher."

"It better," she responded.

I couldn't resist a dig. "I'm sure one of your *friends* would be happy to help you if you needed money. Or a place to live."

She didn't answer me, so I gave her the facts. "It'll most likely start being showed next week, so I suggest you clean it up to make it look its best."

"I'll hire someone," she said airily, as if she were queen of the castle.

"Fine. I'll deduct the cost from your portion. I'll let you know when the first showing is so you won't be there."

"Bailey, wait. I was so glad to see you're doing so well."

"You were?"

My lips twitched because I knew what was coming. Maybe the fact that I hadn't hung up on her immediately allowed her to think I cared. As usual, she didn't disappoint.

"Oh, yes. Your secretary told me how busy you are. Obviously, you must be making enough to live in a fancy apartment in the city, or you'd join a big firm and make even more money."

"Was there something you wanted? Because I really do have to go."

"Wait. Bailey, please. I think you should consider giving me a greater portion of the money we get for the house. After all, you have a high-paying job. I-I have nothing. I'm an older woman, with no man to take care of her. Please."

My head hurt, most likely caused by my eyes rolling so hard in my head from her bullshit. I drew in a deep breath, calming myself.

"Then may I suggest you get a job? The will states fifty-fifty, and that's all I'm prepared to do. Once we receive an offer, I'll let you know. I have to go." There was no need to continue the conversation. Anything further would be more of her whining and crying.

"Bailey, you selfish—"

I didn't get to hear the rest of her loving comments because I ended the call. My heart pounded, and coupled with my headache, I had little desire to keep working. My phone showed five o'clock, and that was my signal to close my files and go meet my incredibly gorgeous, hot, and sexy man for dinner.

How quickly had my life changed since meeting Keston. From zero to one hundred with a single kiss. Because from that first time when he touched me at his shop, I was his.

I entered Inktastic and waved to Jodi, who was cleaning her table and chair, and wandered to stand behind Keston, who was busy working on the shoulder of a big older man. He didn't notice I was there, and it was fascinating to watch him work. While I had no desire to have someone stick needles in my skin, I could appreciate the artistry and talent it took to create and execute the designs.

Keston finished and straightened up, rolling his shoulders. "That's it, Mike. Lemme get you a mirror so you can see."

I spotted the hand mirror on his tray and handed it to him.

"Here."

Keston jerked around, a smile on his face. "How long have you been standing there?" He took the mirror from me.

"Long enough to see how talented you are. And I'm not just saying that because you're my boyfriend." I winked. "And you have a great ass," I murmured.

Muttering, he cast his eyes to the ceiling. Red crept up his cheeks, and he faced his client again, who was busy on his phone. "Mike. Take a look and let me know what you think."

The big man squinted and cocked his head left and right. "Perfect. Exactly what I wanted."

"Great. I'll go get your aftercare set up." Keston left us to gather some items together.

The rest of Mike's arm was covered with other colorful tattoos, but one caught my eye and I stepped forward to peer closer. What I saw sent me reeling, and I pointed to his arm.

"How-how did you know him?"

Mike glanced at his biceps. "Bruce? He was a cop friend. A good man. Helped us on the pile." He flexed and sighed. "I told Keston here that when I heard he died, I wanted to do something to honor him." He ran his fingers over the tattoo. "Too many, gone way too soon."

"What is it? You're white." Standing beside me, Keston moved in closer. "Whoa, wait a second. Is that—"

"My dad." Tears stung my eyes. "Yeah."

Mike's jaw dropped. "You're his boy? He always talked about you. How he was proud you did so good in school and that you wanted to be a lawyer."

"I am." I couldn't take my eyes off the tattoo. Seeing his shield number and date of death sent a rush of love and longing through me. But not pain. No more.

Keston rubbed his face, his wide eyes expressing how overwhelmed he was. "I had no idea that was your father when I did the ink. I remember thinking it was a cool way to pay tribute to a friend. I see so many people, I totally forgot. I'm sorry."

"Hey." I put my hand on his shoulder. "Don't apologize. You didn't do anything wrong. I wouldn't have expected you to connect the two."

"Forget about me." Keston's arm slid around my waist. "Are you okay?"

"Yeah." Warm and secure for the first time in my life, I leaned into him. "I think I am. And I can never forget about you. You're like my own tattoo, only permanently inked across my heart." Keston squeezed me hard.

As Keston treated the tattoo, Mike said, "He's a hero. Worked nonstop when the towers fell and for weeks after. I know he lost buddies as well." Once Mike was wrapped up and had put his sweater and jacket on, he stuck out his hand. "Nice to meetcha."

"Same here. Take care of yourself."

We clasped hands, and after Mike paid, Keston steered me into his office. "Sit for a few while I clean and close up, and then we'll go home."

Jodi had finished up and stopped to say good-bye. "Good to see you again. And again." Her eyes danced, and she closed the space between us to speak quietly. "I know Keston hates when I talk about his private life, but I just wanted you to know I think you've been great for him."

"Thank you. I agree."

Brows together, Keston strode into the office. "Jodi?"

She wiggled her fingers. "Just sayin' good night. Byeeee." Swinging her purse, she left, and I snickered.

"She's cute."

He took me by the elbow and pulled me close. "So're you. Ready to go?"

"Yeah. I'm hungry."

A slow smile spread across his face. "Me too."

A throb of desire hit me. "I am so happy right now."

"Yeah? Something happen?"

Before I could answer, the door opened, and Ambrose came running in. "Oh good, you're here. Bailey, please help Lucas. You're the only one he trusts. His Legal Aid lawyer is just tellin' him to plead guilty. Exactly like the other one."

Keston dropped his arm from around my shoulder. "Didn't Bailey already say no?"

Ignoring Keston, Ambrose continued to entreat me with pleading eyes. "Please, Bailey. He's been screwed once. You know the cops wanna get him."

Dammit. "If I do this and I find out he wasn't wrongfully arrested, are you going to stop hounding me then? I'm not gonna lie."

"Okay. He's in Central Booking. You know where that is?"

I sighed. "Yeah. I'll go and let you know what happens." Keston shifted and huffed by my side, clearly unhappy. "I'm sorry. I can't say how long it'll be. Hopefully I'll be home soon."

"Not your fault. I knew you wouldn't say no."

"I'd better call a car. I'll text you." I kissed him and left.

The ride to Central Booking wasn't long, and I was shown into a conference room to wait for them to bring Lucas in. When they did, he smirked and his eyes lit up.

"Ambrose came through. I knew he would."

"First of all, I'm not representing you or here as your attorney. This is a consultation only. Understand?"

"Yeah, yeah, sure. This is what happened. Me 'n my old lady Tiffany was havin' a fight when that bitch across the hall called the cops."

"What was the fight about?"

His gaze flicked side to side. "Ain't important."

I remained silent.

He huffed and glared. "Okay, I brought some shit to her place, but I wasn't gonna leave it there. I was gonna move it."

Unreal. "And the gun?"

"Listen. The kid was asleep."

My temper exploded. "A child? There was a child there and you had a gun lying around? Are you crazy?"

"Be quiet and just get me out of here."

Fool. "What happened when the police came?"

"I was in the hallway, telling the old witch to mind her business. Tiffany was still yellin' her damn head off at me, and I told her to shut up. The cops wanted to come in, and I said no, even though Tiffany told them yes."

I blinked. "Wait. It's Tiffany's apartment, am I correct?"

"Yeah."

The man was as dense as mud. "She said they could come in?"

He scratched his head, and I wondered if there was anything in there. "So? I said no. And it was my stuff."

"Doesn't matter. She lives there. She gives the consent. You'd better accept whatever plea deal the ADA gives you. Besides, you were fighting, and the police were concerned about a domestic violence issue, which you've been arrested for previously. That right there gave them probable cause. As I see it, you have nothing." I slipped my phone into my pocket and rose to my feet. Lucas, his face a mask of anger, pounded the table with his fist.

"Fuck you. You have to defend me."

"I told you at the outset, I'm not your lawyer, and I'm not touching this case. Drugs and a gun with a baby in the house? That's it, Lucas. Guard," I called out. "I'm ready to leave."

"Bailey," he yelled. "Get the fuck back here. I need you."

I walked out. In the car, I texted Keston.

> On my way home.

> How'd it go? Was it the same as before?

I grimaced.

> Not at all. See you soon.

> I'll be waiting. We'll talk.

And thank God for that. Until that second, I hadn't realized the weight of the burden I'd carried on my shoulders. I hadn't had a chance to tell him I'd decided to sell my father's house. After talking to my mother and then seeing the fireman's tattoo honoring my father, all the energy drained out of me, and I wanted nothing more than a massage, a drink, and my sexy boyfriend. And not in that order.

My phone rang, and seeing it was Belinda, my stomach and heart both squeezed tight. I'd been waiting for this moment for the past few weeks.

"Hi, is everything okay?" I half expected someone from the emergency room to answer.

"Of course. Guess what?"

"What?" As always with Belinda, I had no clue.

"Me 'n Jonas got married! I'm at the airport, leaving for our honeymoon. It's only gonna be a quickie 'cause Jonas can't get off work but wanted to do something, so we're going to Puerto Rico."

My head spun. "Uh, married? When? Where?"

"Yesterday. At city hall." Her happy sigh filled my ear. "And there's somethin' else."

"What?" I was almost afraid to ask.

"You're gonna be an uncle. I'm havin' a baby!"

Despite my shock, I couldn't help my excitement. "Congratulations, Lindee."

She giggled. "Imagine me telling her she's gonna be a grandmother. She's gonna flip."

We shared a laugh. "I'm so happy for you. Honestly. I know I was hard on you and overprotective, but–"

"You were bein' a big brother. I get it. But I'm tryin' to change my life around. I don't want this baby to grow up like me. And I'm not her."

"All I want is for you to be happy and safe."

"Jonas and me go to counseling together. You gotta believe he's changed."

"I'm glad." The car slowed to stop at a red light, a block away from Keston's apartment.

"What about you? Is that guy really not your boyfriend?"

A smile kicked up the corner of my mouth. "Well, maybe things have changed for me too."

"Bailey!" She squealed in my ear. "He's such a hottie. You'll haveta tell me all about it when I get back. We're gonna have a big party."

The car pulled into a No Standing zone in front of the apartment, and I exited. "Have a safe trip. And congratulations."

"Gotta go, they're boarding. Love you."

And she was gone before I could reciprocate.

When I walked into the apartment, Keston was waiting with a cold beer and a warm kiss. "Everything all right?"

"Everything is great." For once, it was the truth. "Only Ambrose isn't going to be happy." I gave him a quick rundown of the facts, and he shook his head, his eyes narrowing with anger.

"Maybe now he'll realize what a dumbass troublemaker his brother is."

"I hope so." We sat on the couch, my head in Keston's lap. "Some people won't ever allow themselves to see another side of a person. They'll choose to see only what they want, even if the person has grown. Like us and our misconceptions about each other."

"Yeah. I thought you were a spoiled, rich smartass." His fingers played with my hair.

"I'm still a smartass."

"*Mmm.* Yeah. Hot as fuck, though, too. That hasn't changed."

With Keston's touch, the tension in my body melted away. "I'm selling my father's house."

Above me, Keston's face reflected worry. "Are you sure? You're not just doing it 'cause you need the extra money for the new place?"

I reached up to touch his cheek. "No. Absolutely not. We have more than enough to get what we want. It was a crutch I was holding on to, and maybe I was being a bit of a bastard to my mother."

"She deserves it," Keston grumbled.

I smiled at his protectiveness. "But I don't need it anymore. Like Dr. Sharpe said, I carry my father's memory with me always. I don't need a house to remind me." I sat up, held Keston, and kissed him. "All I need is you."

"You've got me." Keston's wicked grin sent my blood racing. "We were speaking of a hot and sexy ass, weren't we?" To prove his point, he pinched mine.

"Ow. You're bruising the merch."

"Yeah?" He arched a brow. "I'd better kiss it and make it better."

I grabbed his hand and pulled him to stand with me. "Everything with you is better." I took off running. "Last one naked has to sleep on the wet spot."

CHAPTER TWENTY-SEVEN
KESTON

"I don't wanna go to work," I mumbled, my head buried in Bailey's neck. He wiggled into me, and I hauled him closer.

"So don't. Stay in bed with me all day." He reached out and gripped me. Already hard, my dick swelled to the point of pain, and he grinned. "I love an eager man." His fingers teased and played with me, while his kisses grew heated.

Screw work. I could be late. What the hell was the benefit to being the owner if I couldn't take a little leeway? I slung an arm around Bailey's neck. "On top. I love seeing you ride my cock."

Blue eyes hazy with lust, he grabbed the lube, and I coated my shaft, then palmed his ass, sliding my slick fingers into him. We'd stayed up late, hungry for each other, and he was open and ready for me. I worked him until he wriggled off.

"Enough," he said, and with a face full of bliss, sank onto my cock. With his head thrown back, mouth open and panting, Bailey was the epitome of pleasure, and I let him set the pace, knowing how much he loved this position. I held his ass as he rose and fell, giving him short, quick thrusts.

"God, you're so thick," he moaned. "Fuck me hard. Faster," he demanded, and holding him in place, I drove up, deep and strong, pumping into him at a punishing pace. His ass swallowed my throbbing cock fully, and I lost myself in the white-hot bursts of fire erupting each time his passage squeezed me tighter. I dug my fingers into him, anchoring him as I rolled my hips.

"Bailey," I panted, "Bailey." We'd had sex hundreds of times, but each was like the first. I couldn't get enough of him. I craved his scent, his taste, every twitch and shiver. I grasped his dick, and he cried out, his body racked with spasms as he came. I loved watching him climax—his face grew red and his eyes glowed bluer than ever. I continued to pump into him, and he cried out.

"Keston, oh fuck, you're killing me. Don't stop." He shuddered, the muscles of his ass clasping me like a vise. My orgasm hit, and I clutched him.

"Jesus," I sighed, and he chuckled in my ear.

"Wrong god." Bailey slid off me and rolled onto his side, propping himself up on his elbow, chin in hand. "I wish you didn't have to go in." He kissed my shoulder. "Would you ever consider taking off the weekends, at least one day—I mean, permanently? Watching you yesterday and seeing how intense it is, I hate how you work nonstop. You need a break, Keston. And we need time to be together."

I opened my mouth to say no but thought about it. Why *was* I grinding to the point of exhaustion? Before Bailey, I'd had nothing to look forward to, so I'd stayed holed up in the shop, never taking time off, running on this hamster wheel of go-go-go so I wouldn't have to think of how empty my life was. It was all different now.

"Maybe I should. At least Sundays."

He smiled against my cheek. "I'd like that. I know you make fun of it, but I'd like to go out to brunch with you—the guys have been asking if we could get together, and I keep telling them no because you work weekends."

"If I take it off, it's not 'cause I want to spend time with them," I growled in his ear. "I want you. Like this."

"What, sticky and sweaty?" He sat up and swept the hair out of his eyes. "Come on, you can't still think you don't fit in?" When I didn't answer, of course he pushed. "Seriously? Maybe you feel that way because you don't spend any time with them. I'm telling you, it'll be fun." His gaze skittered away for a second. "After being the third wheel all the time, I'd like the chance to show you off." He hung his head. "At my age, I know it sounds silly, but I've never had a boyfriend to go out with. We stay home so much, and I love being with you, but sometimes it would be nice to see other people too."

Bailey was a much more social animal than me, but I could admit I'd had fun seeing Grady and Lauren for dinner.

"You're right. I can take off Sundays. Jodi can handle the shop on her own, or maybe Ambrose might want to make some extra money. He and Carly want to buy a house."

His face brightened. "Thank you." He flung his arms around me, and I kissed him, then slapped his ass.

"You can thank me later. I gotta get up and shower. I have a client at ten."

Bailey made a face. "I'll get the coffee going. Do you want anything else?"

"Are you offering?" I pinched a cheek.

He snorted. "Down, boy. I meant a bagel or something."

"No, I'm fine with coffee."

He left for the kitchen, and I took my shower. I came out and he had the coffee waiting. I drank it while he talked and read his messages.

"Madison asked if we could look at a couple of places today. Do you have free time?"

Scrolling through my phone, I winced at the texts from Ambrose. "Uh, yeah. I'm free from one through two thirty." In all caps, Ambrose was busy lecturing me on why Bailey didn't know what the hell he was talking about. I decided not to share that with him. "Are they close by?"

He nodded. "Yeah. One's on the same block as your place but in a brownstone. The other's in a prewar building a couple of blocks from here. They're in our price range. Should I tell her we'll meet her at the brownstone first?"

I knew he favored that kind of place, and I wasn't that picky. "Yeah, sure. I'll see you at one."

"Great. Plus, she said she's had a lot of interest in your apartment and is gonna want to show it this week, so I'll arrange for it to be cleaned. She'll do the showing while we're at work, so it won't be disruptive, and if she wants an evening appointment, I told her to let me know."

"Fine, sure." I gulped the rest of my coffee and kissed him. "Bye. See you later. Don't forget to text me the addresses."

"I won't. Bye."

When Carlos died, I never imagined he'd leave me anything. Discovering it was everything he'd owned, I'd fallen apart and cried. Grady had helped me with the probate. Suddenly supposedly grieving relatives popped out of nowhere, threatening to challenge the will. Grady had informed them that the will was valid and they had zero standing. That blood didn't mean they were owed anything, especially as they'd kicked Carlos out and hadn't seen him in more than thirty years. Now, because of his love and generosity, I'd been given a second chance at love and life. I gazed at the clouds scuttling across the blue sky and whispered, "Thank you."

I opened the shop, and without a chance for me to even boot up the computer, Ambrose slammed in, face blazing with anger. "Your boyfriend is a fucking idiot."

Furious, I smacked my hand on the counter. "You know what? Screw this. I'm done. For years I've listened to your shit about Lucas and put up with it because you're my friend. But now? After everything he's done, you have the fucking nerve to call Bailey an idiot?"

Jodi's hands covered her mouth, eyes wide with shock. Ambrose and I had gotten into our share of beefs over the years, but it had never lasted because it was usually due to stupid shit. We'd get in each other's faces, then retreat to our separate corners until we'd cooled off.

Not this time.

"Yeah. I do. He said–"

"I know what he said. And maybe open your damn mind and really listen. Your brother is no good. Get it through your head. I understand it hurts and it's painful, but he's a piece of shit who deserves to go to jail."

A red flush stained his cheeks, but I kept going.

"I'm sick of hearing you stand up for him. He doesn't deserve you. He's a drug dealer, Ambrose. The guy just got out of jail because he was lucky he had Bailey to defend him, and what does he do? Turns right around and starts with the bullshit again. When are you gonna realize he's been using you? And to make things worse, he brings a gun into an apartment with a baby? That's so fucking off the chain, I don't even know what to say. He needs to take responsibility and be locked up for what he's done. Maybe he'll finally learn a lesson." My eyes bored into his, and I poked my finger into his chest. "And if you ever call Bailey an idiot again, you can fuck right off and not come back."

"Are you firing me?" he asked quietly.

"I don't want to," I answered honestly, my chest hurting with each breath drawn. In all the years we'd worked together, we'd never been at the edge of this cliff, ready to jump. "But I won't let you insult Bailey because you have this misguided loyalty to a man you can't seem to understand doesn't give a damn about anything or anyone except himself. Bailey went out of his way as a favor to you last night after working all day. There was never a guarantee Lucas would get off. If Bailey says he's guilty and should take a plea, that's it as far as I'm concerned."

Ambrose slumped into one of the chairs in the waiting area and covered his face with his hands. "I got nobody left."

I sat beside him and put my arm around his shoulders. "What're you talking about, man? You're not alone. Carly loves you. You got Jodi and me." I squeezed him. "I'm not going anywhere, but you gotta see the light. Even Bailey doesn't mind your sorry ass when you're not bugging him about Lucas. C'mon. It's hard to let go, but at some point you gotta open your eyes and see what it's doing to you."

His gaze remained fixed to the floor. "Carly said if I don't stop defending Lucas, especially after this last shit he pulled, she's gonna leave me. But he's my blood. How do you walk away from family?"

Thinking about my own situation, I could relate and speak from the heart. "Sometimes they give you no choice. When you were little, it was easy to look up to him, but he took a wrong path, and I won't let him drag you in the gutter with him."

"He used to care about me. I thought he loved me. We had nobody except each other when we ran away from our grandmother and came to the city. Until he found his crew."

I'd heard his story many times, and it never stopped hurting. Lost kids. There were so many like him...like me. And, unfortunately, like Lucas.

"Neither of us is a winner when it comes to stability, but you have good people on your side. People who really care about you. Family doesn't always have to be blood. Sometimes we get lucky and find people who care about us more. It's the ones who step up and show up with actions, not words." I squeezed him closer. "I'll be your brother."

I heard sniffling and looked up to see Jodi wiping her face. "That was so beautiful. And I love you too, Ambrose. I'll be your sister, if you want one. But Keston is right. Just because Lucas is your brother doesn't mean he's on your side."

"Thanks. I–I guess it'll take a while to learn not to jump every time he calls."

"Why don't you and Carly have dinner with me and Bailey tonight? It'll be good for you to get out, and I want you to get to know each other." Noting the time, I got to my feet. "I gotta get ready for my client. You okay?"

"Yeah," he nodded. "And I'll call Carly about dinner. She'll like that."

I smiled. "So will Bailey."

I worked steadily through the morning on two small tattoos that took about an hour and a half each. I had just enough time to run down the block and meet Bailey and Madison, who were already waiting.

"Sorry."

"Not a problem," Madison said with her brisk efficiency. "This is a two-bedroom, two-bath, mostly renovated. It's a thousand square feet."

"Nice size for the city," Bailey threw over his shoulder as we mounted the stairs. Once inside the apartment, Bailey and I split up—he gravitated to the kitchen and me toward the primary bedroom. It was a nice space, with crown molding and shining wooden floors, nothing I would've noticed if Carlos hadn't taught me.

Bailey joined me and prowled around the room, opening closet doors. "That's the problem with older places. They don't have a lot of space."

I smirked. "I don't have much. You need the room, Calvin Klein?"

"Very funny." He crossed his arms. "What do you think?"

I scanned the rooms. "I don't know. It's not giving me the vibes."

"Is that how it goes? Vibes?"

By now, I was clued in to Bailey's teasing. If he'd really liked it, he'd have begun by pointing out everything he loved about the apartment.

"It goes however I feel it. And I don't think you're loving it, either."

"The light is minimal, and the views are terrible. At least my apartment faced trees. Plus, the rooms are pretty tight."

"Well, the next apartment should solve all those problems," Madison said brightly. "It's a prewar but renovated and has amenities like a gym and a doorman. Shall we?"

We followed her to an apartment building on East 9th, which I knew Bailey wasn't fond of, but I liked the lobby and the prewar aesthetic of wood paneling and older marble walls and floors. When Madison opened the door to the apartment, as strange as it sounded, I felt a sense of home. One wall was exposed brick with the unexpected bonus of a fireplace, and the large picture window let in tons of light across the pale floors. The living room was spacious, easily holding a large sectional couch and other pieces of furniture. There was a small half bath in the hallway.

The kitchen was modern with a big white island we would use as our eating spot. Bailey smoothed his hands over the surface. "Nice vibes," he murmured, meeting my eyes, and I grinned.

"Yeah. Let's check out the bedrooms."

The primary was as large as the one we had now, with the surprise of a walk-in closet. It also had a spacious ensuite bathroom. The second bedroom was a decent size for an office. Hand in hand, we met Madison in the living room and exchanged glances. I nodded, and Bailey spoke.

"We love it."

She beamed. "Wonderful. It's been on the market for a month, so there should be some wiggle room with the price.

The asking is one point two five so let me know what you're going to offer."

Knowing my hesitation from our previous discussions about money, Bailey squeezed my hand. "What are you thinking?"

We'd decided we didn't want a huge mortgage on our heads and were willing to make a large down payment, made possible by the sales of the apartments. I'd never been in the position to buy real estate and had no idea. "I think one point two?" My stomach took a dive to my knees simply speaking that number.

"Let's start at one even," Bailey suggested. "Gives us some wiggle room. Like Madison said, it's been out there for a while."

"All right." Madison took some notes on her phone. "I'll get this to the owner's agent and see what they say. We'll be in touch." She left us on the sidewalk in front of the building.

I checked my phone, and seeing I still had a few minutes, didn't feel the need to rush back to the shop.

"I told Ambrose we'd have dinner with him and Carly tonight. I'd like you to meet her and get to know him better. I know you're all about me getting comfortable in your world, but you need to be the same in mine."

"Uh, okay."

His brows pinched together, and sensing his reluctance, I said, "He's decided to cut loose from Lucas. We had a long talk, and I think he's finally got it right."

"Thank God." Bailey cast his eyes to the sky. "I hope it sticks."

"Besides, Carly works at Sephora, and she can get you a discount on that fancy body wash you like." I leaned in and nuzzled his neck. "I like it too. It drives me crazy."

He kissed me. "I'll stock up so I'll never run out."

**

Later that night, Ambrose and Carly sat across from us at an old-school Italian restaurant in Brooklyn, near their apartment. I was sure Ambrose chose it because he assumed Bailey would feel out of place at a neighborhood pizza joint.

"Me 'n Carly come here all the time. Better and cheaper than anything you can get in the city."

"You know it. This reminds me of where my dad and I would go if I got a good report card," Bailey remarked, scanning the plastic menu. "Oooh, mozzarella sticks. I haven't had them in forever. Let's get some. And a carafe of the house wine."

Ambrose stared hard at him, and I took Bailey's hand under the table and squeezed it. He returned the pressure.

Carly buttered a piece of bread. "I love their chicken parm. Always enough for leftovers."

"Not if I'm eating it." Bailey cackled. "But I'm gonna try something else tonight."

Carly and Bailey had hit it off immediately, talking about their favorite Upper West Side restaurants and her giving him the details on when Sephora would be having their employee special sale.

"Give me a list of what you like, and I'll make sure you get it."

"Fancy-pants and Carly are getting along real well," Ambrose mused.

"Is that what you call him?" I cut into my chicken parm. "I mean, he does look damn good in a suit."

At that moment, Bailey caught my eye and winked, before taking a big bite of his baked ziti Siciliana. "My favorite. Eggplant."

My lips twitched. Life was so fucking strange. A year ago I couldn't have imagined being with a man like Bailey. Like Ambrose, I prejudged him, with his fancy clothes and law-school education, the same way I accused people of looking down their noses at me because of my lack of a college degree and occupation. Now I couldn't imagine life without his teasing, loving, lighthearted nature that I knew hid a wounded soul. Our broken pieces fit each other's jagged edges.

"Bailey," Ambrose said, more serious than I'd ever seen him. "I got something to say."

"Yes?" As if expecting a confrontation, Bailey set his fork on the plate, and I tensed. With Ambrose, I could never tell what might come out of his mouth.

"I know I acted real shitty to you right from the start, and I wanna say I'm sorry. I appreciate everything you did for Lucas, and I know now that he's never gonna change. I tried to visit him, and all he did was call me useless and that I never did nothin' for him. You did what you could. So thanks." Carly rubbed his back.

"Proud of you, baby."

Bailey sighed with what I knew was a mixture of relief and empathy. "I know it's hard to give up on the people who should be there for you, but sometimes we have no choice. Trust me, I understand. You might think I grew up privileged, but I have real-world experience in dysfunctional families." He took my hand and laced our fingers together. "We don't always get the chance to choose our family. We're lucky if we do." Bailey raised his glass. "Here's to being one of the lucky ones."

I clinked my glass to his. "To us."

EPILOGUE

One year later

"How do I look?" I tweaked my tie and stood in front of the mirror. Keston came behind me and kissed my neck.

"Hot as fuck like always. You know I love you in a suit."

"I've never been a godfather."

Keston met my eyes in the full-length mirror. "Well, me neither, but Grady and Lauren said it's like being there for all her special occasions, and if something happens to them, taking care of her."

"God forbid. Imagine us with a little baby."

His gaze turned inward. "There was a time I couldn't have pictured myself being with a guy like you, yet here we are."

I turned and put my arms around his neck. "Yeah. Here we are. A year in this apartment, and I'm happier than I ever thought possible."

He kissed me. "Same. I guess it was silly to worry about leaving my old place and taking on such a huge expense."

I cupped his cheek. "No. Not at all. You've had a tremendous amount of change in your life—Grady, Carlos dying, taking on a business on your own. I tell you all the time, I'm in awe of your resilience."

"Speaking of change, Belinda and Jonas seem to be working out."

"He's been on his best behavior for sure." Since having baby Connor, Belinda had settled down—no more late-night calls or erratic behavior. Jonas came home every night and was the model husband and father. "Do you think I'm wrong to still be on guard?"

The struggle between wanting to back me up yet trying to remain positive was written all over Keston's face. "I think...at some point, you're gonna have to let them live their lives. Belinda is happy, and Jonas is behaving. That's what you want for her, right?"

"You're right. Did anyone ever tell you how smart you are?" I kissed him, his lips softening under mine. "Level-headed, sexy, gorgeous, perfect..."

He held my face a moment before pushing me away. "You're not playing fair," he panted, his eyes hazy.

I grinned. "I'm not playing at all. I meant every word." I patted his cheek. "Let's get going. Don't want to be late." I started whistling "Get Me to the Church on Time."

We entered St. Agatha's Church, and Lauren's sisters were waiting for us. We'd all had a great time partying at Grady and Lauren's wedding, and I'd helped the family with their probate and real estate issues when their mother passed a month later.

Annabella ran toward us. "There they are. The godfathers."

I snickered. "I'm just the *consigliere*. Keston's the boss."

"Don't you believe it," he jumped in. "Bossy is his middle name."

"They're not talking about the bedroom," I whispered in his ear, loving how he turned red.

"Don't say that in front of women." He yanked my hand, and I gave them a wink.

"Where are the proud parents?" I asked, craning my neck. There were some fifty people in the church already, seated in the pews.

"Grady and Lauren are waiting by the altar," Dolores said. "Follow me."

We walked down the aisle and passed by Weston and Brenner, who stood and gave us each a hug.

"Lookin' good, Bailey." Weston squeezed my shoulder.

"Especially with my fabulous eye-candy." I winked at Keston, who rolled his eyes but managed a smile. I knew he still held himself back from the overtures made by Weston and Brenner. We'd gone to brunch with them numerous times, at their apartment and ours, with Grady and Lauren, and without. It didn't matter that I thought he could relate to Brenner, who'd also come from a foster family. Keston simply had a hard time dealing with Weston's wealth, but I hoped the more we saw them, the easier it would get. No matter the outcome, I loved him for making the effort because he knew they were important to me.

Lauren hugged us when we greeted them at the altar. Grady was holding the baby, and little Celia's face peered up at us from the frothy confection of her white dress with pink flowers and matching headband. Grady's sleeve slipped, revealing the tattoo on his wrist he'd gotten with the date he and Keston reunited. Keston had a matching one. It had been an emotional day for them both.

"Bro, you and your daughter." Keston's eyes grew shiny, and my heart squeezed tight. Over the past year, he'd learn to show and share his emotions. "She's so gorgeous. Looks just like Lauren."

"Thank God for that." He chuckled and bent to kiss Celia's tiny nose. The sight of big, gruff Grady with his tiny daughter was enough to make my own eyes blur with tears.

"Hello, princess," I crooned and held out my arms. "Can I?"

"Be careful." Grady gently handed her over, and I gathered her close. "She gets fussy with strangers."

"Not with her Uncle Bailey." I made a funny face at her, and she smiled at me.

"Did you see that?" I asked everyone. "She loves me."

The minister approached, and Grady took her from me. "Sorry, champ, but it's probably gas."

Keston slipped his arm around my waist. "Don't worry. When I smile at you, I promise it's not gas."

"Good to know."

The ceremony didn't take long, and Grady and Lauren had the luncheon at Gigante's. I'd only eaten there once, and Keston had never been. Knowing how overwhelmed he still felt in these types of situations, I stayed close to his side.

"Grady's so happy," he said. "I can't believe he's a dad. A girl dad."

I watched as Grady leaned down and smothered Celia's face with kisses, then lifted her in the air. "He's gonna be a great father."

"He already is." Keston finished his drink and set it on the tray of a passing waiter. "Remember earlier when you mentioned us with a baby? Much as I love Celia, I don't think I could be a parent. Has anything changed for you since she was born? Feeling any paternal vibes?"

"Uh, no, not really. I'm having a hard enough time being an adult and dealing with that."

Keston linked my arm with his. "Glad we're on the same page. Plus, I'm too selfish and greedy to want to share my time with you, especially now that I don't work weekends, except by special appointment."

"And I am eternally grateful for that."

"Yeah. And Ambrose is happy to pick up the extra work with the wedding coming up." Keston shook his head, his glossy black hair falling into his face, but I didn't miss the teasing smile kicking up his lips. "Weddings, babies...I don't know, Bailey. Ever since I met you, all this fun and happy shit keeps happening."

"Awful, isn't it?" I patted his cheek.

"It's not so bad," he murmured against my lips. "Guess I just got lucky."

With the whistles of our friends in the background, I kissed him hard. "Nope. We're both the lucky ones."

FELICE STEVENS writes romance because what is better than people falling in love? Her favorite part of a romance novel is that first kiss...sigh. She loves creating stories of hopes and dreams and happily ever afters. Her stories are character-driven, rich with the sights, sounds, and flavors of New York City, and filled with men who are often deeply flawed but always real.

Felice writes gay romance because she believes that everyone deserves a happily ever after. Having traveled all over the world, she can safely say that the universal language that unites people is love.

Felice has written in a variety of sub-genres, including contemporary and paranormal, and she has a mystery series as well. You can find all her books listed on her website.

Felice is a two-time Lambda Literary Award nominee and a Lambda Award winner in Gay Romance for her book *The Ghost and Charlie Muir*.

BOOKBUB

https://www.bookbub.com/profile/felice-stevens

NEWSLETTER

https://tinyurl.com/y85e69ab

READER GROUP

https://www.facebook.com/groups/FelicesBreakfastClub/

FACEBOOK AUTHOR PAGE

https://www.facebook.com/felicestevensauthor/

INSTAGRAM

https://www.instagram.com/felicestevens

GOODREADS

https://www.goodreads.com/author/show/8432880.Felice_Stevens

WEBSITE

felicestevens.com

PAYHIP STORE

https://payhip.com/FeliceStevensAuthor

TIKTOK

https://www.tiktok.com/@felicestevens

FELICE STEVENS